"God, you are a shrew," he chuckled against her ear, the sound oddly pleasant.

"Because I do not take insults kindly?"

"No, because nothing but vinegar flows from your lips."

"Then I shall spare you further ridiculous conversation," Portia retorted, hot indignation stinging her cheeks.

He chuckled again, the sound rich and throaty as he pulled her even closer. His hand shifted, sliding beneath her cloak to splay against her rib cage indecently. A circumstance she might have objected to could she break her self-imposed vow and speak. Instead, she endured his nearness in silence and denied that her heart raced at the feel of his big hand resting scant inches from her breast—denied that his touch sent waves of heat through her freezing body.

"Something tells me you're unaccustomed to holding your tongue," he murmured, and his hand moved again, closer to her breast. "I don't mind. Talk. I enjoy listening to your voice. So proper. Clipped but soft. Almost breathless, like your corset's laced too tight. You know, I could loosen it for you."

"You—you beast!" Portia cried.

Other **AVON ROMANCES**

SOPHIE JORDAN

Too Wicked To Tame

AVON BOOKS
An Imprint of HarperCollinsPublishers

AVON BOOKS
An Imprint of HarperCollins*Publishers*
10 East 53rd Street
New York, New York 10022-5299

Copyright © 2007 by Sharie Kohler
ISBN: 978-0-06-112226-2
ISBN-10: 0-06-112226-2
www.avonromance.com

First Avon Books paperback printing: March 2007

Avon Trademark Reg. U.S. Pat. Off. and in Other Countries, Marca Registrada, Hecho en U.S.A.
HarperCollins® is a registered trademark of HarperCollins Publishers.

Printed in the U.S.A.

10 9 8 7 6 5 4

For Carlye, my most precious friend—words are not enough.

Acknowledgments

A special thanks goes to all the players on my team: Carlye, Christy, Ane, Leslie, and Tera. As always, you were there for me every step of the way. A bit of each of you lives in these pages. Thanks for pushing me, ladies.

Too Wicked To Tame

Chapter 1

"**I**'m going to carve out his lying tongue," Lady Portia Derring bit out as she surveyed the stretch of empty road nestled among thick, spiny gorse and rocky hills, desperate to catch a glimpse of her errant driver.

An icy wind pulled at her bonnet. Her fingers, stiff and aching from the cold, clung to the frayed ribbons dangling beneath her chin. Even horribly out of fashion, the straw confection was her best bonnet and she wasn't inclined to lose it.

"Looking out that window again?" Nettie asked.

Falling back against the seat, Portia heaved a

1

sigh and announced, "We're stranded. John's not coming back."

"He'll be back," her maid replied with a decided lack of worry as she stretched her generous curves along the threadbare squabs. "Take a nap."

Portia frowned at Nettie. "And let highwaymen take us unaware? Splendid idea, that."

Nettie yawned widely, offering Portia a view of the tonsils far back in her throat. She closed and opened her mouth several times with a vulgar smacking sound before adding, "What's got your nose out of joint?"

Portia gestured about them at the motionless carriage, a feeling of frustration sweeping over her. "In case you failed to notice, we've been abandoned by our sot of a driver." She nodded to the window where the sky deepened to a smoky purple. "I don't relish the idea of spending the night in this rickety carriage."

Nettie lifted a reddish brow and glanced out the window. Portia followed her gaze, eyeing the craggy limestone terrain, then the dark clouds scuttling across the sky, distracted at the sight of such raw beauty. Miles away from civilization. From family and words like duty, responsibility— *marriage*. Her heart lifted, her precarious situation suddenly not feeling so calamitous. The invisible band about her chest loosened, allowing her to take her first easy breath in years.

Nettie clucked her tongue. "You really did it this time for the ol' bird to send you all the way out here."

Portia flicked a piece of lint off her blue merino skirt and stifled the retort that burned on her tongue. "I don't know what you mean," she lied. "I've done nothing. Nothing at all."

"Nothin'," her cheeky maid snorted. "That's about the gist of it. Five years of *nothin'*. Well, your time's run out." She nodded as though pleased. "I heard what your grandmother said."

"Listening at keyholes again?" Portia accused.

"Either you choose or they will. And if you ask me, they should have put an end to your contrary ways long ago."

"No one's asking you," Portia snapped.

Shrugging, the round-cheeked maid looked out the window again, granting Portia a meager moment of peace before demanding, "Ain't there rich enough nabobs in Town? Hardly seems possible any swell lives in this godforsaken land." Shaking her coppery head, Nettie turned to glare at her in a way that left no doubt whom she held responsible for their ejection from Town. "Tell me we're at least almost there."

"John didn't say, but we must be near." Not that her driver had said much before staggering down the road, his vow to return within the hour echoing hollowly even then. Especially when issued through gin-laced breath. "I should have taken the mail coach," she muttered.

Not that Grandmother would have permitted such a thing. A Derring never resorted to public transport. No matter how desperate. There were appearances to be kept, after all. A Derring must not *appear* destitute. Even if they happened to be.

"Bet you wish you'd chosen one of those swells back in Town now, eh?"

Portia stifled a grimace and looked out the window again, careful not to reveal her decided lack of regret. What was one suitor to fend off when she was accustomed to the dozens foisted on her by her family?

She gazed out through parted frayed curtains. The sight of the bleak land, both majestic and deprived, wild with gorse and wind-ruffled heather, washed over her like a balm to the soul. It stirred something deep inside her—in a hidden, secret place that hadn't felt anything in years. The moor was a far cry from the drawing rooms of the *ton* and she was heartily glad for it.

"Not especially," she replied, inhaling clean air kissed by the lips of a vanishing winter. A chance to get away was a rare treat, a much appreciated holiday. Especially when her greatest wish was to travel, to taste the freedom and adventure her mother experienced everyday.

Being forced to entertain the attentions of a new

suitor didn't matter much. Not when it meant escape from the tedium of another Season, from the auction block, from her family's nagging. From a pervading sense of isolation—of holding her breath and waiting, watching, searching every room with senseless hope filling her chest.

Even missing her mother, Portia could understand what drove her to depart for lands unknown. The hot breath of ruin didn't reach so far as Italy, Greece, Spain, or whichever country her mother currently called home.

Portia closed her eyes in one long blink and did her best to shake off the fetters of her world, to let the irons drop and pretend that this was a holiday of her own choosing and not just another foisted courtship.

"Enough of this," Portia announced, arranging her bonnet and repositioning her hatpin through the straw with a determined twist.

"Where you off to?"

"To find help." Portia grasped the latch and pushed the door open. Like an animal lying in wait, the wind attacked the door, whipping it inward again. She caught it with the palm of her hand and pushed, grunting. "Someone must. We can't rely on John." Gathering her skirts in one hand, she added, "You're welcome to come. A brisk walk might energize you."

"I'll be staying here where it's warm and dry,

thank you very much." With a sniff, Nettie curled up on the squabs, heedless of arranging her skirts to cover her plump, milk-white legs.

Glancing at the wild, windswept landscape surrounding them, skies darkening with every passing moment, she experienced a flash of misgiving. Suppressing the feeling, she dropped to the ground, her feet sinking like two stones in water. A wave of mud rolled its way inside her boots. Clutching her skirts high, she wrinkled her nose at the disgusting feel of sludge squishing between her toes. The wind buffeted her, whipping her cloak open and exposing her to the ravaging cold.

"S-splendid," she bit out through chattering teeth, dragging one foot, then the other, through the body-sucking muck. She could ill afford to ruin a good pair of boots. The shops on Bond Street had politely but firmly ceased extending credit to her family. New boots weren't in her near future.

"At this rate you should reach the village tomorrow," Nettie called cheerfully from the carriage window.

Shooting a glare over her shoulder, Portia increased her pace, leaving the carriage and her vexing maid behind.

Suck, drag. Suck, drag. Her lungs expanded, aching from the frigid air filling them. The thought of returning to the shelter of the carriage, to dryness, to a modicum of warmth, tempted her. Yet she did not relish spending the rest of her days trapped in a musty carriage with Nettie. And John—the wretched sot—more than likely lay facedown in a ditch somewhere. With that looming likelihood, she pulled her lips between her teeth and trudged along.

Her cloak's hem dragged behind her, slowing her already crawling pace. Lightning lit the horizon. Portia jerked to a stop. Tilting her head back, she scowled at the sky. A fat raindrop splattered on her cheek.

"Of course," she grumbled. Abandoned. Stranded. Cold. A storm was utterly foreseeable.

Then the clouds opened up.

Rain sluiced her face, obscuring her vision. Icy trails trickled down her neck and beneath her gown, leaving goose bumps in their wake. Too caught up in her misery, she assumed the sudden pounding in the air to be more thunder.

Too late, she realized the air did not shake from thunder. No, the very earth shook. Uneasiness rolled over her as icy as the rain that drenched her. She looked down at her feet as they absorbed the ground's subtle vibration.

"What the—"

Looking up, her words died in her throat.

A horse and rider rounded the bend, emerging

through the gray curtain of rain. Portia opened her mouth to scream. To cry out. But she couldn't so much as squeak. She merely stood frozen, dumbstruck, watching as death charged her.

Blood rushed to her head in a dizzying roar, mingling with the rain's furious tempo. With a choked cry, she flung her hands up—a feeble attempt to protect herself. She jerked sideways, but the mud held fast, manacles at her ankles. Unbalanced, she toppled over in a graceless heap.

Drowning in mud and rain, her gaze swept up, riveted on the massive hooves pawing the air above her. Voice trapped somewhere between her lips and her chest, she clawed fistfuls of wet earth and hauled herself backward, vaguely registering the rider's curses, his wild movements, as he pulled frantically on the horse's reins.

The horse crashed down, its deadly hooves landing inches from her, spraying her with mud. Gasping, she blinked dirty eyelashes and fixed her mud-blurred gaze on the beast's trembling legs, praying they stayed put.

The rider dismounted with a curse that lit fire to her cheeks. Lean, boot-encased legs stopped before her, braced apart as if he stood at the prow of a ship.

Her gaze slowly slid upward, assessing. Muscled thighs. Narrow hips. A broad chest that stretched on forever. Gray eyes as stormy as the sky flashing above.

Gradually, she realized his lips were moving. He was shouting. *At her.* As if *she* had been the one in error. As if *she* were to blame for his wild, reckless riding, for his total disregard for human life.

His dark slashing brows dipped into a frown. "What's wrong with you?" he thundered. "Are you dim-witted? Did you not hear me approach?"

She closed her sagging mouth with a snap. Looking at his lean, ruthless face, her temper flared. The utter gall. Not an ounce of accountability. Not a hint of contrition or apology. Not even a hand to help her to her feet. He was a primitive—a snarling beast. Totally out of control.

She eyed his clothing: buff trousers, wool brown waistcoat, black Hessians. Decent quality. Wet but clean. Mud-free. The heavy black cloak swirling about him looked deliciously warm. He twitched a riding crop against a very solid looking thigh and she couldn't help thinking he wished to use it on her.

"Come now," he coaxed with a breeziness that his storm-cloud eyes belied. "Can you not speak, little Miss Mud Pie?"

Miss Mud Pie?

Her hands fisted into the mud surrounding her, sinking deeper, indifferent to the slime infiltrating the worn cambric of her gloves and sliding thickly beneath her fingernails.

First he nearly killed her.

Now he mocked her.

It was not to be borne. Pulling her bottom lip between her teeth in a determined hiss, she launched a fistful of mud directly at his face, praying her aim proved true.

Chapter 2

The mud slapped the stranger in the cheek, splattering across his nose and mouth with a resounding smack. A lovelier sight she had never seen.

Her satisfaction, however, was short-lived. The look he leveled on her turned her blood to ice.

Panicked, certain he meant to turn the riding crop on her, she struggled to her feet. Squaring her shoulders, she smoothed her gloves, which would never again resemble their former pristine white, over drenched skirts and attempted to strike a dignified pose. To resemble a lady. Even covered head to foot in mud.

Prepared to look him dead in the eye and show him she was no cringing female, she lifted her chin. And blinked. Twice.

Her head barely topped his chin. Unease skated down her spine. She usually looked men in the eye. A definite advantage when intimidating prospective suitors. However, something told her this man did not bow to intimidation.

Wiping a broad hand over the mud obscuring the sharp planes of his face, he snarled, "What the bloody hell was that for?"

"Evening the score," she replied, stumbling back as he advanced one step. Then another. The mud-clogged road posed no difficultly for him. He moved like a panther, closing the distance between them with ease.

"Blinding me with mud accomplishes that?" He reached for her arm. Portia lurched back, jerking away from that grasping hand, and lost her balance. She toppled over. Again. An indignant squeak escaped her mouth as her bottom hit the ground with a loud smack.

He laughed. A rich, boisterous sound that rumbled in the air, mingling with the distant thunder. Scowling, she scooped up a handful of mud, pausing when he wagged a finger. "Don't." The single word dropped into the air like a heavy stone, freezing her.

Thick mud dripped from her fingers as she considered him. From the hard, ruthless look of him, she had no doubt he would retaliate if she hurled mud at his face a second time. The man looked like a pirate. Or a brigand. She shrank further into her wet cloak at the possibility.

"An apology," she demanded. Brigand or not, she refused to back down without the courtesy owed her.

"For what?" he snorted, crossing his arms over his chest. "You're at fault here. The one walking in the middle of the road with your head—"

"Me?" she cut in, pushing to her feet. "Are you mad?"

A change came over him. The barest stiffening. He drew a deep breath that expanded his broad chest. A beat of silence fell, held, stretched as his eyes glittered down at her. Portia waited, breath suspended, staring up at him through the screen of rain.

At last, he replied, his words caustic, a veritable sneer, "If I'm not already, then I'm well on my way."

Suppressing a tremor of nervousness, she retorted, "Well, no doubt . . . for how sensible is it to ride hell-bent around a bend with nary a thought for anyone who might be in your path?"

The muscles along his jaw knotted dangerously. Rain rolled down his face, washing away the last remnants of mud, but his hard gaze never blinked. "No more insensible than someone fool-ish enough to walk in the middle of the road in such inclement weather."

"Rest assured, it's not by choice. My carriage is mired in mud down the road."

The corners of his well-shaped mouth pulled into a frown as he looked beyond her. The wind whipped long strands of hair against his face and neck. The dark, gleaming strands reminded her of a sea lion's pelt.

"Where's your driver?" he demanded.

"I haven't the foggiest notion." Portia lifted her impossibly heavy skirts and adopted her grand-mother's most officious tone. The one she used when addressing someone beneath her dignity. "Now, if you would be so kind as to step aside, I should like to reach the village before nightfall."

He made no effort to oblige so Portia stepped around him and began sludging forward again.

"Wait," he commanded. His large hand clamped down on her arm.

Portia glanced in surprise at the hard fingers encircling her arm. They were surprisingly long and elegant, blunt-tipped. She felt the burn of them through her cloak, into her very skin. Men didn't touch her. Not voluntarily. None presumed such familiarity. She saw to that. Of course this stranger didn't know that, didn't know the rules that governed her.

Looking up into his face, she swallowed a small frission of alarm at how truly alone they were. How very much at his mercy she was. Swiping at the drooping brim of her bonnet, she said in her firmest voice, "Unhand me, sir."

The sound of rain hitting earth and rock increased at that moment, a dull roar that filled their lapse in conversation. His image grew blurry—apart from his eyes. They glowed preternaturally, penetrating the gray screen of rain. "You're a fierce thing, aren't you, little Miss Mud Pie?" his disembodied voice taunted.

Fierce? Never had anyone described her as fierce. Capricious. Eccentric. Even odd. But never fierce. Portia supposed she might be a little like her old dragon of a grandmother after all—perish the thought.

"You can't walk to the village in this storm." His head dipped, assessing her, and she shuddered to think of the picture she made. Almost on cue, the wind picked up, nearly knocking her sideways.

He sighed and seemed to reach some sort of decision. Squaring those broad shoulders of his, he said, "I'll take you there."

"You?"

She blinked against the relentless rain and heard the smile in his voice as he replied, "Yes, me."

Swiping again at her recalcitrant bonnet, she

lifted her chin. "Why would I accept a ride from a self-proclaimed madman?"

His smile slipped and the hard look returned to his eyes. "Because you'll reach the village in ten short minutes rather than the week it will take you on foot."

Hmm. Sound logic for a madman. And truthfully, Portia was too miserable to refuse. Anything to reach shelter. Warmth. Dryness. Ground that didn't shift and sink beneath her feet.

"Very well," she declared, moving past him.

His stallion, hands taller than any horse she had ever mounted, eyed her suspiciously as she approached. Portia stopped, eyed the great beast in turn and wondered how she might mount without the aid of a step. An accomplished horsewoman, she could usually mount unassisted, but not with wet, muddied skirts weighing her down and the spongy ground sucking hungrily at her boots.

She stepped closer, reaching for a handful of sable mane to pull herself atop. The stallion had other ideas. He dipped his head toward her with teeth bared. She jerked back, only barely avoiding the snapping jaws.

"Beast," she cried, shocked and absurdly offended.

Hard hands grasped her waist and lifted her, securing her sideways atop the horse before she had a chance to protest. He swung up behind her, draping her legs over his thighs as if she were nothing more than a cloth doll to be neatly maneuvered.

Heat rushed her face. Settled snugly against him, she recovered her tongue. "W-what are you doing?" she sputtered. Who would have imagined that she, Lady Portia Derring, renowned bluestocking and spinster, would find herself in such an improper position? And with such a virile man?

The stallion craned his neck and tried to take another hunk out of her leg.

"Stop that, you devil," she hissed.

"Iago doesn't care for females."

Iago? How fitting. The beast would be named after one of Shakespeare's most villainous characters.

"Well, would you mind having a word with him?" she asked as she dodged another nip. "Before he cripples me?"

"No need for that," he replied.

Portia opened her mouth to disagree, but he kicked the horse into motion, forcing Iago's attention away from making a meal of her leg. The sudden movement also sent her rocking against him. He looped an arm around her waist.

"What are you doing?" she demanded.

"Delivering you safely to the village." His warm

breath fanned her ear. A bolt of awareness shot through her and her breath caught. "Never let it be said I'm not a gentleman."

She snorted. A gentleman would not ride in the midst of a storm with no thought for life and limb. Nor would he toss her about as if she were a sack of grain. Nor press himself so intimately against her.

True, he possessed a fine horse and cultured speech, but his manners were coarse, his clothing plain, his hair too long, and there was something uncivilized about him. Something raw, elemental, as wild as the rough-hewn land surrounding them. More than likely he was a rustic squire unaccustomed to polite society.

Biting her lip, she told herself not to behave like a simpering miss. The type she rolled her eyes at every Season. Of course she would have to sit closely to him in order to share a mount. Desperate circumstances called for desperate measures.

Closing her eyes, she tried to ignore the firm chest at her back, the hard thighs beneath her. The solid arm holding her close. A slow trembling stole over her.

"You're cold," his husky voice sounded in her ear, and he drew her closer, folding her into him and wrapping his cloak about the two of them, cocooning them together. Far more courtesy than she would have ascribed to the snarling wild man he had first appeared. "You have no business being out in this weather."

She stiffened in his arms, not caring for his chastisement.

"You could catch ill," he added.

"I didn't *plan* on getting caught in a storm," she retorted, "but I'm hardly a frail creature." Indeed not. She stood taller than most of her would-be suitors, was only thin and lacking in feminine curves—as Grandmother frequently criticized. "I have a healthy constitution. A bit of rain won't hurt me."

"In case you haven't noticed, this is more than a bit of rain."

"Wet and miserable as I am, it's hard to ignore."

"Then you should have—"

She twisted her head around, snapping, "I don't need a lecture from someone who can't exercise simple caution when riding his horse."

Portia faced front again, leaning forward as much as she could, too annoyed to let herself relax against his chest.

Silence fell. No sound could be heard save the loud pelting of rain and sucking sound of hooves as they lifted from the quagmire beneath them.

He tugged at her waist, forcing her back against

him. "What's your name?" he asked, his voice grudging, as if he resented asking, resented wanting to know.

She answered in an equally grudging voice, "Portia."

No more than that. No need for him to know that a duke's daughter sat on his lap. Soon they would part company, never to set eyes on each other again.

"Portia," he replied slowly, drawing out her name as if he tasted it on his tongue. "Different."

"My mother named me after Portia in *Merchant of Venice* . . . or *Hamlet*, depending what day you spoke with her . . . and her mood . . . and whether or not I happened to be in her favor at the time." She couldn't keep the bitterness from creeping into her voice. Thoughts of her mother did that to her, even when she willed them not to. Frowning, she wondered why she had volunteered so much to him. An uncouth stranger.

"Not from these parts, are you, Portia?" he asked dryly.

Ignoring his bold usage of her name, she suppressed her impulse to ask after his name and turned her gaze to the rain-soaked terrain, both wild and beautiful.

"No," she answered. Not that she would mind staying. Even awash in rain, this rugged land appealed to her. But this was no holiday. She had a potential husband to scare off—a task at which she particularly excelled. She need only open her mouth and expound at length upon whatever text she currently read. Be it an ancient treatise on Roman engineering, a dramatic work of Sophocles, or the latest commentary on female rights, no one chased away a prospective suitor better.

"London?" he asked, his voice knowing, derision lacing his gravelly tones.

"Obvious, is it?"

"You're not like chits in these parts."

If she had been inclined, she could have told him she wasn't like London ladies either. Vowing never to be auctioned off in matrimony like a cow at market set her apart from the rest of the herd. Not such a difficult task, she had discovered. No one wanted an impoverished bluestocking—even one with an excellent pedigree.

"Indeed," she replied stiffly, certain he did not mean to compliment her.

"Indeed," he echoed, laughter lacing his voice. "Never met someone so haughty."

"Haughty?" she cried. "That's rich. Especially coming from an arrogant brute like you."

"God, you are a shrew," he chuckled against her ear, the sound oddly pleasant.

"Because I do not take insults kindly?"

"No, because nothing but vinegar flows from your lips."

"Then I shall spare you further ridiculous conversation," she retorted, hot indignation stinging her cheeks.

He chuckled again, the sound rich and throaty as he pulled her even closer. His hand shifted, sliding beneath her cloak to splay against her rib cage indecently. A circumstance she might have objected to could she break her self-imposed vow and speak. Instead, she endured his nearness in silence and denied that her heart raced at the feel of his big hand resting scant inches from her breast— denied that his touch sent waves of heat through her otherwise freezing body.

Iago trudged along at a sedate pace, stumbling occasionally in one of the many water-filled ruts in the road. Distant cracks of thunder shook the air. The din agitated Iago, eliciting distressed whinnies.

Behind her, his deep voice hummed gentle murmurings to the volatile stallion and did strange things to her insides.

"Something tells me you're unaccustomed to holding your tongue."

She jumped, taken aback at the sound of that velvet voice addressing her and not the horse.

"I don't mind. Talk," he murmured and his hand moved again, closer to her breast, his thumb almost grazing the underside. "I enjoy listening to your voice. So proper. Clipped but soft. Almost breathless, like your corset's laced too tight."

Portia sputtered. Heat scalded her face all the way to the roots of her hair. He dared make mention of her undergarments? Her outrage mounted as he added, "You know, I could loosen it for you."

"You—you beast!" she cried, struggling out of the shelter of his cloak.

Iago stepped into another rut and they plunged off balance. Portia shrieked and slid off his lap, nearly plummeting to the ground below. A firm arm wrapped around her middle. She dug her fingers into a taut, straining forearm.

"Stop your caterwauling," his harsh command rang out. "You're frightening the bloody horse!"

Biting her lip against another scream, her fingers clawed their way up his forearm to his biceps, desperate to keep from falling. Suddenly the horse reared.

And she was falling. With him. Her fingers didn't release their death grip on his arm as they tumbled to the ground in a tangle of limbs.

Chapter 3

For a long moment, Portia didn't move a muscle—couldn't. Partly due to the large man sprawled atop her, and partly due to the shock of finding herself submerged in mud. Again. At this point, she wondered if she would ever be clean and dry again. Muck coated every last inch of her.

Turning her head, she watched the horse flee down the road, reins whipping wildly in the wind. "Where's he going?"

"Home."

"Home," she echoed, looking up at him.

His face hovered above hers, the chill of his ice-gray eyes the only color in his mud-covered face. If possible, those eyes made her even colder.

"Yes, several miles from here," he bit out.

"Oh, brilliant," she exclaimed. "Splendid horse you have there!"

"Nothing is wrong with Iago."

"No?" she countered, feeling herself start to shake with rage. "He abandoned us."

"With a shrieking witch on his back, I can hardly blame him."

"What kind of horse can't withstand a little noise? A first-rate mount can ride into battle with cannons firing—"

"A cannon, he could tolerate. A loud-mouthed shrew is another matter."

Chest heaving, she shoved at the big body covering hers. The action forced her deeper into the wet, yielding earth. "Care to get off me?"

"With pleasure," he spit out, pushing to his feet.

It was with some satisfaction that she saw he was as filthy as she. He speared her one last fulminating look before turning and stalking away.

"Where are you going?" she shouted, struggling gracelessly to her feet—nearly falling back down when her right ankle collapsed under her weight. Her mouth opened wide on a silent cry. She quickly shifted the bulk of her weight to her left ankle and hopped until she steadied herself.

"The blacksmith can loan me a horse," he called over his shoulder without breaking stride.

Lifting her impossibly heavy skirts, she drew a deep breath and stepped forward—or rather, limped—determined to keep up and not humiliate herself by falling again. Not an easy task. Especially with her ankle throbbing inside her boot.

Wincing, she stifled her pain and worked hard to keep up. Her breath fell hard and fast as she moved her legs. The throb in her ankle intensified, each footfall a bolt of agony.

His figure grew farther and farther away. *He was leaving me.*

Her eyes burned. A deep sob welled up in her chest and she fought to keep up. She gulped air, determined to swallow back the tears. *I will not cry. I will not cry.*

And in that moment, she felt crushed, beaten by life—her family, the mother whose letters were rare and few between, the cloud of poverty that perpetually hung over her, shadowing her every move and breath. And now him. A brute that didn't care if he left her to drown in mud and rain.

The sting in her eyes intensified. Yet she'd be damned if she cried. If she succumbed to weakness. She stopped abruptly. Tilting her face to the sky, she let the deluge of rain wash over her, cooling her burning emotions.

"Keep up," he called.

She dropped her head to glare at his back, wanting to lash out. To hurt. To weep uncontrollably. And that, she absolutely refused to do.

Instead, she dropped where she stood in the middle of the road like a heavy stone sinking to the bottom of a riverbed. Uncaring of her muddied gloves—what part of her wasn't covered in filth?—she buried her face in her hands.

And laughed.

Brittle, shaky laughter rose from deep in her chest. Laughter that she knew could change at any given moment and swing into humiliating tears if she weren't careful. Busy on keeping those tears at bay, she did not hear him approach. Through parted fingers, she saw his boots stop in front of her. Her chest stilled, all laughter gone. With an odd sort of detachment, she studied the rivulets of water running down the gleaming length of his boots.

Dropping her hands, she scanned the long length of his body, her eyes stopping at his face, expecting to see condemnation there—unforgiving reproof for being weak and lagging so far behind.

He gazed down at her blankly, not a flicker of emotion on his stone-carved face. Sighing heavily, he leaned down and reached for her arm.

She slapped at his hand.

Frowning, he went for her arm again.

Again she slapped at his offending hand—this time with more force.

"I can make my own way," she grumbled, determined to accept nothing from him. "Go on without me."

His nostrils flared, his lips flattening into an unrelenting line. A warning she had no time to heed. In one swift, fluid motion, he bent, slid an arm under her knees, and swept her up into his arms as if she weighed a feather. Shocked, she didn't even struggle as he cradled her close to his chest. His long-legged strides cut through the road with seeming ease.

"I can walk," she muttered, holding her arms awkwardly in front of her, wondering where to put them.

"Of course you can," he returned, not looking at her, simply staring ahead, unblinking against the steady fall of rain.

Giving up, she slid one arm around his broad shoulder, her fingers resting lightly at his nape, beneath the too-long strands of hair. His dark hair fell over her fingers and she fought the urge to stroke the rain-slicked strands. Her other hand relaxed against his chest, where the steady thud of his heart beat against her palm.

She studied his profile for a moment, her anger fading as he carried her forth so stalwartly. Suddenly he looked down, his eyes locking with hers. This close she could see the dark ring of blue surrounding his gray irises. Something strange and foreign swelled to life in her chest, trapping her breath deep in her lungs like a bird caged—just as those intense eyes of his trapped her.

Perhaps he wasn't such a brute. A brute would have left her behind instead of sweeping her into his arms like some kind of hero from Arthurian legend.

She gave herself a hard mental shake, reminding herself that those were legends, stories her mother had read to her as a girl. Real knights in shining armor existed only in fairy tales.

A relieved breath escaped her chest when the village came into sight—an assortment of several thatch-roofed cottages, a small stone church, a blacksmith's barn and a large two-story inn that leaned ever so slightly to the left. The cottages, hunkered shapes that seemed to tremble in the biting wind, lured her like a first edition copy of Mrs. Wollstonecraft's *A Vindication on the Rights of Woman.*

The prospect of the warm fires burning behind those meager walls brought home her misery. She'd give anything to be sitting warm and snug in front of a fire, a book in her lap, a steaming cup of tea and plate of honeyed scones within reach.

A clanging carried over the storm, coming from the blacksmith's barn at the edge of the village. They followed the noise, turning full force into the wind. The sharp air lashed at her, stabbing her face and throat. She couldn't imagine how he must feel. He had carried her the distance without complaint, never breaking stride.

Her eyes smarted, tears seeping from the corners and streaming her cheeks, blending with the rain coating her face. She tucked her chin to her chest and averted her face, burying her nose against his chest, seeking his heat, the shelter of his body. Shivering, she burrowed deeper against his chest, pretending not to notice the hard body holding her so securely even as she sank against him, hungering for his warmth.

He carried her beneath a jutting portico. Still holding her in his arms, he stood still for a long moment as if he doubted whether she could stand and support herself.

"I can stand," she murmured, moving her face away from his chest.

Nodding, he released her legs. Her body slid the length of his in agonizing slow degrees. The sensation of her breasts crushed to his hard chest sent a lick of heat curling low in her belly. Flustered at such an unfamiliar sensation she flushed and quickly stepped back.

Though sheltered from the worst of the wind and rain, she felt cold without his nearness, bereft. He kept one hand on her arm, their only remaining contact. From beneath her lashes, she studied the hard, shadowed line of his jaw and accepted what she had tried so hard to ignore. He was magnificent. Even covered in filth. The most attractive man she had seen outside of a ballroom.

He reeked raw, masculine power. From the unfashionably long hair clinging to his face and throat, to the intimidating breadth of his shoulders. *If my family ever thrust a man like him at me, I might think twice before chasing him off.* Following that unbidden thought came the desperate need for distance. No man was worth the shackles of matrimony. No matter how he made her body tingle.

Even yearning for the warmth of his hand, for the burning imprint of those long fingers, she pulled free, severing all contact. He glanced down at her, lifting a dark brow.

Lips compressed, she crossed her arms and forced her attention on the stocky, flat-nosed man stepping out of the building's glowing core. He wiped grimy hands on a leather apron and nodded in greeting.

"Tom, the lady here is looking for her driver."

The blacksmith shook his head, frowning. "Haven't seen a soul since the storm blew in. Everyone's got better sense than to be out in this." His gaze raked them, his expression seeming to say, *everyone except you two fools.*

"My carriage is stuck in a ditch north of here—my maid's still inside." Probably snoring soundly, Portia thought as she lifted her reticule. "I need someone to retrieve both here. Naturally, I'll pay you for your services—"

" 'Course, Miss." The blacksmith turned and called to someone inside the barn. A young man garbed in a matching leather apron joined them. "My son and I will ride out and fetch them for you."

Portia sighed, feeling some of the tension ease out of her shoulders and neck. "Thank you."

The blacksmith gestured across the yard. "I'll find you at the inn, then?"

"Yes," she answered, already visualizing the dry taproom where she could wait and warm herself.

With a nod for the blacksmith, the man at her side took her arm and led her—cautiously, with care for her ankle—to the inn.

Once inside the nearly empty taproom, he settled her at one of the tables, the one nearest the large, crackling fireplace. Her belly rumbled at the tantalizing smells drifting from the kitchen.

She mentally counted the coins in her reticule and debated whether she could afford a hot meal. Grandmother had given her only what she deemed necessary for a journey to Yorkshire and back. Recovery and repair of a carriage had not been part of the calculation.

A few figures sat huddled over their tankards, waiting out the storm. One man lifted his head to shout in greeting, "Heath!"

Heath? Well, she had a name now. Whether she wished to or not, she would forever remember her darkly handsome rescuer by name.

"Clive," Heath greeted.

Clive snatched a knife from the scarred wood tabletop. His thick fist waved it at Heath encouragingly. "Give us a show, eh?"

Heath shook his head. "Another time."

She looked at Heath, a frown pulling her lips. He must have felt her stare. His gaze slid to hers and he shrugged. "It's just a game I played as a lad."

Portia arched an eyebrow at him, curious to see what kind of "show" the locals regarded so highly.

"C'mon," Clive bellowed.

Sighing, Heath strode across the room and plucked the knife from Clive's fist. She watched as he straddled the bench, splayed his large hand flat on the table, and proceeded to stab between each finger in a frenzied blur of movement. She jerked at each thud of the knife in the wood table, certain that he would cut his hand at any moment. Her shocked gaze lifted to his face, to the *bored* expression there.

What kind of boyhood had he led?

Finally, he stopped, and she remembered to breathe again. He rose and sent the knife slicing cleanly through the air. It landed square in the center of a faded and smoke-mottled painting above the hearth.

Clive chortled and slapped the table in approval.

"Do you have a death wish?" she demanded upon his return to their table. "Reckless riding, reckless"—she waved a hand at the table where he had conducted his perilous demonstration, groping for the appropriate words and arriving at—"knife play!"

He replied with aggravating equanimity, even as something furtive gleamed in his gaze, " 'The worst evil of all is to leave the ranks of the living before one dies.' "

She shook her head, frustrated—mystified—at the man before her who quoted Seneca.

"Ain't nothing," Clive called out. "You should see him climb Skidmoor with his bare hands. In winter, too."

"Skidmoor," she echoed.

"It's just a hill," Heath explained.

"A hill?" Clive guffawed, shaking his head. "Right. More like a mountain."

He climbed mountains in the dead of winter?

"Heath," a serving girl squealed from across the taproom.

Portia eyed the woman's scandalously low bodice and instinctively drew her cloak tighter about her shoulders as if she could hide her lack of similar attributes.

"Mary, you're looking well." Heath grinned in a way that made him look suddenly young, boyish. Not nearly so intimidating as the stranger from the road.

Mary sashayed across the room, rolling her hips in what Portia felt certain to be a practiced walk. "Better now that you're here," she purred.

With no thought or regard to her presence, he grinned wickedly at the serving girl, his teeth a flash of white in his sun-browned face. How his skin managed to brown in this sunless country baffled her. No doubt further evidence that he was more devil than man.

The curvy serving girl lowered herself into his lap, tossed her plump arms around his neck and then, for all the world to see, planted an open-mouthed kiss on him.

Portia looked away, embarrassment stinging her cheeks. She studied her hands in her lap, ran her thumbs nervously over the backs, over the cold, puckered gooseflesh of her exposed wrists.

Unable to suppress her morbid curiosity, she sucked in a breath and lifted her eyes to observe the unseemly display.

Her gaze collided with his storm-gray eyes.

He watched *her*—Portia.

Heat flooded her face to be caught staring, as if

she were interested, as if she cared who he kissed. His ravenous wolf's stare never wavered from her face. Amusement gleamed in the gray depths as he kissed the female atop his lap.

She wrenched her gaze away and twisted her fingers in her lap until they ached.

Do not watch. Do not watch. Do not grant him the satisfaction of knowing he fascinates you.

Unable to stop herself, she snuck another look, compelled, beckoned by the magnetic pull of his taunting gaze. His eyes gleamed wickedly, ensnaring her, whispering her name. She gawked as he trailed a hand over Mary's plait, watched as his long, tapered fingers unraveled the rope of hair, twining the tendrils in his elegant, blunt-tipped fingers.

Her stomach clenched and knotted. Something hot and unfamiliar ignited in her blood as she watched him kiss the woman with slow thoroughness, all the while devouring *her* with his eyes.

Was she such a wanton? Her quickening pulse seemed answer enough. Blood rushed to her ears, blocking out the steady patting of rain on the thatched roof, the hiss and pop of the fire in the hearth, the sound of her own excited breath. She moistened her lips with a flick of her tongue and his gray eyes darkened, twin beads of jet as they followed the movement, scanning her face, then dropping to the rise and fall of her chest beneath her soaked clothes.

She lifted her chin and tried to convey her contempt, her absolute disgust at their vulgar display—that she was a lady unmoved in the presence of such wickedness. Yet her breath betrayed her, falling fast and hard from her lips. Her cheeks felt aflame and she worried that color flooded her face.

"Mary," bellowed a man, presumably the establishment's proprietor. "Stop molesting the customers and get in the kitchen, girl."

Mary ended the kiss, a cat's satisfied smile on her face—as if she had just feasted on a bowl of cream. Wiping her lips with the back of her hand, she sent one last glance Heath's way before departing.

Heath rose to his feet, eyes glittering like embers as he looked down at her. Her eyes dropped to his mouth, moist from the kiss of another woman. Her pulse leapt and she looked away, her gaze flitting about the room like a bird looking for a place to land. His boots slid over the dirt-packed floor, scraping to a stop in front of her. She trained her gaze on those soiled boots, not daring to look up at that face, his dark good looks, the heated gaze that for some reason made her squeeze her thighs together beneath her skirts.

He bent, his cheek nearly brushing hers. She jerked and pulled her shoulders back. She stared at him in alarm, feeling like prey trapped in his fixed stare.

A slow smile curved his lips. Then his head dipped. His cheek grazed hers, the stubble on his hard jaw scratchy, sparking a fire in her blood. She bit her lip to stop from crying out, determined that he not see how he affected her. The male musk of him filled her nostrils. Rain, wind, the scent of the moors—of gorse growing wild on rocky hills.

"Did you like that?" he breathed into her ear, his voice sliding over her skin like velvet, igniting a lick of heat low in her belly. "Care to try it?"

She drew a shuddering breath and shook her head fiercely. The image of *her* on his lap, his hand on *her*, flashed through her head, scandalizing her, horrifying her. Thrilling her.

He placed her lips next to his ear and she ceased to breathe. Gathering her composure tightly about her, she replied in her starchiest tone, "I'd rather kiss a pig." She pulled back several inches to measure the effect of her words.

His lips curved in a lopsided grin.

Scowling, she added, "But then, that's what you are, sir. A rutting pig."

He chuckled, the sound deep and dangerous, spiraling through her body like warm sherry.

"Jealous?" His hot breath fanned against her sensitive ear, making her stomach somersault. He cupped the side of her face, his work-roughened palm firm against her cheek. With a forcefulness that stole her breath, he forced her face closer, his fingers sliding and curling around her nape.

Lips, surprisingly gentle, brushed the swirls of her ear as he talked. "You know, I imagined I was kissing your mouth, imagined your tongue tangling with mine."

Ignoring the leap of her pulse, she snapped, "Words that no doubt seduced many a dim-witted maid."

"Not so many," he murmured, his thumb sliding over the curve of her cheek, the line of her jaw, stopping at her mouth. "You'd be surprised."

His feverish gaze fixed on her lips. As if testing its fullness, he stroked her bottom lip. Heat pooled low in her belly and her legs trembled. Somehow she found the strength to bring her hands up to his chest. Ignoring the breadth and firmness beneath the soaked fabric of his shirt, she shoved with all her might.

He didn't budge. She could have been shoving at a boulder.

"Move," she commanded.

He stared down at her for a long moment.

"Move," she repeated, her jaw aching with tension.

"Of course." He stepped back, hands aloft, a crooked smile on his lips.

She surged off the bench, every instinct demanding escape. Even if it meant heading back into the storm. Better than suffering the storm that raged here, between them. A hairsbreadth separated them, and from the heat in his eyes, he had no intention of granting her the space she desired.

"I know what you are," she hissed.

That crooked smile deepened. "Do tell."

"You're a wicked man. A bounder, a—" she stopped, swallowed and continued in a more even tone. "You think to toy with me as though I were some besotted girl happy for the *reward* of your attentions."

Still wearing that wicked grin, he ran a burning trail down her cheek with the tip of his finger. "An hour alone with me and I think I could turn you into a besotted girl happy for my attentions."

"You're disgusting," she spat, fighting the full-body tremble his words produced.

The brute was uncivilized, an absolute primitive. No man had ever spoken to her so coarsely, so vulgarly. Is this how a man addressed a woman he desired? The thought made her feel both hot and cold, both frightened and titillated.

Heath straightened, and with one final soul-blistering look moved off to talk to the innkeeper.

Portia stripped off her soiled gloves and held

shaking hands out to the fire, trying to slow her racing heart. Still, she couldn't stop from watching him beneath lowered lids. At the sound of his heavy tread, she looked up.

"They're preparing a room for you," his voice rumbled through the air, warming her as the fire seemed unable to do. "I explained your circumstances to the innkeeper. He'll send up your maid and things when they arrive."

Her heart jumped, panicked at the expense of a room. The few coins in her reticule wouldn't cover both lodging and the fees due the blacksmith. Annoyance flashed through her. Who was he to make arrangements on her behalf?

"No." The single word fell hard from her mouth. "That's not necessary. I need to move on this evening—"

"Impossible." He frowned and shook his head, dismissing the possibility. "You need a change of clothes before you catch a chill. A warm meal would probably do you some good, too."

Portia shook her head, slapping at the drooping brim of her bonnet. "Really, I—"

"Wet and cold are not a good combination," he said as if he were speaking to a half-wit. "Yorkshire winters aren't for the fainthearted."

Portia stiffened her spine, unsure what offended her more. His overbearing manner or his estimation of her as faint of heart. She'd have him know she had never fainted in her life, not like so many ladies she knew who never strayed far from their smelling salts.

"It's March," she retorted. "Spring."

"Not here."

The rim of her bonnet sagged again, obscuring her vision. With a growl of frustration, she yanked it off her head, uncaring that she exposed her horribly mussed hair. She was done with people telling her what to do. Family, she had to endure. This man—a stranger—she did not. No matter how handsome. No matter how her body tingled in his presence.

"I appreciate all you've done, but I no longer need your assistance."

His face hardened and the intimidating stranger from the road returned. "Very well, then. I'll bid farewell." Turning, he strode swiftly away.

Guilt stabbed at her . . . and something else she couldn't identify. Her chest tightened as she watched his retreating back. Before she could reconsider, she surged to her feet.

He was halfway across the taproom before she caught up with him. Her hand clamped down on his arm. The muscles in his arm tensed under her fingers. He twisted around to look down at her, those deeply set eyes dark, unreadable. She stared up at him, groping for words, unclear why she had pursued him.

"Yes?" he asked.

Portia stood still as stone, frozen for an interminable moment, feeling an utter fool. They were strangers. He had deposited her safely at the inn. They were done. They had no business interacting further.

"T-thank you," she whispered, pausing to swallow, fighting the impulse to look away, to hide from his watchful gaze. "For your help. I did not mean to sound . . . ungrateful."

Portia bit her lip. Her brother would say good manners weren't required from her. That this man's assistance was her due as a Derring. But she couldn't let him go without some kind of acknowledgment.

Opening her mouth, she thought to explain the true reason she could not stay overnight at the inn, then stopped herself. Or rather, pride stopped her. Her explanation stuck in her throat.

A strange light entered his eyes, making her heart pound. Those gray eyes darkened—polished onyx, gliding over her, looking at her in such a way that her blood burned in her veins. He took his time eyeing her muddied person and disheveled hair before returning to her face with a smoldering intensity.

He touched her face then. Warm fingers landed on her cheek with surprising gentleness. She couldn't shrink away. Not as she should have. Not as her mind willed her to. No. Instead she found herself leaning into his hand, turning her cheek fully into the heat of his palm.

Closing her eyes, she forgot herself and let her lips brush his skin. The texture of his palm felt velvet rough against her lips. Her tongue darted out. A quick flick just to taste him. His gasp forced her eyes wide open.

The intense look in his eyes, the way they blazed down at her, no longer gray but a dark, gleaming blue, had her staggering back, distancing herself as if she suddenly found herself in the paws of a wild jungle cat intent on devouring her.

He dropped his hand, holding it before him, staring at it for a moment, turning it over as if he had never seen it before, as if he searched for some answer, some greater truth, carved on the flesh of his hand.

When he looked up, his eyes were the cool gray of before, impassive as stone. Just a stranger.

"Stay warm, Miss Mud Pie," he murmured.

Then he was gone.

The door slammed behind him, wind rattling the crude wood length for several seconds, struggling to gain entrance. Gone with the same suddenness as his entrance into her life. His touch, his pervasive scent, the temptingly wicked man that made her tremble like a fall leaf. Gone. She couldn't help feel a pang of regret. As if she had somehow lost an opportunity. For what she could not say—or dared not.

"Miss Mud Pie," she muttered, gazing at the door for a long moment. Oddly, the nickname failed to annoy her anymore. Not in the almost tender way he had uttered it. Not after the way he had addressed her, looked at her, touched her.

She hugged herself, feeling bereft and troubled by his departure. Cold. Which was absurd. Why should she regret the departure of a stranger? A rough-mannered squire at best? For all his help, he was coarse and ill mannered . . . and made her heart slam against her breast.

Dropping her arms, she headed back to the fire, searching out a heat totally unlike the burn that he had stoked within her. Settling herself on the hard bench, she clasped her knees and waited for the fire's blaze to warm her, doing her best to forget his name, to forget him and the hot invitation in his gaze. She waited for the familiar apathy to settle over her, vowing that by tomorrow he would not even cross her mind.

Heath. Fitting. As wild and out of control as the plant teeming the undulating moorland.

Chapter 4

Heath strode outside, his body cutting through wind and rain as he attempted to block the image of pure blue eyes and long, coal black lashes. Of sweet innocence wrapped in saucy packaging. He walked faster, fleeing the inn and the acute reminder of all he could not have.

Cursing, he jerked to a stop and looked back at the inn's shadowed outline, battling the overwhelming urge to return, to see that she stayed put where it was safe and warm—to hammer at the walls of her ladylike reserve and settle her on his lap for a thorough kiss.

Good God, what was she doing about without a

proper chaperone? She didn't have to say anything for him to know that she was a lady. As blue-blooded as they came. A female as headstrong as that needed constant supervision. The little fool actually insisted on venturing out on a night like this. He only feared she might find someone willing to aid her.

Heath gave his head a violent shake. She wasn't his responsibility. And a proper lady like her damn well never would be.

He spun around and entered the blacksmith's, resisting the invisible string that seemed to connect him to the inn—to her. A few words with the blacksmith and he had a mount. Swinging atop the horse, he stared at the inn again, still feeling the infernal pull to go back inside. She hadn't wanted him to go. She hadn't said the words, but he had seen them in her eyes. He could return. Could see just how strong the walls of her reserve were built. If he were different, perhaps he would.

The old, gnawing bleakness skated through him with the slow insidiousness of a stalking predator. A bleakness he hadn't felt in years. Not since he had learned acceptance. Not since he had trained himself in forbearance. Not since he had ceased wishing for what could never be.

Della. Like a life raft in a tossing sea, her face emerged in his mind. Della would help him forget. Forget the girl that brought forth aching reminders of what could never be his. She would banish the bleakness gripping him. He would make use of her body, sink into her familiar heat and tell himself it was enough.

He urged his mount into a gallop, splashing through the village without a care for his own safety. A man like him had given up concern for his well-being long ago.

Some days he contemplated an abrupt end to it all. Not to mistake that he considered suicide. His mother chose the coward's route and he would not do the same. Yet a random accident, the result of one of his foolhardy risks, would be far kinder than the fate that awaited him.

He pushed his mount harder, determined to get far, far from the inn. And the wisp of girl inside who made him wish things were different, that he was different—not a man bound by duty, responsibility, and a curse that he could never outrun.

Portia entered the dingy taproom the following morning, her brow knitted angrily from her exchange with the innkeeper. *Horrid man*. Not an ounce of kindness.

"At least we can afford breakfast," Nettie said with far too much cheer, pressing a hand to her stomach as if to stave off hunger. "I'm starved. Can't believe you didn't allow us to eat last night."

Portia briefly closed her eyes and stretched her

neck, trying to ease the painful crick, no doubt the result of sharing a too small bed with Nettie in the drafty attic room, the cheapest accommodations to be had.

Heath had been correct. No one could be lured out into the storm last night. Especially since she did not possess coin with which to lure. As a result, Portia and Nettie had spent the night clinging to each other for warmth beneath a scratchy, threadbare blanket. After such a night, Nettie's complaints did not meet with Portia's usual tolerance.

"I explained last night—"

"Yes, yes," Nettie interrupted with a wave of her hand. Her narrowed gaze shot to Portia's wrist. "Too bad you didn't think to offer your bracelet up before. We might not have gone to bed hungry."

Portia clutched her reticule, the weight of coins a painful reminder of what she sacrificed. The idea to barter the bracelet had come to her last night as she stared blindly into the dark, sick with worry over how she would pay the innkeeper come morning.

She rubbed her now bare wrist. Her mother had sent the bauble from Italy three years ago. Portia rarely received correspondence from her mother, let alone gifts. The bracelet had been special. It had been—

Sucking in a breath, she gave her head a small

shake, blinking back the sting of tears. She would not cry over something as inconsequential as a bracelet. Mere silver and stones. Not her mother.

Portia gave the dingy taproom, meager and unwelcoming in the light of day, a sweeping glance, refusing to admit that she searched for someone in particular, hoping beyond hope that she would see *him* again. For some reason Heath had occupied her thoughts long after he left last night. Even when she had managed to fall asleep he had invaded her dreams, his wicked hands and mouth doing to her body all that his hot gaze had promised.

A foolish, disappointed sigh escaped her. No sight of him anywhere. Instead, her gaze landed on a familiar figure. She stiffened.

There, at a corner table, sat her driver, hunkered over a pint of ale.

She stormed across the room, ignoring her sore ankle, paying no heed to the dizziness that swept her from the sudden movement. "John! Where have you been?"

Blinking bleary eyes, he lifted his tankard in mock salute. "Hullo there, my lady. What you doing here?"

"Me? Me?" Portia gave no thought to her raised voice or the pain that lanced her temples, only that John sat before her sipping his ale without a care for the women in his charge—the women he had abandoned. "I ought to horsewhip you. You were supposed to fetch help and return for us *yesterday!*"

"Aye, you bloody louse. Where the hell have you been?" Nettie added as she arrived at Portia's side, at last showing some displeasure over their abandonment.

John lumbered to his feet, jerking his rumpled blue livery into some order. "No need to get your feathers up, my lady. I was on my way to collect you."

"This morning?" Nettie propped both hands on her generous hips. "Right nice of you."

John puffed out his barrel chest, his furry caterpillar eyebrows dipping together as he glared at Nettie. "Now see here, I'll not let a bit of baggage like—"

"Enough. Both of you," Portia commanded, pressing the back of her hand to first one overheated cheek, then the other. Drawing a deep, shaky breath, she ignored the way her head spun and said, "I simply want to reach Moreton Hall . . . as we should have done yesterday." She glanced at Nettie. "Forget breakfast. I want to be gone from here. Now."

For once, the two obeyed and fell in step behind her as she marched out of the inn. Clouds hung low in the sky, either remnants of yesterday's storm or a hint of more rain to come. A cold mist clung to the air and she lifted her chin, glad for it, hoping that it might cool her flushed face.

Once settled in the carriage, she leaned back on the squabs and closed her eyes.

"You feeling all right?" Nettie asked.

"Fine," Portia answered, eyes still closed. A shiver shook her, belying her words.

"You look awful."

"Good." God forbid she should appear attractive to the Earl of Moreton. He might propose.

"Welcome, Lady Portia. We've been expecting you." The Dowager Countess of Moreton glided forward, her perfectly coiffed head held high, a fat, black Persian cat tucked in one arm.

Portia blinked, finding it difficult to reconcile the graceful creature in the elegantly appointed parlor as Grandmother's girlhood friend. Both were of like age, both widows of lofty rank, both determined to see their grandchildren wed. But the similarity ended there. Lady Moreton was slim and elegant, a vision of loveliness in deep blue muslin. Portia's grandmother stuck solely to her widow's weeds, as she had for the past twenty-five years. Nothing save black bombazine hung in her wardrobe.

"Apparently you forgot to inform me we were to have company, Grandmother." The statement came from a woman sitting rigidly on a velvet chaise.

She and a younger woman occupied the chaise. The one who spoke nudged yet another Persian away from her skirts, her expression pinched as she surveyed Portia from head to toe.

Lady Moreton tossed the woman a quelling look. "Indeed, I must have forgotten to mention it, Constance."

A serene smile in place again, the countess faced Portia, keen blue eyes examining her closely. Portia recognized the inspection. Had suffered it time and time again. The critical assessment of her looks, her form, the attempt to determine whether she would satisfy as a bridal candidate.

Portia stifled a sigh, wishing she could put an end to the pretense, wishing she could open her mouth to proclaim that she would never meet the Earl of Moreton's satisfaction. It would certainly spare all involved a great deal of time. But that would never do. She had to frighten him away as she had the others. Had to appear as if she *tried* to be suitable. Her family could never know, must never suspect that she deliberately chased away her suitors. After all, she had plans. And they didn't include matrimony.

"I feel that I already know you from Robbie's letters."

Portia started. *Robbie*? Some of her shock must have shown, for Lady Moreton laughed, a rich, throaty sound so at odds with the very proper picture she made in her high-necked gown. Not a single crease in the heavily starched fabric of her dress. Not a silver blond hair out of place. In her travel-wrinkled dress and mussed hair, Portia felt tattered and untidy in comparison.

"I see that you've never heard someone refer to your grandmother as Robbie."

"No." Portia had never even heard someone use her grandmother's Christian name of Roberta.

"Forgive me. I suppose it is rather undignified." Lady Moreton led her to a brocade-covered settee and gestured for her to sit. "A habit leftover from childhood."

Portia sank down with a grateful sigh. For some reason, her legs felt weak and trembly. Lady Moreton sat beside her. The cat immediately curled up between them and set to kneading Portia's thigh with its paws. Even through her skirts, she could feel the tiny daggerlike claws.

"These are my granddaughters." Lady Moreton nodded to the two young women across from them. "Constance and Wilhelmina."

"I've so been looking forward to meeting you, Lady Portia," Wilhelmina trilled, fairly bouncing where she sat. "Please call me Mina."

Lady Moreton stroked the ear of another cat that appeared as if by magic on the arm of the settee. "Do sit still, child. We don't want Portia to think you ill-mannered."

"It would seem," Constance began in a flat voice, still nudging the cat with the toe of her slipper as it wove in and out from under her skirts, "We aren't all of us surprised by your arrival. That being the case, why not apprise me of a few items, Lady Portia? Where have you traveled from to treat us with this visit? And how long do you intend to stay?"

Treat was uttered with such derision that Portia immediately knew she had already won the disfavor of one Moreton. "From London . . . and please call me Portia." Portia left the latter question unanswered.

Constance arched a brow. "But you'll miss the Season. No doubt you wish to return soon."

Portia frowned, unsure what she had done to earn such immediate dislike. Usually it required a little time and effort on her part.

Lady Moreton cleared her throat and pinned a hard stare on her granddaughter. In that instant, Portia recognized the similarity between the countess and her grandmother, could well understand how the two had formed a bond that lasted fifty-odd years. The two termagants ran roughshod over everyone in their sphere.

"She has just arrived, Constance. Don't run our guest off so soon with your prying questions." Snapping her gaze away, she dismissed her granddaughter as she poured a cup of tea from the impeccably polished service before them. "Come, Portia, this will fortify you. What a ghastly day for travel. You wouldn't believe it's spring."

Lady Moreton's words rang inside her head, reminding her of her exchange with a certain dark-haired stranger and his quick refutation that it was not yet spring. A small smile curved her lips. She wondered if she lingered in his mind the way he lingered in hers, then gave her head a swift shake. Such thoughts were nonsense. Romantic claptrap that had no place in her life.

"Thank you, Lady Moreton." She accepted the cup and took a long sip, telling herself that the warm liquid sliding down her scratchy throat made her feel better. Wrapping her chilled fingers around the warm teacup, she tried to ignore the cat sharpening its talons on her thigh.

A crackling fire burned nearby in a hearth so large Portia could stand in it. At home, they could afford to burn no more than coals. Just the same, the luxury of those fire-burning logs did little to warm her blood.

"You must tell me all about Town," Mina encouraged, her blue eyes shining brightly.

Portia managed a weak smile. "What would you like to know?" she asked, pretending not to notice Constance's glower.

"Everything. Leave nothing out." Mina clapped her hands in delight. "Almack's, Vauxhall, the theaters . . . are the balls really splendid? Have you met our young queen? What is she like?" She scowled. "My brother won't so much as permit me to attend a local assembly. He's an absolute tyrant."

Portia raised a brow as she set her teacup down with a hand that annoyingly shook. The earl sounded like a stodgy old boor. She'd have to re-evaluate her plan for chasing him off. Diatribes on the innovations of ancient Roman road construction may not bore such a profound prig. She may need to rattle on about fashion and the latest *on dit*. Or perhaps current philosophies on female empowerment. That ought to chase off any gentleman averse to society, tonnish ways and free-thinking females.

"And don't think I've had a come-out." Mina went on to say, pressing a hand to her bosom. "Can you imagine? Twenty-one and never a Season. Why, it's barbaric."

Portia could think of countless things more barbaric than that—the poor sanitary conditions in London slums that bred cholera, yellow fever, influenza, and typhus epidemics; women selling their bodies in order to feed their starving families; children working long, exhaustive hours in unsafe foundries for miserly wages—but she held her tongue. This was neither the time nor place to air her many views on societal reform.

"That's enough, Mina," her sister said through tight lips, setting her cup down on its saucer with a sharp clink. Without looking down, Constance gave the cat at her ankles a swift kick. With a moaning meow, the ball of fur darted across the room in a streak of gray.

"Constance, stop tormenting Cleo," Lady Moreton reprimanded, turning an aggrieved look on Portia. "That one is always antagonizing my poor pets."

"My brother *is* a tyrant," Mina repeated, her pretty face scrunched in a scowl.

"We may yet sway your brother into giving you a Season. Your youth has not completely passed." Sighing, Lady Moreton looked to Portia in entreaty. "It's tragic, but my grandson has . . . set notions that have prevented him from granting his sisters their come-outs. How old were you when you made your curtsey?"

Portia wet her lips, hating to be used as an example. "Seventeen."

"And still unwed," Constance leapt to point out, her voice ringing with smug satisfaction. "See, Grandmother, a Season does not guarantee matrimony."

"I have no doubt that *you* are firmly on the shelf, Constance. But Mina?" Lady Moreton gave a swift shake of her head, her shiny sapphire-and-diamond earbobs swinging. "*She* still has prospects."

Color flooded Constance's face and Portia felt a stab of empathy. She had grown well accustomed to the veiled insult—and not so veiled. She knew firsthand how it felt to be scorned by one's family.

Lady Moreton clucked her tongue. "Don't scowl so, Constance. It ages you."

With a rueful smile at Portia, Lady Moreton selected a biscuit from the service, seemingly oblivious to having offended her granddaughter as she began tearing off pieces to feed the cat clawing Portia's thigh. Instantly, cats of all colors and size descended upon the settee. Portia swallowed back her startled cry at the invasion. *How many bloody cats did Lady Moreton possess?*

"It's all horribly unfair," Mina complained, blithely unaware as Portia busily fended off an army of felines. "Before long I, too, shall be firmly on the shelf."

Color spotting her cheeks, Constance muttered, "I'm sure Lady Portia has no wish to hear you prattle on about your life's injustices."

Mina's bottom lip pushed out in a pout as Portia dropped one skinny tabby and then another that looked to be its twin onto the carpet. "I don't mind—"

"Oh, but I do, Lady Portia." The eldest Moreton sister fixed a chilly stare on her.

Portia blinked.

"Oh, cease being such a shrew, Constance,"

Lady Moreton reprimanded over a cacophony of purring.

Portia set her cup down and pressed the back of her hand to her face, dismayed to feel sweat dotting her brow. Especially since she felt so wretchedly cold.

"Are you feeling well, Portia?" Mina leaned forward, her smooth brow wrinkling with concern. "You look a bit . . ."

"Pasty," Constance supplied.

Empathy for Constance rapidly fading, Portia confessed, "Actually, I am quite fatigued. It has been a long journey."

Lady Moreton quickly stood, cats leaping to the floor in every direction. "Of course, how rude of me to subject you to so much excitement. Let me show you to your chamber, my dear."

Portia stood, prepared to follow, when the parlor door flew open.

No. Her heart jumped to her throat and she grasped the back of a nearby chair for support at sight of *him* entering the room.

He paused a moment, eyeing the surprised tableau—most notably her—before his swift, long strides ate up the distance separating them, advancing on her like some kind of dark angel coming to wreak his vengeance.

Heath.

For the briefest, bewildered moment, she wondered why he had come looking for her. Surely he did not intend to follow through on the wicked promise of his hot gaze. Of course not. His glittering eyes held no joy at the sight of her, only grim resolve.

"What in the bloody hell are *you* doing here?"

"Heathston!" Lady Moreton exclaimed while Portia stood silently, her legs wobbly, feeling as though they might give out at any moment. "This is Lady Portia, granddaughter to my dear friend, the Dowager Duchess of Derring, and you would do well to watch your language!"

Realization washed over her, bitter as a cold wind. Heath was the Earl of Moreton. Her suitor. The man her grandmother would have her marry.

His large body loomed in the center of the room, dwarfing the dainty furniture, fripperies, and knickknacks so inherently feminine, making him all the more threatening—male, everything she remembered from the night before.

His storm gray eyes swung to Lady Moreton. "Tell me you did not send for her."

Burning heat seared Portia's cheeks and she dug her fingers into the wood of the chair, feeling a nail crack from the pressure.

"She most certainly did," Constance volunteered. "She wants you to marry her."

His gaze stabbed Portia once again, pinning her to the spot—like that knife he had flung into the painting at the inn.

"Is this all you could find, Grandmother?" His burning gaze scorched her. A sample of Hell, to be certain. "It would take a good deal more than this bit of baggage to tempt me."

Portia gasped, the biting lash of his words as effective as a whip. Even if it had been her intention to chase the earl off, it was another thing entirely to be rejected out of hand in such a humiliating fashion.

"Heathston!" Lady Moreton exclaimed, twin flags of red staining her cheeks as she looked back and forth between her grandson and Portia.

"Rot you, Heath," Mina hissed. "Can you not even pretend to be a gentleman?"

He did not so much as blink in the face of his family's censure. His silvery gaze held her hostage. A muscle in his cheek ticked dangerously. She did her level best to return his dark scowl with one of her own, but feared she only looked cross. No one could look as contemptuous and threatening as the man standing before her. His fury was palpable, searing.

"Hop in your carriage," he began, his voice low and deep as a wolf's growl, "and head straight back to wherever you came from. You'll catch no husband here."

Her rage came boiling to a head. Fury consumed her. Fury at her brother for necessitating that she marry, at her sister-in-law who pestered her to do so, at her Grandmother who sent her on this fool errand in the first place, and at the mother who long ago had promised her a different sort of life.

Most of all, she felt fury at the blackguard who stood before her. The man who yesterday had warmed her blood and filled her with never before felt longing.

Lips compressed, she nodded briskly. The movement sent the room spinning about her and she staggered back from the chair. Opening her mouth, she inhaled a steadying breath to deliver a blistering setdown. To inform the brute that nothing appealed to her more than taking her leave of his hospitality.

Unfortunately, the rush of blood to her head robbed her of speech. She shut her eyes against the spots dancing before her vision. It didn't help. Dizziness swept through her and bile rose high in her throat.

Swaying, she dimly registered exclamations as her legs buckled, and darkness rolled in.

Chapter 5

Heath stared at the girl crumpled bonelessly in his arms, his gut clenching at the sight of her ashen face. He had not been able to forget her—despite Della's most ardent efforts the night before.

Closing his eyes, he cursed beneath his breath, not sure what rattled him more. That she laid sick in his arms or that *she*—the girl he had never thought to see again—laid sick in his arms.

"Satisfied?" Mina exclaimed. "You've killed her, Heath."

"Shut up, Mina," Heath muttered, maneuvering one arm free to check for the pulse at her neck. There it was, slow and steady beneath the soft skin. He brushed the back of his hand against her brow, wincing at her fiery flesh. "She's burning up."

"Quickly, upstairs with her," Grandmother commanded.

Heath readjusted Portia in his arms. Her head fell against his chest as he took the stairs two at a time, his grandmother and sisters fast behind, chattering nonstop.

He proceeded to the Rose room, knowing Grandmother would have sent her things to the most lavish guest chamber.

Mina jumped ahead to open the door.

A copper-haired woman froze amid unpacking luggage, demanding, "What have you done to her?"

Heath smiled wryly. The maid, he presumed.

"Your mistress has fainted," he explained, laying her on the bed.

"Fainted?" The buxom maid murmured, suspicion in her voice as she eyed him up and down. "She isn't the swooning type."

"I imagine not," he replied, recalling her saucy manners from yesterday. "I rather suspect her fever has something to do with it."

"Fever," the maid exclaimed, wringing her

hands. "Oh, the old dragon will have my head if she up and dies."

"And that would be the real tragedy," Mina commented, nodding in mock seriousness.

"She's not going to die," Heath growled, annoyed at the maid's histrionics. Turning, he spied the housekeeper hovering near the door. "Mrs. Crosby. Would you send someone to fetch Dr. Manning?"

"Aye, my lord."

As the housekeeper bustled out of the room, he faced the maid again. "Can I trust you to see Lady Portia into her nightgown?" He motioned to her still form. "She'll need out of her corset immediately."

"Course," the maid bobbed her head and moved toward the wardrobe.

Heath ignored his grandmother's sniff of disapproval at his mention of a corset. Trust his grandmother to get her sensibilities offended at a time like this.

With one last look at the girl stretched out on the bed, he left the room so that the maid could attend Portia in private, and he could struggle to make sense of his spinning thoughts.

His grandmother followed fast on his heels, not about to let him escape so easily. "As soon as she awakens, I expect you to apologize," she demanded.

Heath felt a flash of annoyance at her automatic

assumption that Portia would awaken. People perished every year from fevers and agues. Her large blue eyes, her milky skin, her slimness . . . all hinted at frailty, weakness.

He stopped in the hall and swung around to confront his grandmother. "If anyone owes her an apology, it is you. You're the one who dragged her halfway across the country. And for nothing. You know my position. I will not marry. Ever. Accept it."

Before she could respond, he whipped around and stormed off, too angered to abide the sight of her. For years, she had pestered him, tossing every eligible young lady in the district at him in the hopes that he would marry. But this? He shook his head. This time she went too far.

He wouldn't be his grandmother's pawn. No matter that he found the girl strangely compelling, no matter that she had lingered in his thoughts longer than she should have. Longer than any woman before.

He had responsibilities. Responsibilities that far outweighed his grandmother's desires. Or his own.

Chapter 6

⌒⌒◦∽⌒⌒

Portia opened her eyes and blinked against the invasion of light. She stretched her hands out at her sides, luxuriating in the feel of soft sheets. Looking up, she studied a swath of rich plum-colored damask above her and tried to sort her scattered thoughts. Slowly, she sat up, her gaze sweeping over a large chamber dappled in soft light.

"What are you doing? Back down with you." Nettie pushed her back into the soft mattress.

"What happened?"

"You swooned."

"I never swoon," Portia denied, prepared to

argue further, but stopped suddenly as memory flooded her.

Heath's face swam before her like something out of a dream. Stark good looks. Eyes that glittered gray one moment and black the next. Hair dark as sin, long enough to tangle her fingers in—

Portia halted her wayward thoughts with a swift shake of her head. He should have stayed in her dreams. She had planned to keep the memory of him there—the wickedly handsome stranger who rode like Satan set loose, who knife-played for sport and climbed mountains in the dead of winter, who scandalized her with hot words whispered against her ear.

Only her dream had turned to the stuff of nightmares.

Her anonymous rescuer was none other than the earl her grandmother wanted her to wed. She shook her head, trying to chase away her ridiculous sense of betrayal.

Hysterical laughter bubbled up in her throat. Chasing him off wouldn't be a problem. Not when he wanted her gone.

Sitting up again, she flung back the thick counterpane, humiliation stinging her cheeks as she recalled his wretched treatment of her. "Nettie, fetch my clothes."

"I'll do no such thing. The doctor said—"

"A physician was here?"

"Yes. He said you needed to stay abed until you're well."

Portia shook her head fiercely, an image of Heath's hard features flashing in her mind. In no way would she stay a minute longer under his roof. "I feel better now. Let's be on our way."

Nettie opened her mouth, but Portia waved a hand to silence her. "I will not remain here. Not after the way that brute treated me. Can you imagine, Nettie?" She flattened a palm to her heart as if she bore a mortal wound. "He thinks *I* would want to marry *him*!"

Nettie tossed her hands up in the air. "Fine. Kill yourself—"

"I'm not on death's door." Portia winced when the shrillness of her voice pierced her head. Sighing, she rubbed her throbbing temples. "Truly, I feel much improved. Certainly fit for travel." Her feet dropped down from the tester bed, sinking into the thick carpet.

She made it halfway to the armoire before a brief rap sounded on the door. Halting, she turned and watched Lady Moreton breeze into the room.

The countess froze midstride. "What are you doing?"

Portia twisted a toe in the plush carpet guiltily, feeling absurdly like a child caught at mischief. "Getting dressed."

"You most certainly are not," Lady Moreton declared.

Before Portia could lodge a protest, both women ushered her back into bed, tucking the covers to her throat as if she were an invalid.

"I am really well enough to travel—"

"Travel?" Lady Moreton's eyes rounded. "You're quite ill, my dear. And even if you weren't, you've only just arrived. Why in heavens would you wish to depart so soon?"

Why? Portia blinked at the countess, wondering if she mocked. Did she not hear her grandson demand her departure? "I think it best if I leave."

"Leave?" Lady Moreton glanced at Nettie as if needing confirmation that Portia truly intended to leave. "Why would you want to do that?" Hurt flickered across features surprisingly smooth for a woman of her years.

Portia wet her lips. "Lady Moreton, your grandson made his wishes exceedingly clear—"

"Posh!" Lady Moreton sliced the air with one slender, blue-veined hand. "I invited you. You are my guest. Heath cannot *uninvite* you."

Clearing her throat, Portia tried again. "At any rate, I would be more comfortable taking my leave."

Lady Moreton frowned, pursing her lips until they all but disappeared in her face. A determined glint entered her eyes and a hush fell over the room as Portia suffered her scrutiny. Swallowing, she stubbornly held that considering stare, resisting the inclination to fidget. As with her own grandmother, Portia knew better than to show even a hint of weakness.

"Very well, if you wish to leave I cannot stop you." The silkiness of Lady Moreton's voice made the tiny hairs on her neck stand. "You may leave, my dear. I wouldn't dream of keeping you here against your will." The countess blinked wide, innocent eyes, a hand fluttering to her throat.

Portia waited, breath suspended, knowing more was to come. Lady Moreton stroked the emerald pendant resting in the hollow of her throat.

"Thank you," Portia murmured, sliding the counterpane to her waist. She was on the verge of swinging her legs down when the countess's voice stopped her.

"Of course, I can't permit you to leave until I deem you fit for travel." Lady Moreton drew the counterpane back up to her throat and gave Portia's shoulder a patronizing pat.

"Truly, I am well *now*," she insisted.

Lady Moreton held up a hand, cutting off her protests. "Not another word on the matter. When *I* deem you fit for travel, you may depart and not a moment sooner."

Nettie laughed behind her hand.

Portia sagged into the bed as if a suffocating weight had been placed over her. The counterpane suddenly felt hot, heavy—a death shroud.

Lady Moreton smiled sweetly, as if she had not just sentenced Portia to prison for an undefined amount of time. "Rest. Recuperate. I'll send up some broth."

Broth. Her stomach growled at the mention of food. She could stand a bit more than *broth*. Roast pheasant with creamed potatoes sounded about right, but Lady Moreton appeared determined to treat her like an invalid.

"Very well," she relented, already thinking how she might get Nettie to fetch her some real food—and how soon she might arrange to depart without offending Lady Moreton.

The earl's face emerged in her mind and her chest tightened. *It would take a good deal more than this bit of baggage to tempt me.* Humiliation burned a fire through her at the memory of his words.

Three days. Three days and not a minute longer, she vowed. Then she would leave. With or without Lady Moreton's approval, she would leave. And she would put the earl's hot gaze firmly and forever behind her.

A sudden knock at the door had Portia thrusting her plate of cheese and bread into Nettie's fumbling hands. She anxiously arranged the counterpane around her as she struggled to swallow her mouthful of cheese. Nettie dropped the plate to the carpet and kicked it under the bed. At Portia's nod, she opened the door.

A woman walked in pushing a cart laden with books. "Afternoon, my lady. I'm the housekeeper, Mrs. Crosby." Stopping beside the bed, she bobbed a brief curtsey.

Portia rose up on her elbows, her heart accelerating at the haphazard stack of books. The sight of so many, some whose leather spines never looked to have been cracked, filled her stomach with butterflies.

"What have you there?" Nettie asked.

"Lady Moreton selected these books for Lady Portia."

Portia glanced from the twenty-plus books to Mrs. Crosby, a brow arched suspiciously. "Lady Moreton selected these?" No doubt her grandmother's letters had related Portia's fondness for books.

She reached for one, examining the spine. "Voltaire," she read aloud. Her hand went for another and another. "Austen, Cervantes, Burney, Defoe." Trying to still her racing heart, she slid her gaze to the housekeeper. "Where did all these come from?"

"The library. Perhaps when you feel better you could explore it yourself, my lady. It's quite a large collection." Mrs. Crosby made a tsking sound with her tongue. "Oh, but you'll be leaving, won't you? Unfortunate." In that moment Portia knew Lady Moreton had sent the books deliberately.

Portia reassessed the books, trying to suppress her tremor of delight now that she understood them for what they were—*a bribe*. She pressed her lips into a grim line and crossed her arms over her chest. No amount of books would tempt her to stay. She had her pride. Nothing could keep her here with that brute skulking about the place.

Then she spotted it. Her breath caught in her throat. With a shaking hand, she pulled a thin volume off the top stack. Freshly bound, her fingers skimmed over the smooth leather surface with its shiny embossed lettering. Mr. Edgar Allan Poe's *Tales of the Grotesque and Arabesque*. She had heard of Mr. Poe's unconventional stories.

"Oh, that one came in a few days ago. Lady Constance always sees that the library is kept current."

"Incredible," Portia murmured, her estimation of the stern Constance lifting a notch. She would have had to send away to America for this book. And at no small expense. Who knew what other books awaited below stairs? Likely a veritable treasure trove. Her chest constricted. Unfortunate she had to leave.

A deep yearning to investigate the Moreton library hummed through her veins. Such temptation was hard to resist. Unbearable. Her family's library hadn't been updated in years.

Her fingers caressed the sleek leather, her mind working furiously, searching for justification in staying. The image of herself immersed in books, exploring tome after tome, filled her head until she grew giddy. What better way to spend the Season than far away from Town and a new crop of Grandmother's handpicked suitors? She nodded decidedly. Sound justification. What more did she need? Moreton Hall was precisely where her Grandmother wanted her to be. So what if the earl wished her gone? No threat of him liking her. No threat of him proposing. A slow smile spread across her face.

"I think," she began slowly, "I should like to stay."

Mrs. Crosby beamed. "Splendid, my lady. I shall inform the countess at once. She will be so thrilled."

Portia nodded, ignoring the peculiar look Nettie shot her as she slowly opened the book. The spine gave a small creak and goose bumps broke out over her skin as the smell of ink and freshly cut paper assailed her. "Yes, do that, Mrs. Crosby."

"Certainly, my lady."

For the first time in an age, Portia felt giddy

from anticipation. A good book. Time away from her family. From another disappointing Season.

Even the memory of the earl's hard visage couldn't dampen her spirits.

Chapter 7

━━━⟨◦◦◦⟩━━━

Portia rotated in a small circle in the center of the library, the Persian carpet plush and yielding beneath her bare feet. She had waited until nightfall before sneaking from her bedroom, until a hushed silence fell over the household.

A visit to the library would have been impossible during the day. Not with everyone still treating her like an invalid, and not with Mrs. Crosby standing guard.

Yet standing at the center of the vast, cathedral-like room, she was glad she had waited. It was a reverent moment, almost spiritual. Standing alone with so many books, she didn't want to share the experience.

Never in her life had she seen such a collection. The wind howled outside, rattling against a large mullioned window that looked out onto the moon-washed moor. Portia trembled in her thin cotton gown, half from cold, half from anticipation. The fire burned low in the hearth, and the smell of burning wood mingled with the perfume of leather and parchment. She inhaled deeply through her nostrils. Heaven.

She hugged herself and rocked on the balls of her feet. Mrs. Crosby had not exaggerated. The library was huge. Beyond impressive. Her head fell back, taking in the vaulted, forty-foot ceilings. The books extended to Heaven itself.

Excitement brimming in her heart, she started in one direction, then stopped and turned in another, unsure where to begin. Yet begin she would. All libraries were arranged with some kind of system in mind. Portia vowed to learn the design of this one as quickly as possible.

She had come armed with her reading spectacles. A true indicator of her seriousness considering she abhorred the need for them. Ever since the day she had first donned them and her grandmother recoiled as if confronted with Medusa herself. Pushing them up her nose, she started just left of the door, reverently trailing her fingertips over the leather spines.

"What are you doing here?" A deep voice sounded from behind.

Portia whirled around, stifling a scream. Heath watched her from where he lounged on a sofa—a great jungle cat, all long lines and loosely coiled muscle. Strength and danger lurked beneath his seemingly idle air. How had she not seen him when she first entered the library? How had she failed to notice him?

He stared at her from beneath heavy lids, his wicked gaze liquid dark in the fire glow. Apparently he had watched her from the moment she entered the room—while she gawked and twirled in a circle like a silly child. Her blood burned with mortification.

"I heard you possessed a splendid library." She clasped her hands together in front of her, hoping he did not notice how her voice quavered. "I came to see for myself."

His gaze skimmed the cascade of hair over her shoulders, making her wish she had taken the time to pull it back. "You should be abed."

Wetting her lips, she swallowed and said, "I've slept enough of late—"

"You're ill." His hard gaze fixed on her face as if he could see beyond flesh and bone to all that she guarded. "You should have more sense than to be up and about. Especially dressed only in your nightgown."

Heat scalded her cheeks. Slipping her spectacles from her face, Portia lifted her chin and leveled him a reproving glare. "I wish everyone would cease treating me as though I were a piece of crystal to be handled cautiously."

"You are gravely ill—"

"A mild ague, no more."

He scrutinized her for a long moment, his gaze intense. She stared back and held her ground, chin up. Finally, he shrugged as if her welfare were of no account. And why should it be?

Her face burned as she recalled the way he had flirted with her. The memory of his hands on her body ignited a writhing lick of heat in her belly. A nameless female passing through might have been fit for dalliance—but not a lady his grandmother hoped him to wed. He wanted nothing to do with her. Perhaps he had when he thought her an anonymous female. But not now. Not that he now knew her identity.

"What are you doing here?" Sitting up, he flung one arm along the back of the sofa and gestured about the room with the other hand. "You don't belong here."

"As I said, I wanted to see your library—"

"No. Here. Moreton Hall."

Pressing her lips together, she debated how

forthright to be. He had certainly ended all need for niceties between them when he had ordered her from Moreton Hall with all the finesse of an ogre.

With that burning humiliation in mind, she mocked, "Come now, Lord Moreton. You know why I'm here."

"To snare a husband," he rejoined, his voice hard, cutting. "Me."

"That would be my family's wish, yes." Portia drew a deep breath, ready to explain that he need fear no pressure from her on that score. That she was as much a victim as he, that she had no wish to press him for a proposal. She had no interest in marriage, in handing over what precious freedom she had to a husband.

Only he never gave her the chance to explain.

"Save yourself the trouble," he growled. "I have no intention of marrying. Ever. My grandmother knows this, you understand, she simply can't accept it."

Angling her head, she observed him curiously. She never met a gentleman opposed to matrimony. There were heirs to consider, after all. And family alliances to be made. Intrigued, Portia asked, "You don't want a son? An heir?"

His face hardened, convincing her that she hit a nerve.

"No." The single word fell like a stone, hard, final. Not to be questioned.

"Why not?"

He scowled and even in the dim light she could see a muscle jump angrily in his jaw. "You haven't a clue how to hold your tongue, have you?"

She stared, waiting.

Sighing, he dragged a hand through his hair and confessed, "I can't have children."

Her hand flew to her lips. "Oh, I'm so sorry."

"No," he bit out, rolling his eyes. "I *will not.*" Shaking his head, he demanded, "Did your grandmother not explain the Moreton curse before she sent you here?" He sent her a pitying glance, the kind that seemed to say, *poor fool.*

Portia shook her head, a slow sense of dread tightening her chest.

He smiled cheerlessly. "Ah, the sacrificial lamb. Shall I explain exactly what your family has plotted for you?"

The dread in her chest grew, leaving no room for air. Unable to speak, she nodded jerkily for him to continue, to confess all.

"Your grandmother sent you into the lion's den quite unprepared." His humorless smile slipped and he turned to study the dancing flames in the fireplace. "But then perhaps that was her plan. To have you blink those pretty eyes so guilelessly at me. Such charming naïveté," he broke off with a snort.

Deliberately ignoring his backhanded compliment, she snapped, "You make no sense. What curse?"

"Madness, my dear. Porphyria. As ugly as it gets," he declared, his voice hard as granite. "My father fell victim to it." His expression grew shuttered. "As did my younger brother."

Madness? He had not been jesting. Portia eyed his profile closely, as if she could discern the madness he spoke of lurking beneath his hard exterior, see it in the smoky depths of his gaze, in the unyielding line of his jaw, in the wide mouth and full lips.

He turned then and caught her staring at him. A knowing smile twisted his mouth. "Yes, it's there, runs thick in my blood. Some say it has already surfaced." He shrugged one broad shoulder as if it mattered little.

An image of the wicked man from the road, the one who had nearly run her over with his horse, who flirted outrageously, who played with knives for sport, flashed through her mind.

"Explains much, doesn't it?" he asked, lips curving in a strange, humorless smile. As if he were determined to feel nothing, as if being mad cast no shadow over his life.

Yet his eyes betrayed him. Hot, determined,

they glowed like polished jet, the gray nowhere in evidence. The sight made her heart beat harder against her breast. A purely feminine reaction—one for which she sharply reprimanded herself.

"So you see," he continued, "I *won't* have children. Won't risk future generations."

She rubbed the base of her palm against her temple, struggling to understand why her grandmother would want her to wed a man burdened with such an affliction. "But my grandmother claimed you're a catch—"

"Money, my dear," he cut in sharply, his words echoing within the cavernous room, in the far corners of her heart—a death knell that marked an end to her clinging faith, to the belief that her family regarded her above that of money.

"Many families would gladly forget my tainted bloodlines for a piece of the Moreton fortune," he said, his voice rolling over her like a numbing fog—pervasive, consuming, obliterating.

Families like hers.

Shaming heat crawled up her neck and face.

He continued, "I'm guessing your family is in dire need of funds."

She longed to deny it, to deny that she belonged to such a family—deny that her heart wasn't breaking to think that her grandmother cared so little for her. She opened her mouth, but no sound emerged.

"We might be the Mad Moretons," he went on, not bothering to wait for her reply, "But we've more money than we have use for."

More money than we have use for. That would be her family's sole requisite.

She sank down onto a chair, her shaking legs unable to support her weight. Bile rose in the back of her throat as cold comprehension settled over her. Her grandmother would surrender her to a madman all because his pockets ran deep? Portia had thought she loved her. At least as much as she could love anyone. True, Grandmother strove to see her wed, but Portia had not thought her so desperate, so uncaring. She wouldn't put such a scheme past her brother and his wife. Bertram and Astrid would sell her to the Sultan of Turkey, if Grandmother let them.

He continued, the velvet timbre of his voice doing nothing to soothe her. "Now you know and you can depart and count yourself lucky to have escaped."

Depart? Return to her family?

Lifting her gaze, she shook her head. "No." Absolutely not. More than ever she was determined to remain here. To escape. At least for as long as she could. Grandmother had warned her that this Season would not be like the others—had vowed that Portia would be betrothed by the end of it.

"What do you mean 'no'?" He rose, two long strides bringing him before her.

Evidently she had spoken aloud. Her head fell back to take in the great length of him towering over her. She wet her lips and told herself that he did not intimidate her.

"I have no wish to wed you," she said coolly, striving to sound practical, matter-of-fact. "And you have no wish to wed me. What difference does it make if I remain here? I could use a little escape."

"A *little* escape," he echoed. "What is it you wish to escape?"

"When I return home, my family will begin where they left off, pelting me at gentlemen whose pockets run deep enough to cover my brother's debts." She lifted one shoulder in a carelessly affected shrug, as if that fact did not make her chest tight and her skin itchy. As if she did not feel like a commodity to be bought and sold.

"And money doesn't interest you?" His skeptical gaze slid over her, stopping at her bare feet peeking beneath the hem of her nightgown. "You prefer owning tattered nightgowns with frayed hems?"

Air escaped her in a whoosh. So her wardrobe was a bit shabby. He was no model of fashion.

"The need for funds motivates my family. Not

me." She straightened her spine where she sat, resisting the urge to pull her legs beneath her and hide her unraveling hem. "Is it so hard to imagine that I wish to—"

"Remain a spinster?" he finished for her. "Yes."

Her hands knotted into fists at her sides. "Like you, I have my reasons for eschewing matrimony."

His lips quirked in a scornful smile. He looked down at her in that mocking, skeptical way of his that set her teeth to gnashing. "Madness runs in your family, too?"

It would seem strange to him—to anyone—that she wished to live her life unwed, pitied and reviled by Society. But there was freedom in it. No ties. The freedom in never answering to a husband, in being bent to his iron will. Freedom to pick up and leave when her mother came for her. Perhaps it was foolish to cling to that particular dream. Especially now, eight years later. Yet Portia remembered the mother who had read to her, talked to her for long hours, dismissed the governess so that she herself could teach her daughter her favorite Greek myths. That mother had promised to come for her, promised that they would live a grand life of travel and leisure together. Without husbands.

She raised her eyes to his waiting stare. He would never understand. And she had no intention of revealing so much of herself in order to explain.

"My reasons are my own and none of your concern."

"Convenient," he mocked. "However, if this is some trick or device to stay here in an attempt to persuade me to marry—"

"Don't," she snapped, outrage consuming her, burning low in her belly. "You give yourself too much credit." Was there no end to his arrogance? "Even if I were interested in finding a husband, I certainly wouldn't look to you."

"Not rich enough?" He lifted an eyebrow. "Or you require wealth and a family tree with no threat of insanity?"

No. Those reasons paled in the face of her real fear. Even if it came down to her marrying, nothing would motivate her to choose him, a man who could reduce her to a quivering mass of nerves.

She swallowed and strove for a show of courage. "You needn't be afraid." She flicked her eyes over him, conveying her disdain. "You're safe from me."

"I'm not *afraid*," he gritted, his chest expanding.

With an audacity that even surprised her, she retorted, "Good. Because I've been invited here, and I have no intention of leaving Moreton Hall until I'm well and ready."

His nostrils flared in challenge.

Unable to stop herself, she leaned back in her chair. Tapping her fingers on the cushioned arms, she baited him further, "Best grow accustomed to the sight of me."

"Careful, Miss Mud Pie," he growled. "You may come to regret your decision."

Bristling at the reference to their less than dignified first meeting, she flung out, "Only people who don't know themselves have regrets. I know myself exceptionally well." Pushing to her feet, she thought to depart with that final, ringing announcement.

Yet her breath quickened at finding herself chest to chest with him. Their gazes locked. His gray eyes deepened, blue-black, reminding her of the first time she saw him cursing and spitting mad in the midst of a storm, his eyes identical to the coal gray skies.

He leaned in, crowding her further with the wall of his chest, his primal presence. Her senses filled with him. His musky smell. His towering height. The incredible breadth of chest that seemed to stretch on forever. His intense gaze burned deep into her, searing her soul. Panicked, she jerked back a step. The chair bumped her thighs, preventing her retreat.

"Be warned," he breathed against her ear. "If you stay, expect no quarter from me. You're not wanted here."

She shook her head, bewildered at why he simply couldn't believe her—why he refused to see her as anything but a scheming gold digger. Did she really pose such a threat?

She lifted her hands to shove at his chest, then thought better of it. She all too well recalled how the mere feel of him undid her.

Curling her fingers into her palms, she dropped her hands at her sides. Seeing no other choice, she stepped closer in order to squeeze past. Her breasts grazed the rock wall of his chest. Her nipples sprang to attention, hardened peaks that chafed against the thin cotton of her nightgown. Her stomach plummeted and her gaze flew to his face, to eyes no longer gray but a dark, blistering blue.

Heat suffused her and she crossed her arms tightly over her breasts. With all the grace of a bolting hare, she fled, eyes fixed straight ahead, afraid to look back, afraid that she wouldn't see the earl at all—merely the wicked temptation of one stormy night when she had lost herself in a pair of shifting gray eyes.

Chapter 8

Portia's heart skipped at the swift knock. Pressing the open book to her chest, she stared unblinkingly at the thick oak-paneled door.

For one fleeting moment, she wondered whether the earl had decided to follow her up to her room. Her heart did a full somersault at the possibility.

Then reason asserted itself. A gentleman dead set against matrimony would not risk visiting a lady's room in the middle of the night. Not with his grandmother lurking about, determined to see them wed.

"Come in," she called, closing the book and setting it beside her.

Lady Mina entered the room. "I saw the light beneath your door. Are you feeling well?"

"I'm fine. Merely reading."

Without waiting for an invitation, Mina bounded forward, her single dark plait bouncing over her shoulder as she hopped onto the bed. More bouncing and jiggling followed until she settled across from Portia.

"Then you won't mind me staying for a bit. We haven't had much time to talk. Perhaps you could tell me about life in Town. Especially the Season."

Portia stifled a sigh. The abysmal go-rounds of the Season were not something she relished recounting. "One Season begins to resemble another after a time. There's nothing extraordinary about Town life. I find country living far preferable."

"You would not say that if you'd never been more than ten miles from here." Mina brought her knees up to her chest. "Perhaps I would not mind so much if Heath would let me attend some of the local gatherings." She lowered her chin to her knees and stared at her toes peaking beneath the hem. "I could have at least a small taste of Society, even if not the glitter and bustle of Town."

Portia studied Mina's profile for a long moment, realizing they were not so different. Both were struggling against the strictures foisted upon them, searching for their own happiness, their own kind of freedom.

Feeling a sudden kinship with the girl, Portia grasped her hand and gave it an encouraging squeeze. "Perhaps I can convince your grandmother to invite some neighbors over for tea while I'm here."

Mina shook her head. "Oh, Heath wouldn't allow—"

"I'm a guest here, am I not? Lady Moreton would merely be humoring the requests of her guest."

"You don't know my brother," Mina grumbled, her bottom lip jutting forth. "If he catches wind of it—"

"Then we will simply see that he does not hear of it until it is too late." Portia smoothly cut in. "Trust me. I know all about circumventing authority." How else could she have avoided matrimony for these many years?

Mina's eyes sparkled. "From the moment you appeared I knew things would change."

"Indeed?" Portia asked, smiling wryly. Collapsing in a dead faint did not signify as the most auspicious of beginnings. "If my arrival strikes you as thrilling, then you are quite right. Your life is exceedingly dull. We must see what we can do to add some excitement."

Mina released her knees and clapped her hands. "Oh, you brilliant creature. My prayers were answered the moment you arrived."

Portia smiled grimly. What was the earl thinking, cloistering his sister from the world so that she went into histrionics over a simple tea? He was a tyrant. Clear and simple. No better than her father. Her mother had been unable to wear a gown if it did not meet her father's approval. Everything from clothes to the company she kept had fallen under his inflexible purview.

"Portia," Mina dragged out her name, casting her a sly look from beneath her lashes. "Have you ever . . . kissed a gentleman?"

Portia blinked, taken aback and wondering at the random question.

As though sensing her bewilderment, Mina rushed to explain, her expression solemn and tense, "I only ask because you mentioned excitement."

Excitement? Kissing? Mina equated the two?

Portia pulled back, exasperated. It was the same everywhere. Country or Town—nothing differed. Women looked to men to supply life's excitement. Eligible gentlemen never roused anything remotely close to excitement within her. Portia winced, realizing she could not make such a claim any longer. Not since her path crossed the earl. But then, he couldn't be considered eligible, could he? Or even a gentleman for that matter.

Portia opened her mouth, ready to gently reprimand Mina on her unseemly questions, but then snapped her jaw shut. Mina had been denied quite enough in life. Chastised. Corrected. Bullied. She deserved forthright conversation at the least.

"Yes," Portia began, knowing she was about to dash Mina's romantic notions. "Or to be more accurate, I was the *recipient* of a kiss."

Mina leaned in, her face brightening. "Was he handsome?"

"His name was Roger Cleary. He was sixteen. The vicar's son, and determined *not* to live up to his father's lofty standards." Portia laughed briefly, remembering that winter's day after church in Nottinghamshire. "I was fifteen and didn't see it coming."

"What was it like?"

"It was," she paused, searching for the appropriate words to describe being hauled behind the refectory and subjected to a thick-tongued kiss that tasted vaguely of sardines. "Messy."

Mina's face fell. "Oh. And there have been no others since?"

Portia shook her head, not bothering to explain that she saw to it that no man took such liberties again. When gentlemen looked at her, they did not see a woman they wanted to drag off to some darkened alcove and kiss. She had done her utmost to see they never did. The risk of finding herself shackled in matrimony presented too great a threat. Heath had been the only one to look at her with interest—the only man to make her toes curl and her body tingle and burn in the most shocking, intimate places.

"With the right man," she hedged, "I'm sure kissing is a lovely experience."

Mina pulled a face. "I'll never meet the right man. Not *buried* out here. Heath and Constance will see to that."

"Mina," she began, uncertain if she should say what she felt compelled to, what the fire in her soul demanded. "This is *your* life. You have choices. No one can make you do anything you don't want to. Not even your brother and sister."

Mina angled her head and studied her curiously. "You truly believe that, don't you?"

"I'm twenty-two and unwed." Portia hesitated a moment before confiding, "That's no coincidence, I assure you. My life plans don't involve marriage."

Mina shook her head. "I'm not as strong as you."

Portia smiled. "You've mettle, Mina. Why don't you tell your brother what it is you truly want?"

Mina snorted. "He knows—"

"You must keep telling him until he hears you. Practice if need be." She waved a hand at Mina. "Pretend I'm Heath. Go on."

Mina exhaled, sat up straighter. "I want to go to parties," she announced as if she were tossing down an ultimatum to Heath himself. "To meet people my age. To dance." At Portia's encouraging nod she continued, her voice gaining volume, color blooming in her apple cheeks, "I want romance—and a husband." She fisted her hands at her sides and jammed her eyes shut in deep anguish. "And for one moment I want to live my life free of a stupid curse, to pretend that my father wasn't a madman, that my brother is not . . . that I am not."

Portia cringed at the pain in the girl's voice and asked solemnly, "Can you tell him all that?"

Shaking her head as if suddenly weary, Mina opened her eyes and looked searchingly at Portia. "Does it make me selfish to want things I have no right wanting?"

"No," Portia replied, her voice gentle. "I'd say that makes you fairly normal. You want what every woman wants."

Except you, a voice whispered. Portia desired freedom. Pure and simple. Autonomy. The very things a wife *never* found within the bounds of matrimony.

"Well, if it's so natural, then why can't they understand me wanting these things?"

Portia sighed, unable to answer. She couldn't say whether or not the Moretons should bar themselves from marriage—from procreating. Was it guaranteed their offspring would inherit this affliction? Could the risk be so great?

"I don't know," she offered, wincing at such an ineffectual reply.

"I want love, a husband, children." Mina pulled her slight shoulders back. "You're right, Portia. My brother doesn't rule me, nor does fear of a disease that may or may not strike. I'll show him." With that said, she rose, pressed a quick kiss to Portia's cheek and headed for the door, calling over her shoulder, "Thank you for the advice."

Portia sat up, reached out and grasped air. "Mina, wait. I simply said you should talk . . . to . . . your brother . . ."

But she was gone, the door clicking shut behind her.

Portia fell back on her pillow, an uncomfortable knot forming in her chest. Perhaps she had overstepped herself this time in dispensing advice.

Chapter 9

Heath closed his eyes and settled his mouth over Della's. Moments ticked by as he waited for the familiar haze of lust to steal over him, to thicken his blood and consume him, to block out the rest of the world and free his mind from everything that had driven him from the comfort of his library and across the moors in the dead of night.

Della sighed against his lips, her hands running expertly over his shoulders and down his back.

In the dark night of his mind, however, a face appeared—a minx with flashing blue eyes full of bright indignation.

His eyes flew open, and he tore himself from Della's soft embrace as if he had been submerged in icy water.

"Heath," she purred in a voice that usually succeeded in making his blood simmer. Usually. Except not tonight.

Scowling, he looked down at her face, concentrating on the pert nose and full lips, willing the image of Portia as he had seen her tonight to flee his mind—clad in that damned virginal nightgown with its frayed hem, her ink dark hair sliding like a pelt over her shoulders. He took one long, steadying blink, but she still dwelled in his thoughts, residing in his head, in his blood—the last place she belonged.

Della pursed her lips and slid her hand down his chest and lower still, until that plump palm of hers rubbed the length of him in hard, rhythmic stokes. Such a move would typically have him flinging her on her back, yanking up her skirts and taking his fill. But Portia had ruined that. Damned chit. Now he couldn't even enjoy Della— the one woman he had enjoyed without worry.

Three marriages and no offspring to account for left little room for doubt—Della could not conceive a child. A more perfect mistress he could not have found—someone *safe*, incapable of passing on the Moreton madness. And someone he did not love.

He had dallied with other women—but always

stopped before the final intimacy. The risk was too great. With Della, his passions could flow free. So why not tonight?

More determined than ever, he trailed his tongue over the wildly thrumming pulse point at her neck, intent on satisfying her, intent on raising a reaction in himself, to free himself of Portia's hold. "Just . . . distracted," he muttered.

Della gripped a fistful of his hair and guided him to her breasts. "Well, don't be."

Easier said than done. Even as he turned his attention to Della's bountiful breasts, that dulcet, vexing voice replayed itself in his head. *I have no intention of leaving Moreton Hall until I'm well and ready.* With a groan of aggravation, Heath fell back on the bed. With an arm flung over his forehead, he stared up at the ceiling grimly.

"Heath?" Della leaned over him, her brown eyes wide with concern. "What's wrong?"

He turned his gaze on her, noting with dispassion the fetching tumble of copper waves—frustrating, when he had only ever looked on her with desire.

A deep sigh welled up within him. He had no future. A fact that he had come to terms with long ago. He had accepted his lot in life. It couldn't be changed. Why waste his time lusting for a girl he could never have?

Pulling her nightgown to her hips, Della straddled him. He frowned. The sight of those plump thighs did nothing to tempt him. For the last eight years, those thighs had been enough. Della had been enough. More than enough. Annoying how tonight she couldn't make him forget what waited, lurking in his blood to claim him. Nor could he forget a certain pair of blue eyes and the willowy figure that enticed him as Della's generous curves no longer could. No matter how hard he tried, he could not forget the woman who slept beneath his roof, the bespectacled chit who invaded his library, his home, his blood.

Patting the generous thighs straddling him, he muttered, "Appears I'm not in the mood for company tonight."

Frowning, Della rolled off him and pushed her gown over her legs. "I see," she said coolly. "My mistake."

Clearly, she did not understand. Hell, neither did he. They had a good arrangement. One based on mutual need—sex. After three husbands, Della may have sworn off marriage but not the carnal needs of her body.

He expelled a deep breath as he stood. Reaching for his shirt, he knew he owed her an explanation. He had been the one, after all, to wake her in the middle of the night for a little bed play.

Her gaze searched his. "What's amiss?"

Donning his shirt, he assured her, "Nothing."

"Heath," she said, drawing out his name.

Running a hand through his hair, he sighed. "My bloody grandmother has taken it upon herself to invite the Dowager Duchess of Derring's granddaughter for an extended visit."

Della watched him closely as he slid on his boots. "I don't understand—"

"She wants me to marry the girl," he bit out with a grunt as his foot slid home.

She gave a slight shrug. "So? You've avoided the parson's trap this long. Why is this time any different?"

Heath straightened slowly, gaze fixing unseeingly ahead. Portia, his mind immediately answered. Portia was different.

His grandmother had paraded a slew of girls before him over the years. He couldn't recall a single face or name. Yet they had all been the same—well-bred girls whose families didn't care about the curse, about sentencing themselves or their progeny to violent insanity. His dark scowls eventually conveyed his disinterest and sent them scurrying home.

But not Portia. No, the stubborn chit had planted herself at Moreton Hall. And *she* affected him, tormented him with her eyes, her hair, her scent—bergamot and lemons. The bloody female was dangerous to his senses. Since that first night on the road she had stirred him, roused his desires for a woman beyond his reach. Beyond safe.

"Nothing," he lied, searching for a stronger denial. "Nothing is different except that the girl intends to sit out the Season here."

The smooth skin of Della's brow wrinkled. "No one can make you marry her. Sooner or later she will sense your disinterest and return home. Like all the others."

He laughed dryly. Portia was nothing like all the others. "I've already made known my disinterest and she's not budging."

Della stood and moved to her dressing table. "Interesting." Sitting down, she began brushing her hair in long, quick strokes. "I've never seen you so bothered. Perhaps she's the one."

"The one?" Heath asked, unease skating his spine, warning him that he wasn't going to care for her meaning. "What one?"

"The one to make you rethink this whole curse business. A woman you can marry, someone capable of giving you children." Her eyes lifted to meet his in the mirror's reflection. She set the brush down and added in a subdued voice, "Someone you can love."

Heath stared at her for a long moment before he found his voice. "Come, Della. Love is for the self-absorbed. Fools like my parents."

His lips twisted as old, familiar bitterness

swelled in his chest. The memory of his parents, so in love one moment and at each other's throats the next, reared its ugly head. Yes, he'd seen what love could do. Seen the actions of those under its spell, seen it destroy and consume all in its path— his parents included.

Shaking his head, he motioned at Della and himself. "What we have is better than love." He nodded resolutely. An arrangement of the head, not the heart.

Even if the curse didn't hang over him, a black pall over his life, he wouldn't marry. At least not for love—never for such a destructive emotion as that. His parents' "love" brought nothing but grief and misery to everyone in their sphere: each other, their children, the household staff. No one had been spared the shouting matches, his father's cruel words, his mother's hysterical tears. *Love*— he would have nothing to do with it.

Della laughed mirthlessly. "Spoken by a man never in love."

Heath studied her through the mirror, surprised to hear such a sentimental remark from Della. He had thought her like him.

"I've been married before," she reminded, her light shrug belying the sad light shading her eyes. Setting the brush aside, her manner turned brusque as she asked in clipped tones, "Is she pretty?"

Snatching his coat off the chair, he shrugged

into it, muttering, "Her looks are of no consequence to me."

"Where are you going?"

"Home." He had no intention of discussing Portia with his mistress. That would require digging into feelings best left alone.

"To her."

"Don't be absurd. Lady Portia means nothing to me. Someone to be avoided. Sooner or later she'll become bored." He nodded, as though convinced. "She'll tire of whatever game she's at and head for home."

"Sooner or later," Della echoed in a small voice. "Meanwhile you'll torment yourself, wanting her and denying yourself because—"

Heath sliced the air with his hand. "Enough. Speak no more of it." He pressed a chaste kiss to her forehead. "I'm sorry I woke you."

"Me, too," she replied, watching him with an odd look in her eyes.

As he shut the door behind him, he couldn't help feeling as though he closed more than a door. The prospect of returning to Della's bed any time soon left him cold. A real dilemma since he couldn't turn to the one woman whose mere presence ignited a fire in his blood.

Chapter 10

Heath pulled up short upon entering the dining room the following evening. He hovered in the threshold, shifting on the balls of his feet, debating walking back out of the room as he surveyed the room's occupants. Grandmother, Constance, and Mina occupied their usual seats. Only *she* sat there as well. An unusual presence in every way.

The tempting smell of fried sole and melted butter, combined with the enter-if-you-dare arch of her brow, sealed his fate. He met the challenge of her gaze and took his seat.

She had sauce, he'd grant her that. He would

warrant a lady like her did not exist in all of England. One who would look down her nose at him and declare her intention to stay beneath his roof—whether he wished her to or not.

"Still here, are you?" he asked baldly, snapping his napkin into his lap. With a brisk nod, he indicated for the footmen to begin serving.

That dark brow of hers arched even higher, making her look arrogant and affronted all at once. "Yes, my lord," she replied in clipped tones, "your grandmother deemed me well enough to leave my sickbed."

He opened his mouth, ready to remind her that she had already left her sickbed, then shut it with a snap. No sense revealing that they had been alone in the library last night. His grandmother would seize on that scandalous encounter and insist he marry the girl on the spot. Heath suppressed a shudder.

Leaning back in his chair, he said with more ruthlessness than even he was accustomed, "You don't *look* well. I would have thought you still ill."

A low blow, but he was a bit desperate. Truth be told, she looked better than fine. The sight of her wrought havoc to his senses. With her glossy dark hair swept up, she looked elegant, fresh as the gales blowing in from the mountains to the north. The graceful column of her throat, as slight as a dove's breast, beckoned to be stroked.

Color spotted her cheeks and her gaze dropped. "I feel fine," she insisted, plucking at the edge of the table with her fingers. "The rumblings in my stomach required more than broth." Her gaze, sparkling chips of blue, flew back to his. "Or perhaps you wish to banish me to my room during my stay?"

Intrepid wench. Heath felt his lips twitch but suppressed the betraying smile. She did *not* amuse him. Attractive or not, he would not soften toward her, would not recall that she had beguiled him so utterly on that muddy road.

"The posting inn south of here at Ackersbury boasts a stuffed pheasant that our own cook cannot duplicate. I'm sure you would find it well worth an early departure."

"Enough," Grandmother snapped. "Lady Portia has just arrived. She is not yet ready to leave." Turning her gaze on Portia, she said soothingly, "Don't let him provoke you. He doesn't mean to be cross, my dear. You're more than welcome here."

"No," Heath inserted, gritting his teeth and wondering when exactly he had lost control of the happenings in his own house.

Termagant she may be, Grandmother usually deferred to him. True, she had thrust eligible ladies in front of him over the years, but life had been relatively peaceful of late—the supply of eligible young ladies that he had not frightened away exhausted. His gaze fell on Portia. Evidently Grandmother had to send to the far reaches of England for fresh recruits.

"She is *not* welcome here," he asserted, fisting his napkin beneath the table.

"Pay him no mind, Portia," his grandmother flicked a wrist in his direction. "Like most men, he hasn't any idea what's in his best interest."

"And Lady Portia is in Heath's best interest?" Constance sneered over the rim of her glass. She paused and sipped delicately. "We all know that cannot possibly be the truth."

"Oh, stay out of it, Constance," Mina shot from across the table, rolling her eyes.

Constance's eyes flashed. "I will do no such thing. This concerns all of us—"

"Enough!" Heath bellowed, surging to his feet.

All eyes swung to him.

Tossing his napkin down on the table, he leveled a stern glare on every member of his family before addressing Lady Portia, "You want to stay here? Very well. As long as you understand you're wasting your time. You'll be going home minus a proposal."

Color rode high on her cheeks. Quivering with rage, she sputtered, "Y-you arrogant peacock! You *still* believe I'm in pursuit of you? Were you to get down on bended knee and beg me, I would *never* marry you."

"Good," he snapped, lowering back into his chair.

"Good," she shot back.

Grandmother studied the two of them for a long moment before a slow smile curved her lips. "See, you're agreeing already. I think the two of you shall get on splendidly."

Heath closed his eyes, certain he now knew which side of his family carried the insanity trait.

Portia drew her shawl around her shoulders and gazed at the fountain. The moon's pearl glow gilded the burbling water silver. Beyond the fountain, moorland lay, silent and wild in the twilight. Frost glinted off the heather and gorse, blinking like cut glass in the night. The air smelled fresher, cleaner, hinting at spring, at things to come. By comparison, London smelled stale, stagnant.

Logically, she knew she couldn't hide here forever. Her family waited in the wings, a countless line of suitors on hand for when she returned without a groom. Yet for now, for a little while, she was safe. At peace with her books and a small taste of freedom the likes of which her mother enjoyed.

True, it wasn't her dream of standing before the Parthenon, the Greek sun a warm caress on her face, but it was a small slice of freedom—hers to enjoy for as long as she could abide Constance's dark glares, as long as she could abide one boorish earl.

An image of Heath flashed through her mind. Hawklike features and a storm-cloud gaze. Her skin hummed restlessly like the string of a violin, plucked, awakened, and buzzing with energy. Well, perhaps not total peace, she amended.

She'd not seen him in two days, not since he'd treated her so abysmally at dinner. *She is not welcome here.* Heat burned her cheeks, singed her pride. The arrogant brute. He actually thought she *wanted* to marry him? The insufferable gall.

Two days and no sight of him. Two days of snapping to attention every time she heard the tread of footsteps. Almost as if she hoped to catch a glimpse of *him.*

Lady Moreton complained to no end, expounding at length on the irresponsibility of heirs to their families.

"He's at the dower house," Constance had gleefully volunteered over dinner when Lady Moreton paused amid her diatribe to sip turtle soup from her spoon. "With Della."

"Constance," Lady Moreton had hissed, her spoon clattering to her bowl, "that's quite enough."

Portia had glanced back and forth between the two ladies. "Who is Della?"

"The housekeeper at the dower house," Lady

Moreton answered, her eyes not meeting Portia's as she reached for her glass.

"Yes," Constance had murmured, eyes glinting with amusement. "The housekeeper."

Portia had grasped her meaning perfectly.

Heath was staying at the dower house with a woman named Della.

His mistress.

Exhaling, she hugged herself against the chill, wondering why her sigh sounded so aggrieved. Surely she didn't care that the man kept a mistress. It certainly came as no surprise. A wicked man like him, who went about kissing serving girls in public, would have a score of mistresses. She would not give him another thought.

"What are you doing out here?"

Portia jumped at the sound of the gravelly voice behind her. A shudder ripped through her, and she pulled her shawl tighter. *Don't turn around. Don't turn around.*

"I thought you would have given up by now," he added.

Even loathing his words, his voice rolled through her like warm sherry.

"You expected me to be gone?" Portia asked, pleased at the steadiness of her voice. "Is that why you've stayed away? You thought I'd leave?"

"It occurred to me that a sense of pride might have come over you."

At that, Portia sent him a blistering stare over her shoulder. One that would set him firmly in place.

Yet the sight of him—standing in the threshold of the open balcony doors, the light from the drawing room limning his large physique—snatched the breath from her throat. Attired again in unremitting black, he looked as he did that first night. And like that night, the plainness of his garments heightened his appeal, made him both attractive and dangerous. Irresistible. Not like the gentlemen back home. The ones she found wholly resistible.

"A sense of pride?" she echoed, thinking she had a good deal of pride. Perhaps too much.

If not for her pride, she would have permitted Bertram to bully her into marriage long ago, would have listened to Grandmother's lectures on responsibility and duty and placed the Derring name above that of her own happiness and freedom. If not for her pride, she would have written a score of letters to her mother begging her to return home and fetch the daughter she had abandoned.

And perhaps without pride she would have tossed discretion to the wind and accepted the sinful invitation that one wicked man had recently issued to her in the taproom of a nearby inn.

"Yes," he replied from unsmiling lips, studying her from beneath heavy lids. "To remain where you are clearly unwanted."

"Back to that again, are we?" Portia snapped. "I told you, I have no designs on you. Merely wish for—"

"Escape," he broke in, advancing toward her, his heavy steps thudding onto the stone balcony. "I remember." The wind whipped his too long hair across the planes of his face. "And what does the daughter of a duke need to escape from?" he asked, the sneer in his voice unmistakable.

Being the daughter of a duke, her mind silently cried. A prize to be auctioned off with no thought to the soul sealed within the Derring packaging. To say nothing of the expectations, the unveiled pressure, the countless rules that governed her life, the tedium, the loneliness.

"Teas? Soirees? Rides in the park?" he scoffed.

Yes. And more. Much more. Yet one look at his cold face told her he wouldn't see any of it as a trial. He couldn't. Men never did. They merely expected ladies to do as they were told, to take pleasure in empty pursuits. That was all Bertram expected of her. All her father had expected of her mother. No doubt the Earl of Moreton was cut from the same cloth.

Shaking her head, she looked out at the moor again, at the silent night that asked nothing of her. He was not a man to listen to heartfelt confessions or explanations as to why teas and soirees might be something she wished to escape. He saw nothing beyond himself and his troubles. And at the moment, she was one such trouble.

"You wouldn't understand."

"Try me."

She slid her gaze back to him. Helpless against it, her eyes fastened on his mouth, on those sensual lips that made her insides melt.

Try me.

If he only knew how desperately she wanted to do that. And wouldn't it tickle her grandmother to know she entertained such thoughts. Thankfully, there was no risk of him sharing her impulses. He might still be wicked incarnate, but she was no longer an anonymous lady ripe for seduction.

He stepped closer, crowding her, overwhelming her senses. She leaned back as far as she could, the stone railing stopping her from total retreat. Heart hammering wildly in her chest, she risked a glance up only to find his gaze fixed on her face, his eyes searching, scanning every nuance, missing nothing. He looked at her strangely, his eyes feverish, intense, consuming. As though he had never seen anything quite like her before.

Reaching out, he caught a strand of her hair. Studying the strands, he rubbed them experimentally between his fingers. Dropping the lock, he ran the back of his fingers down her cheek, leaving a trail of fire in their wake.

Her breath caught in her throat, trapped, frozen within her like a bird in the face of its predator. And like prey, she looked away, dropped her gaze, wishing he would step away from her with the same desperate fervor that she prayed he would not.

He inhaled deeply next to her cheek. "You smell so sweet. Bergamot and lemons."

Her gaze lifted, brushed his chin, mouth, nose, up to lock with his eyes. He watched her with fierce relentlessness. She felt as if his gaze alone could strip away everything, all her shields, reveal all her secrets, all that she hid from the world. Perhaps she wasn't such a hard read. Of course, no one had bothered looking before.

"What are you?" he murmured, his voice a wisp of heat on the air, so close he singed her lips.

Closing her eyes tightly, she shook her head, panicked that he should see anything at all when he looked at her.

"N-Nothing," she choked.

"Oh, no," he returned, his voice quiet and smug and much too close as he tucked a strand of hair behind her ear, his thumb caressing her lobe in a deft, sensual stroke. "You're definitely . . . *something.*"

"Heath?" a voice called from behind. "Is that you? When did you return?"

Portia's eyes flew open.

Constance walked out onto the balcony, scowling when she spotted Portia standing beyond her brother. "Lady Portia." She folded her hands in front of her and inclined her head in the barest acknowledgment.

Heath dropped his hand and stepped back, staring at her in that unnerving way of his.

"I'll retire now," she murmured, careful not to touch him as she stepped around him. "Good night."

With an awkward nod for Constance, she hurried from the balcony and headed for the safety of her room, telling herself Constance had not interrupted anything.

She and Heath had not experienced some connection that went beyond what was seemly for two persons avowed against matrimony. She most definitely did not want to experience more . . . did not wonder what could have happened had Constance not interrupted.

Heath stared at the balcony doors, wondering at the ache in his chest—almost as pronounced as the ache in his breeches.

"Heath," Constance said, her voice heavy with warning. "What is it precisely you think you are about?"

"Nothing," he replied, still staring after Portia.

His sister stepped closer. "Then what are you

doing out here? *With her?* It's not wise. Not wise at all. The last thing you want is to be caught in a compromising situation with the Dowager Duchess of Derring's *granddaughter.* Grandmother would pounce on that. You'll have no way out of marrying her then."

"I know." God, did he know. Yet he couldn't seem to keep his distance. Not for any length of time at any rate. For two days he had stayed away, but his thoughts had been filled with her. "It's only . . ." his voice faded, and he rubbed the back of his neck.

"What?"

Dropping his hand, he went ahead and voiced his thoughts. "Incredible as it seems, she claims she doesn't *want* to marry me. And I think I believe her."

Constance laughed mirthlessly. "Of course, she wants to marry you. Why do you think she's here? The Derrings are desperate for funds. Why else would they consider marriage to a Moreton?"

Heath nodded. Yet he wasn't so certain. Portia didn't behave like a marriage-minded lady. For one thing, she appeared too uncomfortable in his presence. She shrank from him. Not the behavior of a woman intent on catching him. Of course that could be her game.

Could she be such an accomplished tease?

Could she actually be playing hard to get, hoping to whet his appetite? If that was her game, then, damn her, it worked. She had his undivided interest. All the more reason to avoid her. Yet here he was, gazing after her like some kind of lovesick puppy.

"Her family is desperate," Constance reminded. "She's here for one reason and that's to make a match. Don't fall for her trap."

"I won't."

Constance studied him carefully. "Heath, I know you don't want to hear this, but I see the way you look at her—"

"Constance," he cut in, growing weary of the subject. "You needn't worry. No woman is tempting enough to make me forget the poison that flows through our blood." Not a day passed that he did not remember. The memory of his father in a mad fit was not to be forgotten. "Nor would I want to marry if I could."

His sister nodded slowly. "Of course. You of all people understand that. I merely wish Mina could."

"She's too young to remember any of it." Heath sighed, wondering if that was somehow a blessing. A blessing to live life with no memories of the bitter fights, of ugly words shouted throughout the house. No memory of his father's slap ringing through the air and his mother's quick cry. What sweet bliss. "Perhaps if she'd been older it would matter to her as it does to us."

"I almost envy that she doesn't remember any of it," Constance murmured, echoing his thoughts.

Ignorance. Blissful ignorance. Yes, Heath envied his younger sister that. Envied the dreams she had that weren't colored by the past and the horrifying knowledge of what waited, lurking to seize them. If only he could have the same peace of mind. Then perhaps he could taste the lips of the woman that kept him awake at nights.

Chapter 11

D ella sighed and closed the ledger with a thud. She usually worked longer. Usually enjoyed the perfect, uniform rows of numbers and found peace in the chore. Hours could pass without her notice. Except today her attention wandered.

Closing her eyes, she rested her elbows on the desk and rubbed her forehead. In truth, her attention had been elsewhere for several days. Ever since Heath had walked away from her—and her bed.

In her experience, that meant simply one thing. Her first husband had been a chronic womanizer. Disinterest had always signified one thing—a new woman. Men were slaves to the flesh. While Heath may not have taken this Lady Portia to bed yet, it was only a matter of time. No matter that his head demanded he resist, his body demanded he succumb. Perhaps even his heart demanded it.

She dropped her arms on the desk and stared around her at the elegantly appointed office. The dower house was the home of her heart, finer than anything a fisherman's daughter from Scarborough ever hoped for. She had thought to spend the rest of her days here. She wasn't interested in remarrying and putting another husband in the ground. Not when she had this lovely home. And Heath in her bed.

She shuddered. Unwilling to consider losing Heath, Della pushed away from the desk. Her abrupt movement slid one of the account books forward, bumping it against the collection of books at the far edge of the great mahogany desk. Three leather bound volumes toppled to the floor, followed by the heavy thud of brass bookends.

Della circled the desk to retrieve them, hoping she hadn't damaged the books. They had belonged to Heath's father and had occupied that corner of the desk ever since her arrival at the dower house.

Bending, she gathered the heavy bookends and set them back on the desk. Then she collected the first two volumes. The final volume lay several feet away. It appeared some of the paper had stripped from its binding.

"Blast," she muttered, crawling nearer.

Upon closer inspection, she could see that the pages had not come loose at all, but rather a note had been tucked within. She pulled the piece of folded parchment free. It crinkled crisply in her fingers, the page yellow from age. She unfolded the sheet and eyed the elegant, feminine scrawl. Her gaze flicked to the bottom of the missive. The signature leapt off the paper. Her heart jumped in her chest and her gaze jerked to the top of the letter, to the beginning. A heaviness settled in her chest, expanding as she devoured each and every word, their significance penetrating her reeling thoughts.

She rose on legs as unsteady as her trembling hand that clutched the letter. The parchment wrinkled hopelessly, brittle as a fall leaf in her white-knuckled grip.

She paced the length of the library and back, her teeth worrying her bottom lip. At last she stopped before the fireplace, staring at the dancing flames for a long moment, considering the twenty-year-old missive gripped tightly in her hand—and all it would signify for Heath. All it would signify for *her*.

Shaking her head fiercely, she tossed the letter into the fire with a turn of her wrist.

"Forgive me, Heath," she murmured, watching

as the paper ignited, curled and vanished into a writhing nest of flames.

"You're brilliant, simply brilliant," Mina gushed, practically dragging Portia down the corridor.

Portia quickened her pace, trying to keep up.

"However did you manage it?" Mina demanded. "I usually only see eligible gentlemen at church, and Constance whisks me away before I can speak with them."

Portia shrugged. "It wasn't so difficult to persuade your grandmother. She hardly strikes me as someone to be denied her social amusements. Not in her own home and not by her grandson. No matter how he tosses his weight about. Lady Moreton is intimidating in her own right."

"True, but Heath's wrath is something to be avoided," Mina explained. "Last time proved that," she added with a shudder.

"Last time?"

Mina's eyes widened. "Oh, it was a fright. Grandmother arranged a luncheon with Mr. Humphrey, the goal being to foist his daughter on Heath."

"What happened?"

"Heath was his usual boorish self, drove off Mr. Humphrey—he was our vicar, you know."

Portia didn't know, but she nodded, prompting Mina to continue.

"The vicar and his daughter stormed out before dessert was even served. The following day they left Yorkshire altogether."

Portia shook her head, shocked. Though she shouldn't be. Heath had proven himself nothing but a blackguard. "I find it surprising that there are even families willing to wed their daughters to him." She cringed, instantly regretting the comment. Of course, there were such families. *Families like hers.*

As if reading her thoughts, Mina replied, "Of course. Isn't yours?"

Portia nodded morosely.

Mina slid her a sideways glance.

Portia swallowed past the lump in her throat, careful to keep her expression neutral. Unwilling to discuss her family's desperate need to be rid of her, she forced a cheeriness she did not feel and returned to Mina's earlier question. "Convincing your grandmother to arrange today's little gathering was not so remarkable. I merely expressed an interest in meeting some of your neighbors."

Mina grinned. "Well, it was no coincidence that Grandmother chose Tuesday afternoon. Clever bird. Constance always calls on the orphanage in Locksley. She won't be back until early evening."

Clever bird, indeed. Lady Moreton had shrewdly organized the tea, keeping both her grandson and

Constance in the dark. Portia didn't know whether to admire the lady or hold her in greater fear than she already did.

Not that this tea was so grand an event. The only nearby neighbors of suitable rank to attend numbered a paltry three. Upon entering the drawing room, the auspicious trio rose to their feet: Vicar Hatley, round and jovial; Squire Milton, a middle-aged widower who blinked about him owlishly, almost as if he were unsure of his presence in the Moreton drawing room; and Baron Whitfield. Portia looked him over appraisingly, thinking Mina's best hope rested here. Flaxen hair framed his youthful face, curling against sideburns a deeper shade of blond. His expression reflected polite interest. Interest, she soon realized, that was reserved for her alone.

"Would you like another cake, Lady Portia?" he asked, proffering a plate of assorted teacakes.

Portia glanced down at the three filling her plate. "No, thank you."

Mina reached for one, a ready smile on her face. "I'd love—" Her voice faded as Whitfield placed the plate back on the tea service, not sparing her a glance. Her hand wavered in the air, an embarrassed flush flooding her face.

Portia glared. Courtesy to a Moreton clearly eluded him. And Milton's manners were little better. When he ceased his incessant blinking, it was merely to engage her or the countess in conversation. Mina he ignored altogether.

Portia strove to discourage their attentions, drawing on her reserve of vapid discussion topics. Nothing, however, deterred the baron. He actually appeared *interested* in early Celtic horticulture—a topic that had always sent prospective suitors diving for the shrubbery.

"I can't say how delighted I am that you chose our little backwater to visit, my lady," Baron Whitfield interjected when she paused amid her diatribe, the only sign that he might prefer a change of topic. "You must be bored senseless here."

"On the contrary. The Moretons are brilliant hosts." Portia smiled at Mina, who returned a wan smile of her own. "Lady Mina is especially delightful, such animated company I've yet to come across in Town."

Whitfield speared Mina a doubtful glance, his nostrils flaring slightly. "I'm sure," he murmured, lips twitching as if she had uttered some joke. Portia's indignation burned even brighter.

Mina averted her face, stirring the contents of her teacup swiftly with a spoon. Despite her brave front, Portia did not miss the rapid blinking of her eyes, as if she fought back tears.

"So you've come to capture our elusive earl,"

Mr. Hatley boomed in ringing tones, seizing Portia's attention. She nearly dropped her teacup. It clattered noisily on its saucer as she cleared her throat, trying to arrive at a suitable reply to the vicar's tactless remark.

"She's the one, Mr. Hatley," Lady Moreton proclaimed, nodding sagely, a smile of approval gracing her lips. "The one we've been waiting for." She leaned forward and whispered in loud tones, "I can feel it."

"That so?" The vicar replied, looking Portia over with renewed interest. "So, you think you'll bring him to heel, eh, my lady?"

"Er . . ." Portia smiled uneasily, knowing to deny him would sound foolish, crazed even. Why else was she here if not to snare the Earl of Moreton? Mr. Hatley watched her, waiting. Moistening her lips, she managed not to choke as she murmured, "I shall do my best in bringing him to heel, Mr. Hatley."

"Good, good," he chortled, holding a sausage-like finger aloft as he quoted, " *'But because of immoralities, let each man have his own wife and let each woman have her own husband.'* "

Immoralities? Portia smiled weakly, unsure how to respond. Did the vicar see through her, deep to the core where sinful thoughts of the earl lurked, a liquid swirl of heat fomenting in her belly at the mere thought of him?

"Well put," Lady Moreton chimed, raising her cup in salute. "Here is to bringing Heathston to heel."

Portia clenched her saucer in her hand, heedless of the delicate china that threatened to snap from the pressure as everyone dutifully echoed Lady Moreton. She stood abruptly, needing escape just as her body craved air.

"It's such a lovely day. Mina, won't you join me for a stroll outside?"

With a relieved expression, Mina rose to her feet.

"Won't you permit me to join you?" Quick as a fox, Whitfield darted ahead and pushed open the balcony doors.

Seeing no way in which to politely object, Portia looped her arm through Mina's and stepped out into the mild sunshine. Whitfield fell in step beside Portia and they descended the stone steps. She shot him a wary glance, vowing he would not slight Mina again. She would not let one overblown gentleman look down his nose at Mina.

"There's nothing quite like spring in Yorkshire," he commented as they strolled along the path, deeper into the vast, mazelike spiny shrubs of gorse. He gestured widely. "Soon all of this will be covered in yellow buds."

"Lovely," Portia murmured, casting a glance at the silent Mina beside her, wondering how to draw her into the conversation. "I can well understand why one would choose country living."

"Do you visit the country often, Lady Portia?"

"Unfortunately, no. It has been quite awhile," she answered.

"Is your family seat not in Nottinghamshire?"

Portia nodded, her gaze narrowing. It appeared he had come prepared. She wondered what else he knew about her.

"It must be lovely. Tell me of it," he coaxed with a toss of feathery curls.

Portia stifled a humorless laugh, wondering how he would react to the truth—that the Derring family seat had been closed tight as a drum for the last two years. That Bertram had released nearly all the staff. That every unentailed item had been sold off. Her mother's rare book collection—long since sold—elicited the greatest pang in her chest. The property, like the house, had fallen to such a sorry state of disrepair, it would take a fortune to return it to its former glory. A fortune they clearly lacked.

"They say Nottinghamshire is beautiful," Whitfield added, pressing closer to her side. "I confess a strong yearning to see if the rumors are true."

Portia swallowed back an unladylike snort at his unqualified gall. Did he actually think such obvious angling would earn himself an invitation to her family estate?

Mina pulled up suddenly, freeing her arm from Portia's. Her gray eyes, so like Heath's, glowed with unshed tears. "F-Forgive me, but I've a vile headache." Her fingers brushed her temple. "I need to retire."

Portia opened her mouth to offer her company, but Mina spun around in a flurry of skirts and sped down the path. She gazed after her friend for a long moment, an invisible band squeezing her heart. Mina had not concealed her high expectations for the day. Apparently her siblings weren't all that prevented her from enjoying Society. Society itself presented its own barriers.

Indifferent to Mina's departure, Whitfield secured Portia's hand more firmly in the nook of his arm and led them deeper down the winding path. Over the many hedges of hawthorn, a fountain could be heard in the distance, its merry gurgling a direct contrast to her somber mood.

"Splendid," he murmured, his low voice conspiratorial as he patted the back of her hand. "Now I have you all to myself."

She averted her face and rolled her eyes, wondering how she might excuse herself from this idiot and return to the house.

"How fortunate am I?" he queried, his thumb moving in small circles on the inside of her wrist. She shivered as if an insect skittered across her skin.

Tugging her hand free, she announced, "I should like to check on Mina."

Whitfield moved quickly, blocking her path. She looked up at the blond Corinthian, her eyebrow cocked in question.

"And abandon me to myself?" With a mock pout, he pressed both hands to his heart as if mortally wounded.

Portia crossed her arms and tapped her foot impatiently. Surely he did not think such a tactic would work. She had been fending off suitors far more charming than he since the age of seventeen. "It would be ill-mannered of me not to look in on Mina."

"I'm certain she is fine—"

"I should like to see for myself." That said, she dropped her arms and stepped around him, not caring if he followed her or not. His heavy tread fell behind her, crunching over the pebbled path.

His beleaguered grumble reached her ears. "And what, pray, does it matter if she is sick?"

Portia stopped and whirled around, convinced she had misheard. "Pardon me?"

He flicked an imaginary piece of lint off his jacket and lifted his chin. In no mincing terms, without the faintest sign of apology in his eyes, he repeated, "What does it matter if she is sick?"

Marveling at his insensitivity, she raked him

with a contemptuous glare and responded crisply, "It matters a great deal to me."

He laughed. A lilting, almost feminine laugh. "She's a Moreton." His look told her that should explain everything.

"Forgive me for being obtuse, but what does that matter?"

He waved a hand before him, as if the gesture would somehow prompt her understanding. "Let's just say that if she is unwell, it's not from any treatable malady."

Portia stared.

Sighing, Whitfield went on, "No doubt she suffers from some sort of fit as a result of her madness. And there's nothing anyone can do to help her on that score."

Trembling with indignation, Portia stepped away from the horrid man, unwilling to place herself close to such idiocy. "Mina is *not* mad."

Whitfield stepped forward and grasped her arm. Her skin crawled at where he held her and she tried to shake him off, but he clung like a tenacious root.

"Lady Portia," he said, his voice slick as oil as it slid over her. "I fear that you've come here under some grave misapprehensions." His fingers flexed, digging into her skin.

"Indeed?" she asked frostily, her lip curling back against her teeth.

"The Moretons are bad blood. Everyone knows it." His mouth twisted in a wry smile and he dipped his head in acknowledgment. "At least everyone in these parts. Apparently not your family. They would not have sent you here to make a match with Mad Moreton had they—"

"I hardly know you," she broke in, unwilling to hear more of his *concern*. "I certainly don't require your advice on such matters."

Portia twisted free, eager to be rid of his skin-crawling touch. She turned, but he recaptured her arm, dragging her around to face him.

"Unhand me," she commanded, her cheeks flaming with temper. She glanced at the hand manacling her arm, her flesh whitening where his fingers dug into her flesh.

"I simply seek to protect you from making a grave error."

"So magnanimous of you," she bit out, knowing his game. Protecting her had nothing to do with it. "Yet I fail to see how I am any concern of yours."

His fingers tightened on her arm, hurting her. "I should very much like to change that, my lady," he murmured, his gaze sliding over her face with a thoroughness that made the back of her neck prickle. "You're clearly on the hunt for a husband. Allow me to offer myself as a candidate. I'm of modest means, but far more suitable than Moreton."

Portia gaped at him. Was it the country air? Or something in the water? First Moreton, and now this wretched man. They both behaved as if she had nothing better to do than find a husband. As if she could desire nothing else out of life. None of the gentlemen in London had come close to their impudence.

Portia flexed her ankle, preparing to stomp down on his foot if he did not release her. Only a quick glance about the silent garden, and she wasn't certain she even knew her way back to the house. This was no London garden. She did not stand a stone's throw from a balcony's door, from people, from safety.

He must have taken her mulling silence for consideration, for he continued, listing his assets as if he were a thoroughbred at Tattersalls. "My bloodlines are impeccable, my mother the daughter of a viscount, my father a hero fallen at Waterloo." He puffed his chest out as if he himself were the one to fall on some distant field in Belgium. "Most would say I've done well in filling his shoes."

"I'm sure," she muttered.

"Most importantly, I can promise never to leap off the banister in a mad fit. The present Lord

Moreton could not promise you the same." He rocked back on his heels with a satisfied air.

She frowned. "What are you talking about?"

"Ah, you haven't heard the story. The old earl dove head first off the banister at the dower house, landed smack in the middle of the foyer. A God awful mess, they say."

Portia closed her eyes, trying to stop the gory image from filling her head.

Whitfield's voice droned on. "And then there was Lady Moreton—shot herself with her husband's pistol. And the youngest son—no one's quite sure what happened to him. He was naught but a babe." Leaning closer, his whisper ruffled the tendrils near her ear. "Rumor has it his death may have been from unnatural causes."

From unnatural causes?

She expelled a deep breath, shaking her head. "Certainly you're not suggesting Lord Heath's parents had a hand in the child's death?"

Whitfield shook his head, his handsome face twisting in derision. "Who said anything about *them* harming the boy?"

"Then who?"

Angling his head, he replied with deliberate vagueness, "They found Lord Heath with the body."

Heath? Heath had something to do with his brother's death? Impossible. She had observed him with his sisters. He would never harm a hair on their heads. And she refused to believe he could harm a brother. To what end? No matter how wicked he behaved, he was incapable of evil that foul.

She tossed back her head and released a brittle laugh.

Whitfield pulled back, a grimace marring his pretty features. "Talk of madness and murder amuses you?"

"*You* amuse me," she said with a lightness that she didn't feel. She would not grant him that satisfaction of knowing his words gave her pause and put doubts in her head. Foul as poison, his words swam through her blood. *They found Lord Heath with the body.*

Inhaling a shaky breath, she continued, "That you would attempt to raise yourself in my estimation by discrediting the earl—"

"I assure you, my lady, the Moreton name has long been discredited. It was quite blackened by the time I was in leading strings. The father was a knave. The mother little better. And all that before the madness."

Portia leveled him her iciest glare and set out to end this conversation once and for all. "Although it's none of your affair, allow me to assure you that I harbor no *tendre* for the earl of Moreton."

His lips slanted into a confidant grin. As if she

had issued an invitation, he stepped nearer, eyes glowing with a feverish gleam.

She hastily slid back a step. "Nor have I any wish to consider your suit. Even if I were so inclined, my family would oppose our match. A man of mere *suitable means* is not a possibility."

His face flushed and he readjusted his grip on her arm, forcing her closer. "That's the way of it, eh? Money over breeding. You want to populate the countryside with future Mad Moretons?"

"You go too far, sir." Hot indignation crept up her neck and swarmed her face.

He shook his head, tossing those golden curls about his face. "I feel I must intercede on your behalf. With your family not present and no doubt unaware—"

She snorted. "I would describe my family as many things, but never unaware."

He stared at her for a long moment, his expression incredulous. She waited patiently for her meaning to sink in.

At last, he exclaimed, "They cannot have sent you here *knowing*—" He stopped cold at her pointed look and shook his head in denial. "No. No one in these parts would even consider binding themselves to a Mad Moreton—no matter his wealth."

"No?" Portia mused. "How very shortsighted. He's rich as Croesus. Owns half the coal mines in

Yorkshire and half a dozen factories in Scarborough. I would think he'd have his pick of ladies."

Whitfield's eyes glittered with spite, as if the mention of Heath's wealth made him loathe the man more. Shaking his head, he growled, "Even so, why would the Duke of Derring permit his sister—"

"That is none of your business," Portia snapped, her last thread of control breaking. She had had quite enough of this arrogant jackass and his meddling . . . and his relentless grip on her arm.

"I couldn't agree more," a voice interjected from somewhere behind, the familiar velvet sound sliding over her like warm sherry, heating her insides in a way totally different from the anger that Whitfield stirred within her.

Chapter 12

Portia looked over her shoulder and swallowed. Heath stood with his arms crossed over his broad chest, legs braced wide, his stone-carved face forbidding as he surveyed her with Whitfield. The mere sight of him unbalanced her. She hadn't seen him since the night on the balcony. Yet she had never once stopped thinking about him. A deep ache throbbed beneath her breastbone each time she imagined him with his mistress. She shook her head. Absurd.

His storm-cloud eyes missed nothing, taking in Whitfield's possessive hold on her arm with one sweep before returning to her face.

"Moreton," Whitfield greeted stiffly, finally releasing her arm.

Portia stepped back, involuntarily rubbing her tender flesh, stopping when she caught Heath watching, his eyes drifting to where she rubbed her arm. His gaze glittered with a dangerous light that made her breath catch, keenly reminding her of the wild, wicked man she had first met.

"Didn't expect you to put in an appearance today," Whitfield drawled, his voice calm, polite, yet she detected a thread of apprehension.

"No?" Heath angled his head, the single word loaded with menace. The dangerous light in his eyes intensified. "I live here." His gaze flicked to her. "And I always see to my interests."

A frisson of alarm—and something else— skittered along her nerves at his words. Surely he did not consider her one of his interests? That would seem contrary to everything he had said since the moment of her arrival, from the moment he sneered at her and called her a gold-digging husband hunter.

Whitfield's gaze shot to her. "It would appear we have similar interests."

The corners of Heath's mouth lifted. A wolf's smile that made her take a hasty step back.

"I'll grant you have nerve showing your face here," Heath murmured with deceptive calm, a muscle ticking furiously in his jaw. "More than I ever gave you credit for."

"Merely looking out for the lady."

"The lady doesn't need you looking after her."

She looked back and forth between the two men. Animosity radiated off them, palpable and thick. The type of animosity that was long-standing, born years ago—before she ever stepped foot in Yorkshire. She felt like a tasty bone in the midst of two dogs long accustomed to fighting.

"Oh, I beg to differ," Whitfield rejoined. "Someone needs to see to her welfare. It appears her family didn't give a thought to sending her into this viper's nest."

"Enough," Portia exclaimed, her cheeks stinging with anger.

"Perhaps," Heath drawled, heedless of her outburst. His gaze drilled into Whitfield with unspoken challenge. "But that someone won't be you."

Whitfield smirked. Shaking his head, he puffed out his chest and faced Portia. "That's the way of it, then? You choose him?"

Portia glared at them both, beyond words. Indignation burned a hot, bilious trail up her throat, coating her tongue. She *chose* nobody, yet nothing she said would convince either one of them of that.

"Very well, then." Whitfield scanned her thoughtfully as he straightened his cuffs, clearly taking her silence as some sort of answer. Turning to Heath, he announced, "She's no beauty, to be sure, but still too good for the likes of you, Moreton."

Heath lunged forward, but Portia reacted quickly, jumping between the two men. She placed a hand on his chest, his muscles bunching beneath her palm.

"That's enough," she scolded. The lines bracketing Heath's mouth remained tight and unforgiving. He made another lunge for Whitfield and she pressed both hands against his chest.

"I said *enough!*"

His gaze dropped to hers, glinting angrily.

Afraid to ease her hands off Heath's chest for even a moment, she spoke over her shoulder, "I think it's time you left."

Giving them wide berth, Whitfield stepped around them.

Heath said nothing, simply held her gaze as the baron's footsteps faded down the path.

His chest, tense with barely checked violence, rose and fell beneath her fingers.

The logical voice in her head commanded she remove her hands. Yet she couldn't withdraw, couldn't part from the tempting feel of his firm chest, warm and male beneath her fingers.

His voice rumbled from deep within that chest, vibrating against her palms. "You should have let me knock his teeth in."

Smiling shakily, she attempted to slide her hands

from his chest but he caught them, holding fast. "He deserves no less." His gaze devoured her, swallowing her whole. "It's not true, you know? You are a beauty, Portia." His intense expression drew into a grimace and he looked away, as though he resented the fact.

She moistened her lips and tried to pretend that his words did not thrill her, did not melt her bones so that she could barely stand.

"That would have been brilliant," she laughed weakly, giving her hands another tug. Still he clung, warm fingers pressed over hers, the thud of his heart steady and strong beneath her quivering palms.

Striving for a calm she did not feel, she continued, "Striking a guest in your own home . . . everyone would expect no less of Mad Moreton."

"He was not *my* guest." His eyes stared accusingly—as if she were somehow responsible for Baron Whitfield's presence in his home. "The gathering in my drawing room wouldn't be because of you, would it?"

Her face flushed and she dropped her gaze.

"I thought as much," he growled, his thumb pressing harder upon the pulse point at her wrist.

Refusing to feel guilty because she helped arrange a simple tea—perhaps even put the notion in Lady Moreton's head—she snapped her gaze back to his. "Your sister and grandmother deserve a taste of society, my lord. However small."

"Don't speak to me on the needs of my family."

"Oh, I wouldn't dream of it. You know best."

"I do," he said from lips so tight they barely moved. "If you won't return home, then at least cease your interference when it comes to my family."

"As you wish," she mocked, "I'm merely a guest here, after all. I wouldn't want to presume too much. Am I even allowed to converse with your sister?"

"A guest," he growled, shaking his head in evident disgust. "You're much more than that." He scorched her with a blistering glare, leaving no doubt that he did not mean to compliment her.

His gaze shifted from her eyes, scanning her hair, her face, stopping at her mouth. Her tongue darted out to moisten her lips. His smoke eyes darkened, as fathomless as the sea at night, ready to drag her under, suck her down into the depths.

Her breath caught in her chest, fluttering there helplessly like a butterfly trapped beneath glass. It took every ounce of will to stop herself from leaning into him, toward the heat of his gaze, the beckoning wall of his chest.

The burn in her blood bewildered her. How could she hunger for a man who so clearly disliked her? How could she hunger for a man at all? Such a mind-set would get her trapped in marriage if she weren't careful. Her plans for living a glorious life abroad would be lost. Places like the Parthenon would remain something read about, never visited, never seen with her own eyes.

Inhaling, she extricated her hands, tucking them behind her back. Lifting her chin, she stared at him and told herself that he was no mesmerist to enchant her. He was nothing more than a flesh-and-blood man. A boorish brute. And one rumored to be unbalanced.

He considered her for several moments, his head angled to the side as if he studied a strange creature, a rare specimen that he had inadvertently stumbled upon. Then, with a small shake of his head, his voice broke the silence, almost startling her in its swiftness, "What were you doing out here with Whitfield?"

She gave her own head a shake, as if needing a moment to make sense of his words. "We didn't set out alone. Your sister accompanied us."

"She left you alone with Whitfield? Why?"

Portia swallowed uneasily. "I fear her feelings were hurt when the baron paid her little heed."

"The bastard wouldn't," he ground out, his fingers diving through his longish hair, dark as a raven's wing. "She has stared calf-eyed after him for years. Why will she not listen? Does she think I'm a monster to forbid her to fraternize with lackwits like Whitfield? I know what they see when they look at her. The same thing they see when they look at me. Another Mad Moreton. Today is a small taste of what she would face if I allowed her to enter Society. I don't want her hurt. Only the most desperate of fortune hunters would pay her court. All else would spurn her."

"You love her," Portia mumbled, unable to hide her absolute surprise.

He swung her a sharp glance, a crease forming between his dark brows. "Of course I love her. She's my sister."

She averted her face, feigning interest in the tall hedge of blackthorn to her right. He sounded so offended. As if she had questioned his very honor. Not at all like someone capable of murder. Regret filled her for allowing Whitfield to place such a doubt in her head.

She snagged a branch and plucked a twig from it, dismissing her guilt as she rubbed a thumb over a loosening bud. So Heath wasn't a murderer. He wasn't even a depraved and selfish brother. *Of course I love her. She's my sister.*

"Portia?"

With a deep breath, she faced him again, trying to view him as the heartless brother she had thought him moments ago. Yet she no longer could. She attempted a smile but felt it falter and die on her lips. "Yes?"

He drilled her with his gaze, seeking answers,

a truth that she was unwilling to reveal. "A brother's love is so remarkable to you?"

She laughed, the sound strange and brittle to her own ears. "Indeed."

"Your brother—"

"My brother," she interrupted, "cares only for what I can bring him." She gestured about her. "Hence my presence here."

The hard gleam in his eyes faded. "Perhaps your brother knew nothing of my family's affliction."

She lifted her shoulders in a careless shrug. "He wouldn't have cared." Portia paused to fill her lungs with steadying air. "And Grandmother had to know. She corresponds regularly with yours. She knew and didn't care. So, you see, my lord, I know nothing of a family's love. At least," she amended, "not the kind of love you share with yours."

With a brisk nod, she flung the twig down and started down the path in swift, forceful strides, hating the thickness of her throat, the heaviness in her chest, the infernal burn at the backs of her eyes.

Heath fell into step alongside her. "What of your parents?"

Fighting back the lump in her throat, she rounded another hedge of blackthorn and stopped in the midst of a small courtyard, a burbling fountain at its center. "How the devil do you get out of this labyrinth?"

Smiling almost kindly, he pointed to another

path that led from the courtyard. "That way."

With a single nod, she started down the path. Heath's solid tread followed, as did his prying questions. "Come, what of your parents, Portia?"

"My father died when I was fourteen," she tossed over her shoulder.

"I'm sorry," he murmured, the velvet glide of his voice sending a flutter through her heart.

"Don't be. He never took any special note of me," she replied, not daring to look at him, afraid that he should read more behind her casually uttered words.

"That must have hurt."

"Not especially." In truth, she felt spared. Her father spent most of his time subjugating her mother, examining her social calendar, approving her friends, her charities, everything to her wardrobe.

"And your mother?" he asked. "Did she neglect you as well?"

"No," Portia answered quickly. "She was attentive."

"Was. Is she gone too?"

"No."

"Then—"

Portia stopped abruptly and spun around. "My mother left for the Continent exactly one week after my father's funeral. Just long enough for her to make the travel arrangements."

"Eight years ago? Has she not returned for a visit?"

Portia bristled at his pitying look, feeling every inch the abandoned daughter, cast aside and forgotten.

"She writes." So what if the letters grew less frequent with every passing year. Her mother loved her. Portia did not begrudge her for pursuing her own life. She lifted her chin a notch and strode ahead. "She promised to come back for me. We're going to travel the world together. I'm going to see the Parthenon," she declared, wondering why her voice sounded defensive. As if he had somehow told her she could not.

"I see," he murmured.

She cut him a glance.

He continued to look at her in that irksome way—as if she were a deluded child who believed in fairies and magic.

Eager to shift the subject from her and rid the pitying look from his face, she said, "I understand you're trying to do what's best for Mina, but I don't think you realize how determined she is to have what she considers a normal life."

He grasped her arm and turned her to face him. She could see the house now, looming above the overgrown hedge at Heath's back.

"Normal?" He lifted one dark brow as if he had never heard the word before.

"Yes. Beaus, courtship, marriage, children."

Heath stared, his gaze scouring her face, before muttering, "*Normal* is not our lot in life. Mina must accept that."

He nodded as if that put the matter to rest.

"Because you say so?"

"I know what's best for my sister."

"She'll be miserable," she warned, ignoring the muscle ticking dangerously in his jaw. "Do you want that on your head?"

"Life isn't fair," he snapped a mere moment before he captured her by the back of the neck.

She released a small squeak as he hauled her closer, thinking he meant to kiss her. His mouth descended, then stopped a disappointing hairsbreadth above her lips.

"We rarely get what we want," he whispered, drawing his words out in agonizing slowness, his breath a warm puff against her trembling lips. "Or haven't you learned that yet?"

Without another word, he released her and disappeared around the hedge. She fell back against the hedge, a boneless, sagging mass. Her fingers pressed to her lips as she willed the flutterings in her belly to cease.

We rarely get what we want. Portia wondered if she wasn't a little bit determined to prove him wrong.

Chapter 13

Heath ascended the top of the stairs and advanced down the hallway, stopping short at the sight of his grandmother leaning weakly against the corridor's wall.

"Grandmother?" he asked, hurrying to her side. "Are you unwell?"

She glanced up, smiling wanly. "I couldn't sleep, so I thought I might fetch a book from the library to take my mind off the pain."

"Pain?" Heath demanded, grasping her by the arm and leading her back to her bedroom. "What hurts? Shall I send for the physician?"

"No, no." She fluttered a hand through the air.

"Merely spent too much time on my knees in the garden today. Afraid these bones aren't as spry as they used to be."

Heath studied his grandmother closely, noting the tiny lines around her mouth and eyes. She looked tired—old—he realized with a start. The thought caused him some concern. As much as she aggravated him, he could not imagine not having her around. He'd experienced his fair share of death. William. His mother. His father. And none of it simple. No peaceful departures, any of them. Grandmother had been his one constant.

Gently grasping her elbow, he guided her to her bed. "Off your feet," he ordered.

With a mumble of agreement, she slipped beneath the counterpane. "I so had my heart set on a little reading. It usually puts me to sleep. Would you mind fetching a book for me?"

"Of course not," he replied, the feeble tremor in her voice striking worry to his heart. "Anything in particular?"

"Hmmm." She rubbed her forehead wearily, her eyes half closed. "A novel would be lovely." She dropped her fingers. "I would not mind rereading Ms. Austen's *Persuasion*."

"Certainly. I'll be right back."

Giving her hand a pat, he made his way back down the stairs to the library. The double doors stood parted and he pushed one open with the flat of his palm.

Like a moth drawn to flame, his gaze flew to Portia, reclining on a chaise, one calf propped on a bent knee. Her bare foot bounced idly, her pink toes as slight as the rest of her. His chest tightened at the sight.

He stared at her a long moment, eyeing the exposed length of calf, the subtle arch of her foot, his gut twisting. Logic urged him to turn and leave, to simply tell his grandmother he could not locate the book. He released a silent sigh. She would likely send him back for another one.

Resigned, he cleared his throat.

She shot into a sitting position, wide eyes falling on him as she anxiously tucked her legs beneath her nightgown.

"Availing yourself of the library again, I see."

She nodded jerkily, her gaze wary as she hugged the book to her chest.

"I'm fetching a book for my grandmother," he offered, as if he needed to explain his presence.

He walked to the side of the library where Constance kept the novels. After several moments of staring at book spines, he heard her approach. How could he not? He was attuned to every movement she made, her every whisper of sound. He even imagined he heard the soft fall of her bare feet on the carpet, the pounding of her heart behind him.

"What are you looking for?" she asked, her voice soft, uncertain. And why wouldn't she be? Their last encounter in this room had been less than cordial.

Of course, he had been convinced that her motive for remaining at Moreton Hall was in trapping him. Now he was not so certain. He didn't know what went on in that head of hers. If she wasn't a husband-hunting gold digger, then what kept her here?

He glanced at the library doors, barely parted, and felt a stab of alarm. Getting caught in a compromising situation with her would be foolish. Nothing good could come of that. Comprising situation or not, he would not wed her. Too many reasons prohibited that. The curse only one of them.

He looked over his shoulder, eyeing her slim, elegant form, far too tempting in her prim nightgown. Her unbound hair gleamed black as a seal's pelt in the lamplight and his palms tingled, itching to take their fill, to experience for himself the strands he knew to be soft as lambskin.

Disgusted and angry at harboring such thoughts, he shook his head and directed his anger on the nearest and most appropriate source—her.

"You shouldn't be here. Not with me." He gestured to her person. "And not dressed so."

Her chin lifted and her eyes shot blue fire. "*I* was here first."

"This is my house," he snapped. "I've been here long before you."

Her bottom lip quivered ever so slightly. "I'm a guest."

"Not mine."

"Back to this again, are we?" she huffed, tossing her hair over one shoulder. Shaking her head as though wearied of him, she went on to say, "I'm here by your grandmother's invitation. I suggest you accept my presence and learn to be civil."

He studied her coolly. The insufferable lift of her dark brow aggravated him endlessly. Then she smiled. Twin dimples dented her creamy cheeks—a burst of sunshine lighting the room. He felt that smile like a blow to the gut. Oh, she was dangerous. No doubt she knew the power of that smile. Constance's words echoed in his head: *She's here for one reason and that's to make a match.* Of course. He mustn't let her fool him otherwise.

She gestured to the books behind him. "Now," she began in a very governesslike tone, "do you want my help finding the book? I've become well acquainted with your library."

"If it will get me out of here faster, then by all means." He stepped back, gesturing for her to search among the shelves.

With a slight tsking sound, she stepped forward, asking starchily, "The title, if you please?"

"*Persuasion*, by Austen."

Angling her head, she examined the shelves in front of her. Tapping her lips, she murmured, "I don't think I've seen that one."

"You hardly looked. The book is here. Grandmother has read it before."

She slid him an annoyed glance. "As I said, I've grown acquainted with your library, and I would have noticed. Look, here's *Sense and Sensibility*, *Emma*, *Pride and Prejudice* and *Mansfield Park*. *Persuasion* is not here. Your grandmother must have been mistaken."

An uneasy feeling began to settle deep in his chest. "You say you've been spending most of your time here?"

"Yes."

The uneasiness spread from his chest to his stomach. "At my grandmother's encouragement, no doubt."

Her brows knitted together. "Of course. She saw me venturing in here shortly before you arrived this evening. I confess some embarrassment at being caught in my nightclothes, but she put me at ease and insisted that I stay."

With a groan, he ran his hands roughly through his hair.

"What? What's wrong?"

"Cunning old bird," he muttered, glancing at the door, wondering if she lurked beyond with a parson in tow. "I should have known."

"You're not implying—"

"That my grandmother deliberately sent me down here to fetch a book she knew wasn't here? Yes."

Portia gaped.

"She deliberately sent me on a goose chase because she knew you would be here."

"Deliberately," she echoed, color flooding her pale face. "Oh, you don't mean . . ." her voice faltered.

He nodded grimly. "She is set on the notion of you and me."

"B-but I told her that we wouldn't suit—"

"No matter. She went through the trouble of getting you here. She's not about to give up." Heath grimaced, imagining such machinations were not about to end. "Of course you could leave. That would put an end to her schemes where you and I are concerned."

She looked about the room, her gaze sweeping the books in clear longing. "Come now," she chided. "I don't need to flee back to Town simply because we may find ourselves alone every now and then. It's not as if either of us harbors a *tendre* for the other. Who cares if we're thrown together on occasion?"

He looked at her sharply, wondering if she mocked him, if she knew how mightily she tempted him. "I care," he ground out.

"You still don't think I have designs on you, do you?"

Laughter brimmed in her eyes, and it galled him.

He had desired her since the moment they met, before he even knew her identity. Dare she pretend indifference? He had seen the flare of lust in her eyes at the inn and knew he affected her still.

Foolish as it seemed, he felt the need to prove she was not so immune to him. Perhaps ego drove him, perhaps the madness surfaced at last, whatever the case, he stepped nearer, closing the distance between them until a mere slice of air separated them.

Until he stood so close he could breathe the scent of her: bergamot and lemons.

Her eyes rounded, enormous and blue in her pale face. She jerked back a step and collided with the wall of books at her back.

There was no escape. He knew it. So did she.

"Don't you?" he asked. "Admit it. You're here for one reason."

"No. I am not." Her voice came quickly, a hushed utterance.

"You've no wish to wed me?" he challenged, watching her eyes dilate as he crowded even closer. Her gaze flew over his face, reminding him of a wild bird in flight, afraid to land anywhere for too long.

He trailed his thumb along the downy soft skin of her jaw. "I think you want . . . something."

She shook her head fiercely. "I—I have self-control—"

"Is that so?" he asked, seizing her words, the first hint that perhaps she was not immune. "You need self-control around me, then?"

"Yes, n-no," she stammered, wrenching her gaze away from his face. "I don't know."

"Shall I tell you?" he asked silkily, staring at that very pink bottom lip trapped between her small, white teeth.

She lifted wary eyes to him and gave a single nod.

"Very well," he murmured, his gaze still fixed to her mouth, his gut tightening as her tongue moistened her lips. He drew a ragged breath. Casting good sense and years of restraint to the wind, he growled, "Never mind. I shall show you."

Dipping his head, he seized her lips and kissed her. And knew true madness. True, head-spinning insanity. Swallowing her startled cry in his mouth, he deepened the kiss. His arms came around her, lifting her off her feet and pulling her closer. Starved, past denying himself, he drank from the mouth that had tormented him for days. With a groan, he let himself go, gave in to the impossible impulses he had felt from the start, since the moment he laid eyes on her—soaked in rain, covered in mud, her viper's tongue lashing out at him.

Mouth fastened on hers, he slid his hands from her back up to her breasts, cupping them through the sheer nightgown. He kneaded the mounds, firm warm flesh that fit perfectly in his hands. Her nipples pebbled against his palms and she whimpered, kissing him back. Tentatively at first, then more aggressively, sliding her tongue against his as he rolled her nipples between thumbs and index fingers, aching to strip off her nightgown and feel their texture for himself. To taste their sweetness, bite and nip at the rigid little peaks.

He wedged his knee between her legs, pushing her higher against the bookcase. She pressed herself against his thigh with an untutored ardor. The core of her burned through his breeches into the flesh of his thigh, branding him. His hands released her breasts and cupped her face to better angle her head for his questing tongue.

She kissed him back, matching the thrusts and

parries of his tongue, her small hands clutching his shoulders. He tangled his fingers through her hair, luxuriating in the silken tresses.

He couldn't stop. Couldn't get enough of her, couldn't prevent his hands from roaming every inch of her. Down again they slid, skimming the slim line of her spine to cup a deliciously full bottom. He groaned and massaged the tight cheeks, bringing her burning sex against him.

A desperate, wild need to rid them both of their clothes seized them. But the restraint and discipline that had ruled him through his life obediently reared its head, and he withdrew, removing his leg from between hers. Then his hands. Then his mouth.

Glassy blue eyes gazed up at him. She raised her hand to touch her lips, moist and bruised.

"Enough," he managed to get out, the tremble in his voice betraying him, exposing her mind-weakening affect on him. He had set out to prove she was not immune to him and had only succeeded in torturing himself. His painfully hard erection attested to that.

She nodded, her dark hair falling wildly about her, mussed from his hands. He stepped back, the sight of her still far too tempting. The taste of her still far too fresh on his lips.

"Good night," he murmured. "I'll leave you to your books."

Even as he departed, frustrated and aching with desire, it comforted him to know that his library wasn't all that she enjoyed here. Despite her claims. Whether she cared to admit it or not, she wanted him. As much as he wanted her. Yet he'd be damned if he let her dig her claws into him any deeper.

Chapter 14

"**G**ood morning, Lady Moreton, Mina," Portia greeted, her face burning at the memory of last night's debacle in the library—and the countess's hand in it.

Averting her face, she turned and surveyed the surfeit of food on the sideboard. After selecting a large honeyed roll, she seated herself, still avoiding Lady Moreton's gaze, afraid that one look and all would be revealed. Surely anyone could see that she had been kissed senseless last night? She hadn't slept a wink, too busy reliving that kiss. Her lips still tingled. Her head still reeled.

A footman stepped forth to pour her tea.

"Thank you," she murmured, her eyes scanning the table, mildly surprised to find Constance absent. Constance's glowers over breakfast had become quite routine.

A plate sat at the head of the table. Piled high with food, it loomed rather conspicuously.

Mina followed her gaze. "Heath," she explained, over the rim of her cup. "He stepped out for a moment."

A frission of alarm rushed down her spine and she eyed her roll, wondering how quickly she could consume it without making a spectacle. Heath never breakfasted with them. Could this have anything to do with last night? It couldn't possibly mean he wanted to see her again. He had practically run from the library last night.

"Drat," Lady Moreton exclaimed. "This won't do, won't do at all."

"Is something amiss, my lady?" Portia asked, stirring her tea.

Lady Moreton chewed her bottom lip as she studied a sheet of parchment next to her plate. "I'm devising tonight's menu, and I can't remember if we have any Haute-Brion left in the cellar."

Mina frowned. "But Heath—"

"Mina," Lady Moreton quickly cut in, her voice sharp as a whip, "don't speak with your mouth full."

Mina snapped her mouth shut and chewed

slowly, blinking from her grandmother to Portia.

"We're having turbot with lobster sauce for dinner and I wanted to honor your visit with a claret I've been saving," Lady Moreton paused, pinching the air. "The Haute-Brion is perfection." She looked directly at Portia, her gaze keen. "I certainly couldn't trust one of the servants to fetch something so dear."

"I see," Portia murmured, wondering why Mrs. Crosby couldn't be trusted with such a task. It fell within her duties.

"Indeed not."

Portia fidgeted beneath the weight of Lady Moreton's pointed stare. A stare that clearly conveyed that Portia should somehow rectify the matter.

After a long moment of silence, Lady Moreton added, her stare no less intense, "I simply cannot abide fish without the proper claret."

Setting her napkin aside, Portia asked uncertainly, "Would you like me to fetch it from the cellar?"

"Would you?" Lady Moreton asked as if she had not been angling for such an offer. "That would be splendid."

Mina made a choking sound that she quickly muffled, pressing her napkin to her lips.

Portia rose to her feet. "Which way to the cellar?"

"Through the kitchens," Lady Moreton directed, "and do be careful with the bottle. I believe we only have one left."

Exiting the dining room, Portia hurried into the kitchen, her nose following the warm, yeasty fragrance of rising bread. All activity and chatter ceased the moment she entered the stifling room. Several pairs of eyes fastened on her.

"Er, the cellar, please?" she asked in the sudden silence.

"Through that door, my lady," a harried-looking woman volunteered, no doubt the cook from her stained and spattered apron.

"Thank you." Everyone parted a path for her as she approached the narrow oak door. Her hand closed around the latch. The iron hinges creaked as she pulled it open.

Cool, stale air assailed her. Trailing one hand against the stone wall to her left, she descended into the gloom, feeling as though she were perhaps tumbling into a dungeon of old. A soft, flickering glow of light dwelled far below, reassuring her that she was not sinking into a chasm of total blackness.

A loud slam sounded from above, reverberating through the stale air, startling her into nearly losing her step. She swung her gaze back to the top of the stairs.

"Who's there?" a voice called from below. A

deep, familiar voice that had invaded her dreams only last night.

For a moment, she hovered there, biting her lip as she considered fleeing back up the steps, away from that voice, away from the man that stirred impossible longings deep inside her. But that would be cowardly.

She would simply locate the claret she had come to fetch and be gone. She would prove to him that they could be alone together, that they could behave sensibly, above such base emotion as lust. This time she was prepared, resistance sheathing her heart like a suit of armor.

Squaring her shoulders, she took the final steps that brought her to the cellar floor. Chin high, she faced him, expecting his immediate rebuke. No doubt he would think her presence here another attempt to stalk him.

Surprise flickered in his eyes. He stood beside a tall rack of wine, one of several lining the cavernous cellar. He held a dust-covered bottle in one hand.

"What are you doing down here?" he demanded.

"Your grandmother sent me to fetch—"

"Claret," he finished for her, returning the bottle to its home among the others with a violent shove.

"How . . ." she began, then stopped, the cold hand of realization stealing over her.

"That's why *I'm* here. Fetching the Haute-Brion for her." His lips thinned into a grim line.

She closed her eyes in one long, mortified blink. "She did it again," she whispered.

And this time Mina had been involved. Portia's supposed friend. She must have known Heath had left to fetch wine but held her tongue anyway.

"Damn fool," he muttered.

"Me?" she demanded, heat washing over her face as he swept past her and stormed up the stairs, each pounding step making her flinch.

"Bloody hell," fell from above a moment later, followed by the hard pound of boots back down the steps.

He halted in front of her, legs braced apart, his broad chest heaving with barely checked fury.

She watched him warily, resisting the urge to shrink back.

"Locked," he growled, his storm eyes burning with accusation as they raked her.

"Don't look at me as though I had some part in this." She pressed a hand to her stomach in an effort to stave off the sudden queasiness. "You can't think I wanted to be stuck down here with—"

"Damned convenient for you to decide to visit the cellar when I happened to be here."

"Your grandmother asked me to fetch wine for dinner."

"And it's commonplace to send a guest on a servant's errand?" he sneered.

"She sent you, didn't she?"

"Because she wouldn't cease on the subject until I offered."

"Precisely." She shook her head, frustration bubbling deep inside her. "I confess I thought it odd, but what was I to do? Refuse the dear lady when—"

"Dear lady," he snorted. "That *dear* lady just locked us down here."

Portia glanced back up the shadowed steps uneasily. She squinted, trying to make out the door at the top of the stairs. "Surely one of the servants will come along and—"

"Risk losing their employment?"

"Your grandmother would not be so callous. Furthermore, are you not their employer?"

"Yes, but Grandmother could make their life very unpleasant if they thwarted her will." A shadow of a smile shaded his lips. "She's quite good at that. And in case you haven't noticed, her current agenda is for us to wed, so I suggest you tread carefully about her and read more into her seemingly innocent suggestions." His eyes narrowed and he mocked, "Especially since you have no wish to marry."

A maddening sense of *déjà vu* swept over her. "How many times must I say it? I truly have no designs on you." She groaned in exasperation. "You act as though you fear I'll ravish you."

"On the contrary." His eyes slid over her in a way that made her belly tighten and twist. "Just know that if word leaks out of this—or any other rendezvous Grandmother orchestrates—I won't marry you. No matter how many tongues wag. Perhaps you should forget your little fantasy of escape. It could end badly for you."

Little fantasy. As if a chance to escape, a chance to experience a small taste of freedom, amounted to nothing.

Her fists curled at her sides. Could he not understand? He knew what it felt like to be badgered at every turn, to live in the shadow of another's expectations. To never measure up.

The glow from the solitary candle lent shadows to the hollows of his face, making him look menacing, sinister—far too handsome.

Portia swallowed and looked around the cellar, trying to overlook the canopy of cobwebs hanging from the beams above. How long would they be stuck down here? To one side of them racks of wine, all perfectly aligned, stretched into forever, disappearing into the hushed shadows. On the other side, enormous vats undulated like dark waves into the depths of the cellar.

She shivered and briskly rubbed her arms, trying not to imagine what kind of vermin lurked beyond the candle's glowing sphere. "How long will she keep us down here?"

"If she had her way?" He paused and gave her a wry look. "Until you're with child."

Shocked at his outrageous words, and horrified at the lurid images that popped unbidden into her head, she dropped her gaze to her hands, turning them over and examining her cuticles. After a moment she looked up to find his gaze, steady and relentless as ever, fixed on her.

His lips twisted into a semblance of a smile. "We haven't any food," he reminded and glanced at the rack of wine nearest to him. "But I suppose we won't perish of thirst." He tapped one bottle. "Perhaps we should drink the Haute-Brion?"

A laugh bubbled in her throat. "A fine claret, I'm told."

"Would serve the old harridan right."

Portia smiled, imagining Lady Moreton's reaction when she discovered her precious claret consumed.

Silence fell between them, awkward and tense following their moment of levity. Still smiling, Portia studied her hands again.

"God, you're lovely when you smile."

Portia whipped her gaze back to his, her heart lurching to her throat. "I—I beg your pardon?"

Was that her voice? Small and tremulous as a feather drifting on a breeze?

"You're lovely when you smile," he repeated.

He reached out. One blunt-tipped finger stroked her cheek, close to her quivering lips. "You have a dimple here." His finger moved, drifting a hairsbreadth over her mouth. So close but not touching. His finger came down on the other side of her face, soft as a butterfly landing on a petal. "And here." His gaze locked with hers. "They only come out when you smile."

She moistened her lips, her stomach churning at his seductive words, his gentle touch. The man was dangerous, indeed. He captivated her with disturbing ease. She trembled. Partly from how he made her feel. Partly from how much more he could make her feel if she let him. If he let himself. She would be nothing more than clay beneath his expert hands.

His finger lingered on her face, brushing one dimple, liquefying her bones with the heat of his touch. She stepped back, pulling her face from his hand, from his tempting heat. Straightening her spine, she asked again, "How long do you think she'll keep us down here?"

His hand fell to his side and he stared at her in brooding silence before answering. "I'm sure she has no wish to starve us. She'll release us for dinner."

Dinner? Panic seized her heart, its cold fingers squeezing. How could she abide being locked away with him for a full day?

"Of course," she replied, doing her best to appear composed. "Dinner." Interlacing her fingers before her, she paced a short path, making certain to remain within the circle of light. "I have to commend your grandmother for her initiative." She tried for a laugh but failed miserably. Twisting her fingers, she went on to say, "She could certainly teach my grandmother a trick or two."

Heath lowered himself, his boots scraping the ground as he stretched out his long legs in front of him. "Perhaps she's not yet desperate enough."

Not desperate enough? Portia paused and let the possibility sink in. The nagging, the pressure, the criticisms that wounded like the slice of a blade. And of course there was her ultimatum. "Hard to fathom Grandmother as anything less than desperate. She has threatened to choose a husband for me this Season if I do not."

Bending one knee, he propped his arm over it and studied her beneath hooded eyes. "And yet you're here."

She lifted a shoulder. "Difficult to make a match if no one proposes."

"True," he murmured, "but aren't you worried who your grandmother will choose for you?"

"I'll deal with that when the time comes. You'd

be surprised how easy it is to chase off a would-be-husband."

"You're experienced in that endeavor, I gather?"

"Quite."

He studied her in mulling silence and she wished she knew his thoughts. "Well, don't expect a peaceful stay here." He waved a hand about them in demonstration. "Grandmother won't stop at this."

Portia shook her head, grumbling, "Why don't you give her what she wants and marry someone?" It weren't as if gentlemen lost anything by marrying. He would still keep his freedom, could pursue his dreams with no one interfering.

He narrowed his eyes on her and she hastily assured, "Not me."

"I'll never marry."

"The madness," she concluded.

He stared, saying nothing.

A certain suspicion filled her, one that she couldn't shake. Angling her head, she asked, "You *still* wouldn't marry, would you?"

She nodded, convinced she had discovered the truth. "You're afraid of marriage."

He stiffened where he sat, his expression appalled. *"Afraid?"*

"There's no shame admitting it. I'm afraid of marriage," she announced in a flat voice.

"Indeed?" he asked.

"I've no interest in granting a man total power over me. The day a woman says 'I do,' she surrenders herself. I have precious little freedom as it is. I'm not about to hand it over."

"You can't be serious," he murmured, his eyes raking her from head to toe as if he had never quite seen her before.

"Indeed I am." She quickened her pacing. "Husbands dictate where their wives go, how they dress, what they read, eat, topics they may discuss." Stopping, she gave a shuddering shrug. "No, thank you."

He laughed, the sound chafing simply because it mocked her greatest fear. "You've described a marriage the likes of which I've never seen."

Portia halted and settled her hands on her hips. "No? Well, I've seen it."

"Have you now?" His laugh quieted. "You think a man would dare run roughshod over you? Surely you know yourself better than that." His amused eyes flitted over her, measuring. "You'd likely strangle the poor fool."

She sniffed, smoothing an imaginary wrinkle in her skirt, unsure whether to feel complimented. "I simply do not plan on ever putting myself in the position where I must wrangle my freedom from a husband."

He studied her for a long moment, his gaze probing. "Your parents' marriage, I take it?"

She shrugged as if it were of little account. "My mother could scarcely breathe without his permission."

Heath tapped his knee thoughtfully.

Before he could probe further, she forged ahead, saying, "Why don't you wed? Marriage is no hardship for a gentleman. No one says you must have children."

"A name only marriage to silence my grandmother? Is that what you're suggesting?" he demanded, a hard glint entering his eyes.

"Precisely."

"I don't know many ladies who would agree to that kind of marriage."

Portia fluttered a hand. "Oh, I'm sure they exist."

"Are you volunteering for the position?"

Her hand dropped to her side. Their eyes clashed. Something in the air shifted, thickened. Tension swelled between them. She crossed her arms over her chest, dropped them and then crossed them again. "Of course not," she answered in a voice she hardly recognized as her own.

"Good. Because it would never work. Not with you, at any rate." He slid those smoke-colored eyes over her again—a slow, languorous perusal that made her limbs feel as unsteady as jam.

Lifting her chin, she muttered, "Of course not. You would be the controlling type of husband I precisely wish to avoid."

Throughout their conversation, the light had grown dimmer, his face more deeply cast in shadow. Portia glanced at the candle and bit her lip, noticing with some alarm that it was close to dying.

His husky voice rolled over her like the drag of silk across her flesh. "Not scared of the dark are you?"

"No," she replied, the word falling hard and fast from her mouth. No. She wasn't scared of the dark. Merely of being *alone* in the dark with him.

He knocked the ground with his knuckles, the sound jarring her from her thoughts. "Hard as a rock and cold as ice. I wouldn't mind settling myself into something soft."

Heat washed over her, scorching her face all the way to her hairline, and she wondered if he were aware of his innuendo, if he meant to scandalize her. He looked her over, his blistering gaze stripping her bare.

Of course he knew, the wicked man.

Nervous, her fingers moved to toy with the tiny rosettes fringing the scooped neckline of her dress.

His eyes followed the gesture, the gray deepening to slate, the precise color she had seen last night, moments before he kissed her, ravaging her mouth. Ears burning, she dropped her hand from her bodice, fisting the skirt of her dress as if it were a lifeline capable of saving her from all he stirred inside her.

He looked away, to the steps, his expression echoing the desperation wringing her heart. His head fell back on the rack behind him, rattling the bottles.

She studied him in the flickering glow of light.

"Better settle in," he muttered. "The light's almost out."

"Perhaps we should try pounding on the door?"

"No one will come." He gestured at the steps. "But if you'd like to try, by all means."

Expelling a deep breath, she lowered herself to the ground a few inches from his side. In a cellar where all manner of vermin likely resided, she didn't wish to stray too far from him.

Settled beside him, she watched the sputtering flame in silence, both dreading and eager for the coming darkness. Eager for her gaze to cease wandering to his long, muscled legs splayed before them on the floor, to the broad hand with its long, blunt-tipped fingers that rested atop his muscled thigh. At least she would be free of the sight of him, free of the temptation to turn and feast on the mouth that had plundered hers just last night.

The flame died, a whisper on the air, plunging them into gloom with such suddenness that a gasp spilled from her lips.

Chapter 15

$\sim\!\!\infty\!\!\sim$

Darkness enveloped them—a blackened tomb sealing them in from the rest of the world. Portia filled her lungs with the stale air, a strange sense of detachment stealing over her. She felt as though she were imprisoned in a dream—a dark, dreamless slumber.

"Portia? Are you all right?" Heath's disembodied voice cut through the blackness, thrumming over the air like the vibrating key on a harpsichord.

Her senses sprang into aching, singing alertness at that deep voice so near her ear.

"Fine." Her voice sounded strangled, a mere

croak, and she closed her eyes. At least she thought she closed her eyes. Blackness swirled around her, so thick and tangible she couldn't tell whether her eyes were open or shut.

A violent shiver rippled over her, leaving goose bumps in its wake. She brought her hands up to rub her bare arms briskly. Her fingers caught on one of the bottles behind her, rattling it noisily on the rack, jangling her already taut nerves.

"Sorry," she muttered. "Just a bit cold."

He shifted beside her, his every sound heightened—the rustle of clothing, the slide of his big body over the dirt-packed floor, the warm puff of his breath as he drew closer, stirring the wisps of hair that had fallen loose and tickled her throat.

His body radiated warmth beside her. So close. Her fingers twitched at her sides, tempted to reach out and discover precisely how close. His smell filled her nostrils—earth, wind, and man. The scent of him imparted energy to the stale air, filling her with a restless vigor that had her pressing her thighs together.

The rustle of his clothing grew louder. "Here. Take my jacket." The low growl of his voice sounded directly in her ear and made her jump.

She hesitated, unwilling to extend her hand. No telling what she might brush in the darkness.

He sighed impatiently. "Take it."

She stretched out her hand, groping air.

Their hands touched, collided, and her heart constricted.

She jerked back, stung. He snatched hold of her clumsy fingers, the rough pads of his fingers sliding the length of hers. His touch felt warm, sure—reverent as a lover.

Time suspended. Her mouth dried. Her breasts tightened. She couldn't draw air as he held on to her hands. Her satin to his steel. Finally he released her, shoving his jacket in her hands.

His voice scratched the air, rough, strained. "Put it on."

She leaned forward and slipped his jacket over her shoulders. Her nostrils flared, the scent of him encircling her. Settling back against the rack, she willed the tension to ease from her rigid body.

Suddenly, a scrabbling noise sounded nearby.

She stiffened. "What was that?"

"Nothing."

He didn't sound very convinced. The sound grew closer, until she was quite certain she knew it for what it was—nails scurrying over ground.

"Rats," she cried, flinging herself against him. He grunted from the force of her body.

Embarrassment burned her cheeks. Still, she was not about to disentangle herself from his protective bulk with rats lurking nearby. She didn't care how cowardly she looked.

His hands flexed on her arms, burning through his jacket and the capped sleeves of her gown and into her shoulders. She wrapped her arms around his neck and pressed close. That disembodied voice floated over her, a broken whisper that added to the unreality of the moment. "Portia."

She wet her lips and opened her mouth. No sound emerged. Instead, she snuggled deeper against him, her hand snaking around his broad shoulder, brushing his hair. She no longer knew or cared what had sent her vaulting into his arms. Unable to resist, she stroked the gossamer strands. In her mind she saw the dark hair sifting through her pale fingers.

With a muttered curse, he gripped her waist and lifted her so that she straddled him. Her skirts pooled around her knees. Shocked at the intimate position, she dropped her hands to his hard chest, ready to push away.

Then he said her name. "Portia." A hoarse plea—a benediction she couldn't deny. Didn't want to.

Her hands ceased pushing.

Darkness beguiled her, tempting her to forget what was real. Who he was. Who she was. And why they had no business sitting together touching each other like this. It had to be the darkness. It couldn't be the man himself who held such power over her.

Swallowing, she flexed her fingers against the soft lawn of his shirt, her hands overflowing with the hard sensation of him. His chest muscles danced beneath her palms and her belly fluttered.

She gasped when his hands came down on her thighs, sliding her skirts to her hips. With a rough yank, he untied her garters and pushed her stockings below her knees. Cool air rushed over her knees.

She fought to control her breathing. Impossible when his large hands covered her bare thighs, squeezing, fondling, his calluses rasping her tender flesh. His thumbs descended, inching closer and closer to the center of her that ached.

His hard chest pushed against her breasts and the peaks tightened, pebbled. Mortified, she prayed he did not notice, did not feel the evidence of her desire.

He dragged his coat from her shoulders; it dropped behind her in a whisper of sound. His breath fanned her ear a moment before his lips closed on the lobe, biting gently, sending her pulse into a fury.

Releasing her lobe, he shifted his head so that the warmth of his cheek scratched hers. Meanwhile, his big hands roamed. Over her shoulders. Down her back. His fingers skimmed her spine, and she squirmed, detesting the thin barrier of muslin.

The suffocating darkness magnified his touch. The anticipation of where he would touch next tightening every nerve into singing alertness. She felt the hot fan of his breath against her lips and leaned forward, hungry for his lips. Ravenous for another taste of last night's kiss.

His tongue flicked over her bottom lip. Once. Twice. She moaned and parted her mouth even more. He seized her lips, thrusting his tongue inside. His hands gripped her thighs. The dig of his fingers in her soft flesh filled her with a deep, primal thrill and she pressed closer, desperate for more, desperate for him.

As his hands clung to her thighs, his tongue parried with hers. The bulge of his manhood pressed against the burning center of her, prodding her through bunched skirts. She pushed against his hardness, frantic to assuage the ache.

"Heath?" a voice suddenly called, its peevish quality a cold douse of water.

He wrenched free and Portia moaned, bereft from the sudden loss of his lips, his nearness—his hard body rocking against hers.

"Heath?" the voice called again.

A soft glow of light invaded their sanctuary. Reality had arrived, nosing its way into her passion-clouded head. Heath rose, hauling her with him. Portia blinked and looked about, her head fuzzy as wool.

Feet pounded down the steps and she turned to watch Constance halt at the bottom step. Portia's stockings slipped past her knees and she squeezed her legs together to keep them from sliding to her ankles.

Constance held her candle aloft and surveyed them suspiciously. "Sorry to interrupt your little *tête-à-tête.*"

"Constance," Heath replied, his voice surprisingly steady, all things considered. "Good of you to unlock the door for us."

His sister snorted. "Grandmother is furious with me."

"I'll deal with her," Heath vowed with quiet assurance.

Portia slid him an uneasy glance. The hard set of his mouth almost had her feeling sorry for Lady Moreton.

"Come along, then," Constance said, turning on the step.

"We need a moment," he stated, holding out his hand. "The candle, if you will."

Constance frowned. "Heath—"

"Thank you. That will be all, Constance." His voice rang flat, final. Not to be contested.

Still frowning, Constance stepped down and handed him the candle. With a quick glare for Portia, she turned on her heels. Her lavender skirts swished noisily as she took the steps forcefully, each jarring step reverberating on the air.

Portia faced Heath. "She doesn't much care for me."

Without a response, he dropped, squatting at her feet.

"What—aaaah," she squealed as he shoved up her skirts. She staggered, grabbing his broad shoulders for support.

"Hold your skirts," he commanded, his muscles bunching beneath his fingers.

Finding her balance, she released him to grab fistfuls of skirt. She dipped her head to watch him. One warm hand closed around her left knee, circling it until his fingers teased the sensitive back. Her gaze snapped up, staring straight ahead even though the sight of that hand on her knee burned its image on her mind.

Her throat tightened. She swallowed fiercely, trying to open her airway. That hand slid up, taking her stocking with it. He lifted his head and locked gazes with her burning stare, searching into her very soul. His fingers trailed a flaming path along the inside of her thigh. Up, up, up . . .

Moisture gathered between legs and her face flamed, scandalized, certain that he knew his touch made her throb, ache.

With her heart hammering wildly in her chest,

he deftly retied the garter before moving on to her other leg and repeating the same bone-melting process. He took his time, toying with her, torturing her with his tantalizing touch. His dark head dipped, pressing a moist, open-mouthed kiss on the inside of her thigh. A small squeak of pleasure escaped her at the teasing swipe of his tongue.

Then his mouth vanished. Back on his feet, he looked at her with eyes more black than gray. The intimacy of his action, the familiarity, left her shaken, speechless, achingly aroused.

"You can drop your skirts now."

Gasping, she released her skirts, letting them flutter back to her ankles. She stood frozen, rooted to the ground. Her eyes scanned his face, devouring the sight of him, wondering how he could shut off his emotions like that.

No man ever made her feel this way. No man had tried. Fool that she was, she had thought herself immune, thought herself different, better than all those other debs tittering and batting their eyelashes for every gentleman that cut a fine figure in his evening attire.

Her gaze traveled the length of him, stopping at the hands knotted at his sides.

Her heart loosened. Apparently, he wasn't unaffected. "Your hands are shaking," she whispered before she could think better and hold her tongue.

Abruptly, he turned, removing his hands from

her view. His voice floated on the air, the command so soft she barely heard it. "Go."

She eyed the broad expanse of his back.

"Go," he barked, making her jump.

Without another word she fled up the steps as fast as her legs could move. Wicked man. Making her feel this way—making her want him. Her fingers brushed her tingling lips. Lady Moreton could never know.

"Heath! Where are you going?"

Heath stopped in the foyer at the sound of that shrill voice. He stood frozen as stone, reining in his temper before slowly turning to face the woman responsible for turning his world upside down.

His grandmother approached at a sedate pace, eyeing him with keen, narrowed eyes. He fixed a neutral expression on his face.

She stopped before him and folded her fine, blue-veined hands primly in front of her. A smile played about her lips as she took note of his clenched fists.

He immediately relaxed his fists, letting his hands hang limply at his sides. She would mark that as a sign, an indication that his captivity with Portia affected him. If she had even an inkling of how much he desired the damned chit . . .

He shook his head, both amazed and horrified. For once, remarkably, his grandmother had gotten it right and managed to thrust an eligible female beneath his nose that he found hard to resist. He could never let her find out.

"Where are you off to?" she asked in clipped tones.

Knowing the one response that would vex her the most—and perhaps convince her of his disinterest in Portia—he replied, "The dower house."

A colossal lie that. He had not visited Della since the night he turned from her bed, contrary to what his family thought. He couldn't bring himself to see her again, to face the questions that were sure to rise when he couldn't bring himself to touch her. Lately, he had stayed at the old lodge. He didn't have to face anyone there.

His grandmother's nostrils flared as though she smelled something foul. "With your strumpet?"

He smiled coldly. "I have no idea to whom you refer."

"That Fletcher woman."

"Della manages the dower house," he said with mock innocence. "And a better housekeeper I've never run across. I've actually considered bringing her here and retiring Mrs. Crosby to the dower house. She's getting on in years—"

"That woman will never step foot in this house." His grandmother's voice shook.

Heath shook his head. Grandmother had always blamed Della for his bachelor status. As if Della were the reason he never married.

"Fortunately, this house belongs to me," he replied. "Perhaps you would like to take up residence at the dower house? Mrs. Crosby could accompany you."

"I'll move to the dower house when you take a wife. As is proper." She inhaled deeply through quivering nostrils. "And on that matter." A pregnant pause filled the air before she accused, "You were in the cellar with Lady Portia for an unseemly amount of time."

"And you know why," he ground out, having a good idea where she was heading and still astounded at her unbelievable gall.

"I only know that you have placed yourself and Lady Portia in an untenable situation."

"Cease your games. We both know how Portia and I came to be in that cellar, and I'm sorry to disappoint you, but there is no need to post the banns."

Her controlled features cracked for the barest moment, revealing the frustration that simmered just beneath the surface. "Just the same, a gentleman would do right by her and make an offer."

Heath laughed, the bitter sound echoing in the cavernous foyer. "Never mistake that I'm a gentleman, Grandmother."

Angry splotches of color broke out over her face and her voice dropped to an enraged whisper. "You're a disgrace to this family."

Heath laughed more, the hard sound welling up from deep in his chest. "I'm such a blight, am I?" he demanded, thumping his fist to his chest.

His grandmother snorted in disgust. "You're a reprobate with no consideration for duty, just like your father—"

Hiding the sting her words inflicted, he shook his head fiercely, his words biting as he spit out, "Dear lady, I'm doing my duty, whether you see it that way or not. I'll make certain that I am the last Mad Moreton to ever live."

"Mina," Portia bit out, her voice swift and sharp as she entered the dining room.

Her face still burned from the liberties she had allowed Heath. She doubted she would ever forget. Doubted she could ever close her eyes and not recall the teasing brush of his fingers at the backs of her knees, the burn of his hands on her thighs.

A quick survey of the dining room revealed that Lady Moreton had departed. Wise woman. No doubt she would reappear once the smoke cleared . . . ready to mount another campaign in the war to see her grandson wed. Yet this time Portia would not be so unsuspecting. The old lady would not get the upper hand again.

Only Mina remained, face flushed with guilt as she fiddled with the handle of her teacup. "Portia," she greeted. "Where have you been?"

Inhaling deeply, Portia asked as calmly as she could, "Why did you not tell me your brother had already gone to the cellar?"

"Grandmother wouldn't permit me to speak." Mina shrugged, smiling weakly.

Portia pursed her lips, refraining from pointing out that Mina was not the most obedient of souls. "You are aware that she locked me down there with your brother?"

Mina gave a guilty nod.

Betrayal stung Portia's heart. Absurd, she knew. Mina owed her no loyalty. Still, she thought they had forged a friendship, thought them kindred souls, two spirits searching for their own sense of freedom and happiness.

Portia shook her head, struggling over Mina's role in the scheme to rob her of that freedom. "Why would you—"

"Would it be such a terrible thing for you to marry my brother?" Mina blurted, her eyes bright and alive as she set her teacup down.

Portia blinked, a resounding *yes* reverberating through her head. Terrible to marry a man who made her feel totally powerless, who turned her blood to molten lava, who reduced her to an incoherent, quivering mass?

He would run over her with frightening ease, trample her will until nothing but ashes of her old self remained. Her dream of standing free and independent before the Parthenon would be forever lost. She would exist as a ghost, like her mother when Portia's father had lived, drifting through life more dead than alive.

But his hands on your body night after night would make you feel alive. Portia shook her head, driving out the insidious voice that would have her seeking out the wicked earl and casting aside her inhibitions . . . and her dreams for freedom.

"Do you not find him attractive?" Mina asked, her gaze searching Portia's face.

Portia opened her mouth to reply, but Mina rushed ahead, her voice insistent, "Do not deny it. I have seen the way you look at him, and he does his share of watching you, too. Perhaps Grandmother is right and Heath simply needs his hand forced."

Portia snapped her mouth shut, recognizing the fervent gleam in the young woman's eyes. Portia knew that look. Had seen it countless times on the faces of those who presumed to know what was best for her.

Mina had clearly joined ranks with Lady Moreton to see that Portia and Heath wed. Contrary to *their* wishes. Like everyone else, Mina had become someone to guard against. Weariness settled in, a weight on her heart.

"A terrible thing?" she asked in a paper-thin voice. "No, to you I suppose it wouldn't be."

Turning, she walked from the room.

"Portia! Portia, wait!"

Ignoring Mina, she continued walking, wondering if the day would come when someone took her wishes into account.

Chapter 16

despite the ...

Portia stepped into the stables, grateful to
leave the biting wind behind. Her gaze swept
the rows of gleaming wood stalls as she loosened
her shawl around her shoulders. Not a soul in
sight. Yet she had seen Mina enter the stables from
her upstairs window.

After two days of avoiding her, Portia decided it
was time to face her. Surely Mina now realized
how misguided her efforts? Besides, Portia couldn't
very well ignore *every* Moreton family member.
Not while she resided under their roof. If that were
the case, she might as well go home.

And despite everything, Portia wanted to remain. She loved looking out her window each morning to the windswept moors. She loved losing herself for hours in the Moreton's inexhaustible library. She felt more alive here than anywhere else. And not, she told herself, because her blood burned in the presence of a certain man.

"Hello?" she called out, her voice tinny and small in the cavernous heart of the stables. No groom rushed forth, so she walked deeper into the shadowed interior, thinking perhaps they couldn't hear her if they worked somewhere toward the back of the enormous building. Perhaps Mina was fetching her mount in one of the stalls. Heath's sister didn't strike her as the sort to wait for her horse to be fetched for her.

A horse stuck his head over a nearby stall door, whinnying for her attention.

"Hello, lovely," she greeted, stroking her gloved hand over his velvety nose.

The beast snorted his warm breath into her palm.

"Looking for a treat, are you?" she crooned. "Perhaps next time, hmm?"

A whimper—or rather, a moan—diverted her attention. Angling her head, she listened. And heard it again. Definitely a moan. Dropping her hand, she walked ahead, peering over each stall door.

Finally, she arrived at the last stall. Rising on her tiptoes, she peered over the door.

Her gaze fell on Mina. Atop a pile of hay and buried beneath a young, virile-looking groom. The strapping fellow had wedged his body between her legs and was fondling her breasts through her bodice with the industriousness of a cook kneading dough.

Portia's mouth dropped. The impulse to flee and pretend she never saw anything—never saw Heath's sister rolling in the hay like a common crofter's daughter—battled her urge to march into the stall, yank the groom off Mina, and give both a stern lecture. She shifted her weight back and forth between her feet, indecision twisting her stomach into knots.

The image of herself with Heath in the library—in the cellar—flashed through her mind and her own hypocrisy made her cheeks catch fire. Who was she to lecture on propriety?

With a curse under her breath no lady should know, she whirled around and headed back down the narrow alley lining the stalls. Her feet beat the ground in hard, agitated steps. It was none of her business with whom Mina cavorted. Goodness, it was none of her business whether Mina cavorted. Still . . .

Portia jerked to a halt and looked back toward the stall. Mina could very well be losing her virtue. *In a stable.* Did not her own recent carnal activities grant her some authority on this matter? Grant her the firsthand knowledge that decisions should never be made under the influence of passion?

Portia bit her lip until she tasted the coppery tang of her own blood. Indecision warred inside her. She had never stood by the notion that young ladies should be coddled and prohibited from enjoying all the freedoms and pursuits that young gentlemen were allowed. But did Mina truly want this? Or was this an act of defiance, a rebellion against the strictures imposed upon her. Would she one day regret tossing up her skirts and losing her virtue in a pile of hay?

With a deep sigh, Portia lifted her skirts and marched back toward the stall with fierce steps. As embarrassing as it would be, she had to save Mina from herself.

The sound of hooves pounding on earth reached her ears, growing steadily louder, freezing her in her tracks. Turning, dread filled her heart as she watched Heath, riding at his usual breakneck speed into the yard, pull his mount to a stop before the stable. He dismounted in one fluid movement. The moment he spotted her, his lips compressed in a hard line.

"Portia," he greeted, standing several feet from her, legs braced wide. He made no effort to close the distance. His mouth was drawn firmly, resolutely. He clenched his reins in one fist as he stared at her, his eyes unreadable. Sunlight glinted off his dark head and her eyes squinted against its glossy brilliance.

"Lord Moreton," she returned, clinging to the formality of his title, a much needed barrier.

One corner of his mouth lifted, her formality clearly amusing him. "What are you doing here?"

"I . . ." her voice faded, dying on her lips. She shot a quick glance over her shoulder to where Mina conducted her tryst, wondering what to tell him.

With a gulp of air, she strode forward and looped her arm through his. Laying her hand on that hard, muscled arm, she said, "I thought I saw Mina step outside. Apparently, I was mistaken."

He looked down at her arm looped through his, at her pale fingers resting on the dark fabric of his jacket, and arched a brow.

She flushed, realizing how forward he must perceive her. No doubt he thought she welcomed his attentions. Perhaps even craved more of the type he had lavished on her in the cellar. Swallowing her pride—and her own instinct to flee him and the fascination he stirred within her—she batted her eyelashes in the manner she had observed from countless coquettes. "Won't you join me inside?"

His brows drew together and he looked at her strangely, as if she had sprouted a second head. "I don't think so."

"You must be parched from your ride," she nee-
dled, suppressing the pride that demanded she
cease such shameful cajoling. "I can send for a
tray of tea. Or perhaps you would care for something a little more fortifying?" She wet her lips,
slowly, deliberately.

His eyes darkened as he stared at her mouth
and she felt a stab of satisfaction.

Giving his head a hard shake, he muttered, "I
need to tend to Iago." He tried to shrug free of her
arm and advance into the stable, but her fingers
clung harder, panic seizing her.

"Oh, pooh." She thrust out her bottom lip and
lightly slapped his chest, fluttering her lashes.

He scowled down at her with narrowed eyes.
"What the hell's gotten into you?" he demanded,
clearly past patience. "And what's wrong with
your eyes?"

Portia ceased batting her lashes and fought
back a scowl of her own. Deciding another tactic
in order, she leaned heavily against him, com-
plaining, "I'm not feeling quite well." Her fingers
dug into his muscled arm, clinging for support. "I
must not be fully recovered. Would you escort me
to the house, my lord?"

His piercing gaze drilled into her and she held
her breath, waiting for him to either accept or reject her little charade.

At last, he nodded slowly and she remembered to breathe.

"Certainly. Perhaps you've overtaxed yourself these last few—"

A sudden giggle tinkled over the air, twisting into a sharp, feminine gasp of pleasure.

"What was that?" he asked, craning his head to peer into the stable.

"I didn't hear anything," she replied, her hands fastening tighter on his arm as she attempted to pull him along with her. He plucked her hand from his arm and started down the wide aisle.

She rushed to keep up, still bent on distracting him. Pressing her hand to her forehead, she tried again. "You know, I'm suddenly feeling very feverish, my lord."

He didn't so much as look her way. A quiet rumble of voices drifted from the end stall. Why were they talking? Couldn't two people caught in the throes of passion put their mouths to better use? Heat flooded her face and she suddenly did feel feverish. She briefly considered dropping in a swoon at his feet. Yet with her luck, he would fail to catch her.

Heath advanced on the stall, Portia fast on his heels.

"That's it, love," a deep voice encouraged. "There you go, that's it."

Portia closed her eyes, afraid to know what Mina did to elicit such ardent approval. Opening her eyes, her stomach dropped to her feet as Heath stopped before the last stall door, his dark head cocked at a dangerous angle.

Feminine laughter floated over the door, so incongruous to the dismay hammering in Portia's heart.

"Mina?" he murmured, apparently recognizing the laughter. Laying a hand flat on the door, he gave it a push. It swung inward with a slight creak of iron hinges.

Wincing, Portia forgot to breathe as her gaze landed on Mina—with her hand in the groom's trousers.

Heath charged into the stall, blocking her from seeing more. A relief, to be certain. Portia would likely be haunted by the unwanted image for years.

Heath yanked the groom to his feet. Mina bounced to her feet, pulling her bodice over jiggling breasts as she babbled incoherent explanations.

The groom managed a few warbled words before Heath's fist made contact with his face in a sickening smack of bone against bone. Portia jerked, startled at the unrestrained violence of the blow. The groom careened backward into the hay, limbs flailing, blood spurting from his nose like a fountain.

"Pack your things," Heath snarled, fists flexing as he stood over the hapless young man. He kicked violently at one of his jutting boots. "I want you off my property. Never show yourself in the area again. If word should ever leak of you and my sister—"

The groom nodded his head vigorously. Blood, thick and crimson, seeped between the fingers of the hand he clutched over his nose. With eyes averted, he staggered to his feet again and fled the stall.

Mina, eyes round as saucers, looked from her fleeing would-be lover to Heath before uttering with quiet intensity, "I hate you."

Portia grimaced, her hand fluttering to her heart, the stab of Mina's words burying themselves there as effectively as a well-aimed arrow. Her gaze flew to Heath. A flash of raw emotion flickered in his eyes. A deep vulnerability that revealed itself for a mere instant before the familiar gray fog rolled back in, obscuring his exact thoughts.

Before he could respond, Mina tore out of the stall.

Heath bellowed like an outraged bull behind her. "Mina, get back here. I'm not finished with you!"

His sister ignored him, dashing for the house like a hare in flight.

Portia moistened her lips and inched her way out of the stall, not about to be left alone with Heath in his present state of ire. Her eyes fixed longingly at the leaves scuttling across the ground outside the stables.

"*You.*"

Portia froze.

"Yes?" she asked in a small voice. Turning, she faced the full blast of Heath's glare, as bitter cold as a glacier wind.

He advanced on her, face stark and jagged as the wind-carved countryside. "You knew she was in here."

Nodding, she backed up until she collided with a stall door. Hard wood at her back, she trembled as if she stood outside the shelter of the stables.

"You *knew* and attempted to distract me," he accused, closing in like a deadly jungle cat. "You tried to get me to go inside with you."

She held up a hand as if she could ward off his blistering accusations. "I merely wanted to save her from getting into trouble with you. I would have come back for her and put a stop to it."

"And in the time it took to get rid of me, my sister could very well have been ruined."

Portia flinched. She was *not* responsible for Mina's tryst, nor would she permit Heath to place the blame at her feet. Not when a good portion of the blame could be attributed to him. If he had allowed Mina some freedom, she wouldn't have gone to such extremes.

"So your sister wants a little adventure." She flicked her hand in a gesture of impatience. "Not so surprising. You've prohibited her from meeting and courting gentlemen of her station, prohibited her from marrying. How else is she to satisfy her desires?"

Heath shook his head. "You think her behavior acceptable then? Do *you* satisfy your desires with servants?" he pressed, stepping closer, his eyes intense, feral as a predator.

"Of course not," Portia snapped, discomfited by his nearness, his encroaching heat, the way her skin warmed as if too near the hearth. "But I understand *you* do." She slapped a hand over her mouth, wondering what had possessed her to say such a thing, true or not.

His jaw thrust forward. "That is neither here nor there. Gentlemen are held to different standards."

She dropped her hand from her mouth. "Which is absolute nonsense. If gentlemen are free to sew their wild oats, then why not women?"

"Gently bred ladies do not have wild oats."

"Posh."

He blinked. "Posh?"

"Posh!" she repeated, voice firm.

Heath frowned and cocked his head, a challenging glint entering his eyes. His gaze raked her as if seeing her for the first time, as if she were some strange creature, a species never before sighted by man. "I'm not so certain I should permit you to associate with Mina. Your notions are nothing short of scandalous." His voice dipped dangerously low. "Have you sewn your wild oats yet, Portia?"

She swallowed nervously. The memory of his kiss surged forward and made her lips burn. She sucked in a fast breath and pushed the memory out of her head.

"No. But that's not to say I wouldn't do so. I've simply not been tempted yet." She grimaced, praying he would not call her out on the lie. He need merely fling her wanton behavior in the cellar to remind her that *he* tempted her. Shaking her head, she added, "It's not my place to judge Mina's behavior—although had it been a brother in the stall with a kitchen maid, I doubt we would be having this conversation."

Heath opened his mouth to protest, but she held up a hand, stalling him. "Your sister is bored, lonely." Her mind searched for the apt word. Arriving at it, she exclaimed with relish, "Oppressed."

"Oppressed?" His eyes flared wide, an unholy light gleaming at the center of his pupils.

Portia nodded. Who better than she understood such feelings, after all? She had felt oppressed ever since her grandmother pushed her through her first Season at the tender age of seventeen.

"I'm the great oppressor, I take it?" he demanded.

"Who else?"

"So you're saying my sister will likely continue on this ruinous path until I give in and grant her a Season?" His jaw tensed, muscles knotting beneath the taut skin.

Her fingers twitched, itching at her sides to reach out and smooth the flesh into evenness. She laced her fingers together in front of her, locking her hands lest they betray her.

"All I'm saying is that you need to *talk* to your sister. Don't bark commands. Don't issue edicts. Come to an understanding. She has to be allowed to pursue her desires to some degree or else her life is no better than a slave's."

"And what of you, Portia?"

She looked at him, feeling the skin of her brow knit in confusion.

"Come now, Portia," he chided, his mocking voice grating. "Your family doesn't permit you to pursue your desires, do they?"

She frowned, wondering if any member of her family even knew what it was that she desired. Certainly no one had thought to ask.

His eyes drilled into hers, relentless, probing. Knowing. He already knew the answer to his infernal question. Still, he demanded to hear her response, demanded to hear her say that what she expected of him, her own family could not deliver.

Thrusting back her shoulders, she answered him. "No. My family has never taken my wishes into account."

"Precisely," he said in that exasperating, smug voice of his. "Most fathers and brothers do not. Our world doesn't work that way. Fathers and brothers make the decisions, and daughters dutifully obey."

Obey. Never following her heart's yearnings, never following her heart. Bearing no more freedom than a slave. Releasing her hands, she pressed her fingers to her temples, suddenly feeling a headache threaten.

Heath's voice continued, a cold douse of reason. "Yet you expect me to be different."

"Yes," she shot back, a fire sparking deep in her chest, rising its way up her throat to inflame her tongue, "Because you are—you love your sister."

His eyes softened for the barest moment before

hard resolve filled them. "Love or not, if Mina desires a tumble in the hay, she's not getting her way. In fact, she may find herself cloistered in a convent."

"Then you'll lose her," she pronounced, saddened for Mina, for him, for herself who felt every bit as trapped as Heath's foolish young sister.

Something that looked alarmingly close to pain flickered in his eyes. "I can live with her hatred if it means protecting her." With that said, he turned and walked away.

She stared after him, feeling bewildered but mostly sad that no one could ever claim to love her that much.

Chapter 17

"Did I ever tell you about the time my brother forced me to ride through the park with Lord Melton?" Portia pulled a face. "Eighty-eight years old. Creaky joints. Wooden teeth. Smelled of mold." She glanced at Mina, hoping to see some reaction in her implacable expression.

Mina did not so much as blink. The tight set of her mouth brought Heath to mind. Did they even know how alike they were? Stubborn fools.

Their mounts ambled along side by side at an easy gait. Clouds hung low overhead, large puffs of dirty wool. Portia tightened her fingers around her reins and tried again. "Or the time he forced me to dance with Lord Houghton, renowned for his lead feet? My toes still bear the scars."

Mina stared ahead, her expression unaltered.

"And then there was Sir Lionel—"

"Enough. Point taken," Mina finally burst out. "I appreciate what you're trying to do, but nothing you say will make me forgive my brother. I shall never speak to him again."

Portia nodded slowly. "Very well. You're entitled to your anger . . . but, then, perhaps so is he."

Mina shot her a mutinous look, her lips twisting.

"Do you love him?" Portia asked gently.

"Who?"

"Your young groom, of course."

"Edgar?" Mina laughed awkwardly. "No. I mean, I find him attractive, but . . ." Her voice slid into a sigh. "No, I don't love him. I hardly know him. Is that so horrible? I suppose I should have at least *believed* myself in love to permit such liberties." Mina's lips trembled. "I simply tire of no gentleman considering me good enough."

"You're not horrible, Mina. And you're good enough for any man." Moistening her lips, she couldn't resist imparting one final bit of advice. "You're luckier than you realize. Your brother cares for you. He merely seeks to protect you from the Whitfields of this world."

"Why are you defending him?" Mina demanded, her gaze searching Portia's face. "You don't even like him."

"Regardless of how I feel about your brother, he's good to you."

And when he kisses me, he makes the world disappear. I become as wicked as he—as yielding as a serving girl in his arms.

Heat suffused her face and she pressed the back of her gloved hand to one overly warm cheek, then the other. Drawing in a ragged breath, she stared ahead, feigning interest in the rocky terrain closing in around them.

Praying Heath's sister would not wonder at her flushed face, she suggested, "Perhaps we should head back? I smell rain."

"It always smells of rain."

"Well, it *looks* ready to rain."

"It always looks ready to rain. Don't be such a city girl," Mina taunted. "I had hoped we might do some serious riding today."

Portia quirked a brow. *"Serious* riding?"

A devious light twinkled in Mina's eyes. "Yes. Up for a little race?"

Portia appraised Mina for a moment, then shrugged. Why not? It had been years since she could ride anywhere other than the boundaries of Hyde Park. A slow grin curved her lips. "You've no idea who you're challenging."

Mina lifted a single brow, the jaunty feather of her hat bouncing in the wind. "I admit you sit a horse well." Her smiling eyes raked Portia. "But a city girl can't think to best me. I was born in the saddle."

"Let's see, then." With an exultant shout, Portia jabbed her heels and hurtled ahead.

"No fair," Mina shouted behind her.

Portia laughed over her shoulder. The pounding of hooves on earth filled her ears, spurring her on even faster. It had been too long. Too long in Town. Too long limited to sedate rides on Rotten Row under Astrid's watchful eyes.

Without glancing back, she gave herself up to the thrill of the ride, heedless of her bonnet flying from her head. The wind clawed her hairpins loose and her hair trailed behind her. She whooped in delight. Tears smarted in her eyes from the wind's sting, but she didn't care; she felt alive. Free.

After several minutes, she slowed her pounding pace. Assuming she had won, she looked over her shoulder, prepared to tease Mina mercilessly.

Craggy limestone terrain stared back. Gorse and wild blackthorn shuddered in the wind, but no Mina.

"Mina?" Portia pulled on her reins and came to a complete stop.

No sight of her anywhere. Frowning, Portia

turned in every direction. "Mina!" she called, worry hammering her heart.

The wind howled back like a beast in the distance, heightening her sense of isolation. She spun her mount around, her unbound hair whipping into her face, blinding her. Wiping the dark strands from her eyes, she scanned the horizon, searching even as she tried to steady her racing pulse. Nothing. She thundered back in the direction she had come.

After several moments, she stopped again, acknowledging that she was well and truly lost. Believing Mina behind her, she had not paid attention to landmarks.

"Brilliant," she muttered, her eyes scanning the barren landscape. Opening her mouth, she called Mina's name until she grew hoarse. The dark clouds looked close to bursting overhead. She was in for another soak if she didn't somehow find her way back to the house.

Prodding her mount into motion again, she set a halting pace, surveying her surroundings as she went along.

The first raindrop landed on her cheek. So softly she barely felt it. Several more followed, growing in volume and intensity. Tilting her face to the skies, she muttered an epithet no lady should know.

* * *

Heath sat in his office the precise moment the storm hit. Wind and rain buffeted the tall mullioned windows at his back. He lifted his head from the ledgers scattered across his desk and turned to glance out the window behind him, hoping his sister and Portia had returned from their afternoon ride.

He had seen them head out over an hour ago—had considered putting a stop to it. With yesterday's debacle so fresh in his mind, how could he not consider putting an end to their time together? As far as companions went, Lady Portia was entirely unsuitable. Impeccable pedigree or not, she wasn't a lady with whom his sister ought to keep company. Mina had never given him as much trouble in her entire life as she had since Portia's arrival. Still, he couldn't concentrate until he knew they were safely inside. Shoving to his feet, he strode from his office.

He'd just reached the foyer when Mina burst into the house, soaked to the skin, jabbering so fast he could hardly make out a word.

"Heath," she panted between gulping breaths. Her wet fingers latched onto his wrist. "I've lost Portia!"

"Lost?" he demanded, his heart leaping against his chest.

"What's this?" His grandmother called from

the top of the stairs, one of her many cats tucked in her arm. The animal's yellow eyes glittered in seeming mockery.

"I lost Portia." Mina shook her head, wide eyes a mixture of awe and worry. "Who knew a girl from Town could ride like that?"

"Well, Heath," his grandmother drawled, "you'll have to go after her, won't you?"

A sound request. Logical. Except his grandmother's eyes gleamed with a victorious light. She angled her head, her shifty blue eyes watching him, waiting.

The hair on his arms prickled. He pinched the bridge of his nose, convinced more than ever that he wouldn't have a moment's peace until Portia was gone. Still, losing her somewhere on his estate was not the way to rid himself of her.

Inhaling deeply through his nose, he said, "Tell me precisely where you last saw her."

Mina's shoulders sagged in clear relief. "You mean you'll find her?"

He felt his lips twist. Dropping his hand from his face he met his grandmother's triumphant gaze, asking, "Was there ever any doubt?"

Rain fell in torrents. Portia squinted against the downpour, giving up any attempt to guide her horse through the quagmire that threatened to drag them down. She let the reins fall lax in her hands and simply trusted that the animal desired shelter as much as she did.

"Come on, boy," she muttered through chattering teeth. Crouching low, she clung to the horse's neck as he wrestled his hooves from the marshy ground. "Take us home."

A cottage materialized through the gray curtain of rain as if her words alone had summoned it. Her mount, clearly no stranger to the dwelling, bypassed the cottage, trotting straight for the nearby stables. He halted at the closed doors, snorting loudly enough to be heard over the heavy thrum of rain.

"Not precisely what I had in mind," Portia grumbled as she slid off the horse's back and trudged through the mud to fling open the doors. Still, it was shelter, and she couldn't begrudge the beast from delivering them safely from the storm.

Her mount needed no prodding. He barreled past her in his haste to get inside. Muttering beneath her breath, she followed after him. Her gaze swept over the interior as she tugged off her clinging gloves. A quick survey revealed no animals and little in the way of equipment. Barren stalls stared back at her. Her horse sauntered in and out of these, snuffling and devouring the hay littering the ground.

She followed the horse into one stall. Removing

his saddle, she snatched a blanket that hung over one of the rails and rubbed the animal down.

Satisfied that she had tended the horse to the best of her ability, she gave his rump one last pat and darted back outside, a hand shielding her face in a feeble attempt to ward off the deluge.

After three swift raps, her hand went for the latch. Thankfully, the cottage door was unlocked. Gasping, she stumbled inside. Closing the door behind her, she eyed the room.

This was no meager crofter's cottage. Contrary to the humble exterior, the inside was well appointed—an elegant sanctuary.

Wringing water from her hair, she moved to the center of the single-room dwelling and turned in a small circle. Her gaze fell on the large tester bed, the type found in any fine home. An elegant dining table, accompanied with high back chairs, sat before the shuttered window. A large desk, littered with books and papers, occupied one corner. A chintz-covered sofa was angled before the fireplace, allowing room for a large sheepskin rug, the mere sight of which already made her feel warm. Her gaze landed on a stack of wood in a basket.

"Yes," she breathed, her breath fogging the air. Already she imagined the heat of a fire soaking into her bones and ridding her of foggy breath. Hurrying forward, she arranged the logs in the fireplace. Her cold fingers stumbled several times, stinging from both cold and the abrasive wood, until at last she coaxed a fire to life.

Her trembling hands then attacked the buttons of her habit, eager to be rid of the clinging wet fabric, eager for the fire to do its work and warm her bones.

Stripped bare, she draped her clothing over the backs of the chairs. Shaking in the frigid air, she snatched the blanket off the bed and drew it around her. Wrapped tight, she sank onto the rug before the hearth, the soft lambskin a heavenly cloud beneath her chilled body.

She stared into the dancing flames, feeling rather satisfied with herself. Bathed in the warm glow of the fire, she felt at peace in the unexpected solitude. Freedom at last, even if short-lived.

She had contemplated running away before. Escape from responsibility. From the pressure of insurmountable debt. From a constant sense of inadequacy. If her mother could escape, could take leave of all expectations placed upon her, why not her?

Sighing softly, Portia rested her chin on her knees. She flexed her toes in the soft wool. Her eyelids grew heavy as she watched the flames stretch and sway in the hearth. Lethargy crept into her bones and her thoughts drifted back to her mother. Did the daughter she left behind never intrude on her thoughts? Portia gave her head a violent shake and wiped at the sudden dash of tears on her cheeks, refusing to let such thoughts rob her of this rare-found tranquility.

She snuggled onto her side, loosening the blanket so that it draped over her. With the soft wool cushioning her body, she could almost imagine she floated in the heavens. Popping sounds from the fire and the steady beat of rain lulled her. She closed her eyes and let her muscles sink and melt into deep sleep.

Chapter 18

Heath rode like a demon, calling Portia's name over the howl of wind and rain. He lost all sense of time as he searched, scanning the horizon, his voice growing hoarse from shouting.

Tracks could not be found in this weather, so he scoured the countryside, pushing Iago hard, oblivious to the cold, to the rain that chilled him to the very marrow of his bones. As the minutes rolled into an hour, fear wormed its way into his heart.

If she gave her horse its lead, it should know its way back. His fear heightened. Unless she had lost her horse, had been thrown—like their first meeting. She could be on foot—or worse, lying unconscious somewhere.

Words shuddered from his mouth, from lips that had long gone numb. Gradually, they began to take meaning in his head. *God, let her be safe. Let her be safe. Don't take her, too.*

For the first time since boyhood, he prayed to God for intervention. The same God that had cursed his family with a blight that haunted their every day, a specter from which he could never escape.

His horse plunged down a steep incline, and Heath stopped at the bottom, realizing he was near the lodge. His retreat. The sanctuary he had fled lately, preferring it to the dower house and the questions he would undoubtedly find in Della's gaze when he could not bring himself to touch her.

Hope burned low in his gut, hot and hungry as he thundered into the yard, pulling up hard at sight of the stable door swinging in the wind. Digging in his heels, he rode into the barn, discovering a mount from his stables snuffling the ground for hay in one of the stalls.

A hiss of breath escaped him. Portia was here. Safe. He dismounted and made short work of unsaddling Iago and securing him in a stall next to the sorrel. Tension knotted his shoulders, winding a path up the back of his neck. He stalked through the yard, his relief dissolving in place of anger. Anger at her. Anger at himself for the fear that had gripped him.

He halted at the door, hand poised over the latch. *Was this another trick?* Another device to force him alone with her? He scowled, recalling his grandmother's satisfied expression as she looked down on him from the top of the stairs.

Constance had warned him. And he had not listened. He had, instead, let fathomless blue eyes gull him. He stared at the door, watching rain sluice down its plane, knowing to go inside would mean utter isolation with a woman he craved with every fiber of his being. Last time Constance had interrupted. His sister would not arrive to save him this time. No one would. He had only his willpower on which to rely.

Inhaling deeply, he flung open the door, telling himself he could resist one marriage-minded female.

He truly must be mad to have allowed things to come this far. To let his heart soften toward any woman. Soft hearts bled, and in their pain they caused grief and havoc. His parents had proved that.

Yet he could set things right. Starting now. He would do what he should have done from the beginning. Whether she wanted to or not, Portia's holiday was at an end.

Like a moth to the flame, his gaze found her—asleep on the lambskin before the fire. He approached, blood rushing to his groin as he eyed breasts so pert his hands itched to palm them, to take the tight, pebble-sized nipples into his mouth.

If he had any doubts, they fled in an instant. Lady Portia Derring would do whatever it took to get him to the altar.

Portia whimpered at the sensation of cool air crawling over her breasts, shriveling her nipples and stroking her belly with icy hands. Her eyes fluttered open and she stared in confusion at the murky room. Firelight flickered over the walls like demons writhing and twisting in some kind of primeval dance. With a shiver, she closed her eyes again and pulled the blanket back over her nakedness, grasping at the fleeing scraps of her dream.

She had been standing beneath a warm Athens sun—the gleaming columns of the Parthenon stretching to a sky so blue her eyes ached to look at it. Her mother stood beside her, her face glowing as she talked. The sun beat down on Portia's bare head until her scalp tingled. A breeze, fragrant and balmy, kissed her face. For a brief moment, in the sanctuary of her dream, Portia had everything she ever wanted.

Closing her eyes tightly, she breathed through her nostrils and concentrated, trying to recapture the scent of sweet, honeyed air, trying to glimpse marble columns gleaming in the afternoon sun. All to no avail. It was gone. Lost. A frown tugged at her lips.

A drop of water fell on her forehead, cold and irritating. She brushed it away with the back of her hand. Another followed, as cold and irritating as the last, and she opened her eyes, hoping that the roof didn't have a leak.

No leak, she registered with a strange sense of detachment as she gazed up at the shadowy figure of a man, immense and looming above her. A scream lodged in her throat. Clutching the blanket to her chin, she sank deeper into her bed of wool.

"Get up," he growled.

"Heath?"

"On your feet," he demanded, the force behind each word a gouge to her heart.

Tucking the blanket beneath her armpits, she rose, bringing herself flush against him. She attempted to step back but his hand clamped down, quick and brutal on her arm.

Filling her lungs with a fortifying breath, she attempted to speak, "How did you—"

"Was this part of the plan?" His gaze scraped her like a freshly sharpened blade. Eyes she knew to be gray were now black as night. Deadly as a viper's stare. "Waiting for me naked and sleep-warmed?"

She looked down at herself, at his hand on her arm, at her blanket-swathed body, and had a pretty good idea of how he saw her. A woman lying in wait, a predator primed to seduce.

The fire at her naked back felt almost too warm. No doubt her skin glowed pink, flushed. Her eyes sleep clouded. Her hair—she didn't want to imagine its condition. It must look a mess. She dragged a hand through the snarled mass, tucking several loose strands behind both ears in a feeble effort to restore it to order.

"Oh, you're good," he sneered, dropping her arm as if burned. "I almost believed you. Believed that you were as much a victim as I to all of Grandmother's machinations. But this has been your game from the start, hasn't it?"

Portia shook her head fiercely. "No. You're a fool if you believe that." She lurched back, uncaring that her back grew uncomfortably warm. She would step into the flames of hell itself if it put distance between them. She waved an arm toward the door. "You think I had some part in arranging the storm that stranded me here?"

He ignored her and glanced about the cottage,

his gaze stopping at the chair where her clothes draped. "Get dressed."

She looked at her clothes. "They're still wet."

He thumbed behind him to the door. "Since we're going to ride back out into the rain, wet clothes won't matter much."

Portia shivered. "Can we not wait until the weather clears?"

His lips curled back from his teeth. "Oh, you'd like that wouldn't you? More time alone with me." He advanced, stalking her like a jungle cat, his eyes gleaming wickedly. "And just how far would you go to trap me?" His eyes dropped and she felt them burn a trail over the tops of her bare shoulders. "Who's to say I won't take what you're offering and still not wed you?" His hand rose, brushing the slope of one shoulder, sliding down until the backs of his fingers grazed the swell of one breast.

Her breath caught, and not entirely from fear. She should loathe him and the suggestive gleam in his eyes, the wicked bent of his thoughts. How could she feel anything but contempt for a man who thought so ill of her? Who thought her dishonest and conniving?

She watched his mouth as he continued to talk, hypnotized by the slow, seductive movement of his lips, the way they moved to form each and every word—regardless that his words were poison. "Are you prepared to wager all, Lady Portia, on the chance that I will come to scratch and wed you?" He angled his head. "It's a wager you'll lose, but I'll accommodate you. I wouldn't mind a taste of what you're flaunting."

With a snort of disgust, she twisted away from his roving fingers, suddenly feeling as though foul insects crawled across her flesh. "Get your hands off me. I'm offering you *nothing*."

She blinked rapidly, wondering at the sting in her eyes, the awful thickness in her throat. He would *not* reduce her to tears. Swallowing, she lifted her chin. "I'm not about to be dragged across the countryside simply because of your deranged notion that I've designs on you. When will you get it through that thick skull of yours that I am not in pursuit of you?" She raked him with a withering glare.

His chest lifted on a great inhalation as if gathering strength and patience from some deep well within him. As if *he* were the one being tested and pushed beyond aggravation. "We are not about to stay here together. This rain could very well continue on through the night."

"Then leave." She flung a hand in the direction of the door. "Feel no obligation to remain. Heaven knows you're not *safe* with me. Why, I might ravish you." Rolling her eyes, she stomped toward the table and pulled out a chair. Securing her blanket more tightly about her, she planted herself in the seat. Lifting an eyebrow, she dared him to force her to move from her spot.

He could leave. She was staying put.

He took his time replying, looking from her to the door as if he debated hefting her bodily from the chair. She held her breath, willing him to leave—willing him to quit this absurdity and believe her. At last, he sighed and muttered, "I can't leave you here by yourself."

"Pesky gentlemanly honor," she mocked. "Picks the most inopportune times to surface."

He cocked his head and studied her through narrowed eyes. "Sarcasm doesn't suit you, Portia."

"No, my lord, you don't suit me," she countered.

One corner of his mouth lifted. "Ah, but we know that to be untrue."

Memories intruded. The taste of his kiss, the velvet slide of his tongue in her mouth. She pushed aside the unwanted memories and reminded herself of his total misjudgment of her. How could she crave a man who thought so little of her? Where was her pride?

She stifled the urge to howl in frustration. "What you *know* couldn't fill the inside of my boot."

"God's teeth, you've a viper's tongue. No wonder you can't find a gentleman to wed in Town."

The barb stung and she stiffened, fighting for composure.

He looked away, too—to the single window, where wind and rain rattled noisily against the shutters. He sighed, and the sound resounded through her.

Swallowing, she strove to appear poised, unaffected—the precise way she didn't feel at the prospect of a night alone with him.

"I'll sleep on the rug," he finally said. "But don't think my staying changes anything. You're not so tempting I can't resist you for a single night."

Heat scalded her cheeks. She surged to her feet, every inch of her quivering with fury. He had delivered his final insult. Her hands clenched about her blanket, her fingers stiff and bloodless. "I'll sleep on the rug. I found it quite comfortable before you woke me."

With stiff movements, she marched back to the lambskin rug.

"Portia," he began, his hand falling on her arm. "I'll sleep—"

"Unhand me," she snarled, wrenching free. "I'll sleep on the rug. You take the bed. No need to make a pretense of good manners now. Your true colors have been revealed. You're no gentleman." Clutching the blanket about her as if it were a shield, she looked him over as if he were some bug lying very small and insignificant at her feet. Holding herself stiff with dignity, she tossed down, "You're nothing. Nothing at all."

She whirled around, choking down the sob rising from her chest, desperate that he not suspect how that single lie shattered her. Sinking onto the soft pelt, she wished her words were true, wished it didn't matter what he thought.

Chapter 19

Heath surged upright in bed, blinking against cold blackness. He gazed blindly into the dark, still caught within the tight fist of a nightmare that never fully left him—even when awake. The dream had burrowed itself into his soul with relentless tenacity, surfacing off and on throughout his life, reminding him that he was never in full possession of himself.

Absurd as it was, when the nightmare beset him, he turned into the boy he had been—the impulse to call out for his mother burning on his tongue. Ironic considering she had never responded to his calls when he'd been a boy.

From the moment of his brother's birth, the curse already had him in its terrible hold. Everyone knew William's fate—the fate of another Moreton lost to madness. It broke his mother, thrusting her into some dark place from which she never returned.

He dragged a shaking hand through his hair. His heart lodged somewhere in his throat. He fought to swallow it back down. Nothing save the occasional crumble of burnt wood in the hearth could be heard. A faint light glowed there, not enough to suffuse the room, but enough to remind him instantly of where he was. The lodge. His refuge of late when he craved escape. Except his refuge had now become the site of his torment.

He released a shuddering breath, unaware until that moment that he had been holding it deep in his lungs. Almost as if he feared the nightmare real and not a thing of the past. As if he had awakened, twelve years old again, the tormented screams of his baby brother engulfing him and his own fragile sanity. Every keening wail a knife thrust into his heart, driving Heath closer and closer to a madness that lurked like a beast in the dark, waiting to strike and drag him into the abyss.

He rose, dropping his feet on the cold, bare wood floor. Taking care not to glance at the figure asleep on the large rug, he made his way to the hearth. Stubborn female. He would have given her the bed.

Giving the rug a wide berth, he knelt and added some logs to the fire, then stoked it until it crackled and emitted a steady glow of light throughout the room. His downfall—for when he turned around, his gaze sought her, feasting on the sight of her like a man starved.

His feet moved, advancing on her where she slept, curled on her side like an innocent babe asleep. Yet she was no innocent. He could no longer believe her blameless, that she had fallen in so unwittingly with all his grandmother's schemes. That her sole purpose in remaining at Moreton Hall could possibly be to escape the Season. What a fool he'd been to ever consider it.

He hovered over her sleeping form, hands flexing at his sides. Tension thrummed through his muscles. Anger coursed his blood—anger at himself for being drawn to her despite all he knew her to be.

He didn't know which urge the strongest: to pull her in his arms or shake her until her teeth rattled in that stubborn head of hers. She thought him *nothing*? Damned if that didn't wound him to the core, didn't leave him staring at the rafters long after her breathing had grown slow and even in sleep. And what was she, the one that had duped him with her pretty denials. He had even begun to feel empathy for her.

She shifted, rolling onto her back, her hair a

dark puddle around her. Her shoulders gleamed like pale marble above the blanket's edge. His mouth went dry at the sight. Only a thin barrier of fabric hid her nudity from his eyes. A few feet separated him from the unhindered sight of her, from total access to the body that had haunted his dreams for nights. And his mind for days.

A soft sound escaped her lips, and her eyes fluttered open. She stared up at him though unfocused eyes. A soft, dreamy smile curved her lips. Then she blinked. The smile vanished, right along with the dreamy look. With a startled cry, she lurched up, forgetting the blanket, forgetting her nudity.

His breath escaped in a hiss as he devoured the sight of her small, pert breasts, the dusky nipples, the gentle slope of her belly. It was too much. The sight undid him, made his legs weaken and buckle beneath him.

He dropped to his knees before her, greedily drinking in the sight of her.

She followed his gaze to her breasts, gasped and made a grab for the blanket pooled around her waist.

A growl sounded from deep within his chest and something hot and primal erupted low in his gut. Without thinking, he tore the blanket from her and tossed it aside, forcing her to lay before him in all her naked glory.

She made a small sound of distress and tried to cover herself with her hands, but he seized her wrists, his fingers flexing around the delicate bones. Bones so fragile the barest pressure would snap them.

His gaze ran the full length of her body, roaming over the sleek lines and gentle curves. She tucked her knees in an attempt to cover her most secret part and the move, so basic, so womanly, enflamed his desire to have her, to give up the fight and fall—to descend into the very depths of the abyss he had spent a lifetime fighting.

He had always preferred his women buxom, voluptuous like Della. Yet Portia's coltlike slimness possessed its own beauty. Achingly feminine, soft and graceful as a willow bending in the wind, her body demanded worship, praise from his mouth and hands. There was no fighting it, no strength left in him to resist.

Releasing her wrists, he grasped the smooth and supple outside swell of one hip. His breath hitched and he slid his hand around, cupping the fullness of one cheek. Her gasp reached his ears, different than any sound he'd ever heard, ripped from some place deep in her throat where pleasure hid.

His fingers flexed, digging into the roundness of her bottom, forcing her closer, until her legs unfurled, opening her like a flower to him. He pressed his full length against her, moaning at her softness, her silken limbs, her warm body.

Her wide eyes locked with his, the luminescent blue glowing like precious gems in the firelight. "What are you—"

He silenced her with a violent shake of his head.

No time for words. For logic. Logic had clearly fled if he would come to this woman. If he would take her in his arms, clutch her lissom figure against his as if he had some kind of claim on her.

Closing his eyes, he curled his fingers and trailed the backs along the sleek flesh of her back, over each tiny bump of her spine. Delicate, tantalizing—he wanted to skim his mouth over each and every one.

His hands continued their exploration, roaming every inch of her. The tender hollow of her navel. The delicate shape of each rib. The soft curve of her belly that quivered under his fingertips. His hands grazed the underside of each breast, testing their slight weight. He brushed open palms over her hard nipples. Her breathing grew harsh, arousing him nearly as much as the silky feel of her.

Unable to stop himself, he closed a hand over each breast, gripping the firm, petite mounds, squeezing, kneading, rolling the distended peaks. Her desperate keening filled the air, knifing through him, making him burn, banishing any lingering reservations. A strangled laugh rose up in his throat. Not that he had any notion of stopping.

Her hands grabbed his forearms, her nails cutting his flesh in a pain that bordered pleasure. "Heath," she whimpered, begging, pleading.

Releasing her breasts, he delved one hand between her thighs, brushing feather-soft curls damp with need. He tested her readiness, stroking the folds of her sex, already slick for him.

Her fingers dug like talons into his arms and she leaned forward, resting her damp forehead against his chest as he worked his fingers feverishly along those folds, back and forth, back and forth, each time brushing nearer and nearer to that tiny little nub. Finally, he touched it, rubbed his fingers over the pearl in fast, little circles. Her body tensed and she released a shuddering cry.

He drank in her rapturous expression, branding that look in his mind, never wanting to forget it. Then, as the waves of her climax were still washing over her, he parted her legs and put his mouth to that exquisite pleasure point and sucked, tasting her passion.

Arching her back, she came up off the rug releasing a cry as sweet as any songbird. His eyes devoured the breasts quivering above him, golden in the firelight as her climax tore through her.

She collapsed back on the lambskin, her sinuous body panting and humming from her release.

He never took his eyes off her as he stood to shuck off his clothes, his movements as eager and clumsy as a lad.

Her eyes lifted, searching his. "Heath?" she asked, her voice a hoarse rasp.

He shook his head, one boot hitting the floor, then the next. Naked, he stood over her. Her eyes flitted over him, flaring wide. He held her wide gaze, daring her to object.

"This has been coming from the start," he muttered, determined that nothing veer him from this course, determined that common sense not rear itself and put a stop to the very thing he had wanted to do since first laying eyes on her. "Since we met on that muddy road. There's no going back now."

He was past reasoning, past caring about all the reasons he couldn't do this, why she was the last woman on earth he had any business taking to his bed.

He'd finally descended into the abyss.

Chapter 20

There's no going back now.

Portia heard the words, heard their challenge and knew a part of her should be annoyed, perhaps even afraid of the naked giant looming over her. The very man who had accused *her* of trying to trap him into marriage was now bent on ravishment.

Yet when she looked into his eyes and saw the question in his feverish gaze, the desperate need, she knew he waited, knew he wanted her to decide . . . in spite of his bold proclamation.

His arms, taut bands of steel braced on each

243

side of her, trembled with restraint. She marveled that someone as formidable and powerful as he could waver in his strength. And the greatest shock of all was that *she* did that to him. Beyond finding herself naked in a man's arms, *she* was the object of his desire. She had never considered herself capable of producing such a visceral reaction in a man. Not her—a woman who had passed five Seasons without an offer of matrimony. And not with him—a man with every reason to avoid entanglements with gently bred females.

She drank in the sight of him, the shadows pooling in the hollows of his face, the play of his sculpted muscles. Her gaze fell lower, eyeing his manhood springing from between his legs, daunting in its size. The hard length pulsed before her very eyes, seeming to summon her touch. Instead of feeling the apprehension she should, her stomach clenched in response. The place between her thighs throbbed. Her breathing grew labored.

Could that part of him make her feel as wonderful as his marvelous mouth had? Her eyes shot back up to his, heat flaming her face at her lurid thoughts.

"Oh, yes," he muttered, as if he had the ability to read her thoughts. "Touch me," he commanded.

His rough voice, combined with the desperate intensity of his gaze, would have her do anything he asked.

She reached out and touched the center of his chest with one finger. Smiling tentatively, she trailed that finger down his sternum, over the flat plane of his hard stomach, her nail slightly scraping the firm skin. His breathing grew harsh.

Her finger inched lower, hesitating a moment before arriving at his jutting manhood. She touched the head of him, intrigued at the tiny bead of moisture that rose to kiss her fingertip.

He groaned.

Emboldened, she closed her hand around his throbbing length and gently squeezed, both amazed and delighted at the soft texture of him— silk on steel in her palm.

"Portia, I can't wait any longer." His jaw clenched, the muscles knotting, demonstrating his hard-fought control. "Tell me you want this."

Her smile deepened. It thrilled her to see her power over him, to know how badly he wanted her, to know that he held himself back, waiting for her to say the word. Despite the infernal curse hanging over him—a perpetual storm cloud that influenced his life's every action—he couldn't resist her. So much that he would put aside the fears and habits of a lifetime for her. All for her. Her heart swelled.

Arching her spine, she rubbed her bare breasts against his chest.

"You mean you could stop?" she purred.

His hands clamped down on her hips, positioning her beneath him. The head of him probed her entrance and she sucked in a breath.

His breath caught in a hiss as he pushed inside her slowly, one inch at a time. Her muscles stretched to accommodate him.

His gaze, fathomless as a midnight sea, mesmerized her, lodging deep in her soul as he held himself still as stone over her.

"Heath," she whimpered, her fingers digging into his tense forearms, urging him on, desperate for more, not understanding what *more* could be but knowing it hung there, elusive, just beyond her reach. "Please."

"I don't want to hurt—"

"Heath," she moaned, instinctively opening her legs wider and angling her hips to take him in deeper.

A choked cry escaped him. "Portia," he muttered, his breath fanning hotly against her throat. "You don't know—"

Portia shook her head from side to side on the rug, the throbbing burn in her core desperate to have all of him.

She let go of his arms and slid her hands down his back, skimming the smooth skin until she clutched his firm buttocks with both hands. Guided by instinct, she dragged him closer, impaling him deep in her womb.

Their cries mingled, filling the air: his exultant, hers shocked at the pleasure-pain of her rendered maidenhead—at the overwhelming feeling of completion, of never again being anything except a part of him.

His body pressed heavily upon her, comforting and thrilling in its weight.

"Portia?" he gasped in her ear, chest shuddering atop her. His arms came around her, holding her as if she were some gentle, precious creature that might vanish at any moment.

She didn't answer, couldn't. Could only move, writhe beneath him. Rotating her hips, she tightened her inner muscles and clenched him tightly, her body begging for more, for an end to the incredible fire that he had stoked within her.

"Oh, God," he groaned and moved, withdrawing himself nearly out of her before thrusting back inside. Ripples of white-hot pleasure washed over her as he repeated the action, pumping in and out of her. The feel of his hardness hammering into her, the strong fingers digging into her hips, anchoring her for his amorous assault, drove her over the edge.

Her head came off the rug, a scream rising from deep in her throat, hovering on her lips. His frenzied stroking stoked her passions higher, created a maelstrom of desire that at last wrung an air-shattering shout from her lips.

He pumped several more times, the violent smacking sounds of their bodies coming together thrilling her in the deepest, primal way. With a brief shout, he pulled from her body, leaving her suddenly bereft.

Portia watched as he spilled his seed into his waiting hand. She looked from his cupped hand, a tightness gripping her chest as she studied his face. The heavy fall of his dark hair obscured his eyes, yet she longed to see them, longed to gauge his exact emotions and understand how he could even possess the foresight to withdraw his body from hers at the peak of passion.

Suddenly he looked up, flinging the hair back from his face, and she found herself pinned beneath his searing gaze. And there, in his eyes, she saw it. Everything that would forever keep them apart. Curse or no, he'd never let her have his heart. The Earl of Moreton refused to love. Not her or any woman. She tormented herself to think otherwise.

She dipped her gaze, determined that he not read her pain—the inexplicable, unreasonable pain that clawed her heart.

Heath rose and walked away. Portia sat up and hugged her knees to her chest, resisting her sudden sense of desolation, fighting the desire to follow him with her eyes, her heart.

"Portia."

She turned at the sound of her name, a hush on

the air. He handed her a damp cloth. She stared at it for a moment, puzzled, and then she winced, understanding.

"Thank you," she murmured, accepting the cloth. She looked from him to the linen, an awkward flush creeping up her neck. Absurd considering what had transpired between them.

"Do you mind?" she asked in a small voice, careful to keep her eyes on his face and not his nudity. She motioned for him to turn around. He shot her an annoyed look.

Snatching the cloth from her hand, he commanded, "Lay down."

"W-What?"

"Lay. Down." He must have read her bewilderment, for he softened his voice. "Let me do this for you, Portia."

She slowly fell back on the rug. Throwing an arm over her eyes as if she could hide from the intimacy, she spread her legs for him, forcing her muscles to relax as he cleaned her, eliminating the evidence of her rendered maidenhead. She only wished the memory of what she had done could be wiped out as easily.

The linen felt cool and abrasive against her tender flesh, each swipe unhurried—sweet agony to her oversensitized skin. She bit her lip to stop a whimper from escaping.

She heard the linen hit the floor and sighed

with relief—glad for an end to the torment—only to gasp when he curled his big body next to hers.

"What are you doing?"

"Going to sleep," his voice sounded beside her ear, fluttering strands of her hair against her cheek.

He did not intend to return to the bed now that he had taken his pleasure? Her thoughts whirled. Why had he made love to her? The very woman he suspected intent on trapping him? And why was he still here? Beside her? Pulling her to him as if he had every right, as if she belonged at his side?

"Sleep," she echoed, her every nerve stretched tight, achingly alive. Sleep. Elusive as smoke circling overhead.

His hand splayed over her hip possessively, as if anchoring her to him.

She wet her lips, searching for her voice, pretending that the slight touch did not affect her. "Tomorrow," she began, pausing, relieved that her voice did not quake as her insides did. "Your grandmother will prove difficult."

"Isn't she always?" he said against her neck, the moist fan of his breath making her belly flutter.

"We will have been alone together"—her voice tore, twisting into a sharp gasp as his teeth bit down on her earlobe. Desire, hot and savage, spiked through her, melting her bones and burning her blood as she fought to finish her sentence— "all night."

"Yes," he breathed in a voice warm as sherry, thick with promise. He raised his head to look at her. "All night." His hair fell forward, a dark curtain on either side of his face. Light and shadow flickered over his features—sunlight on wind-rippled water, casting his face into sharp lines and hollows.

Her hand wobbled hesitantly on the air before pushing the heavy skein of hair back from his face. His eyes gleamed down at her, those dark fathomless pools, pulling her in, swallowing her whole. "What will we do?" She moistened her lips. "What will we say?"

He tensed and took his time responding. For a moment, she thought he would not answer at all—or if he did, it would be to heap the familiar abuse on her head.

Then he spoke, and in a voice that bore little resemblance to the intimate huskiness of moments ago. This voice rang with decisiveness, gravity. "Nothing. Nothing has changed. I know why you came here, Portia. What you expect."

She opened her mouth to protest, but he placed a finger against her lips, silencing her with the single feather-soft touch. "And I know what it is we've done," he continued, "but I cannot marry. You or anyone. Ever."

Nothing has changed. His proclamation echoed in her heart, her soul. And she had to confess that a secret part of her wished things had changed—wished he had. Yet he would never wed, not as long as he believed his destiny rested in madness . . . and he closed his heart to love.

"Can you accept that?" His gaze burned into her, demanding she understand. And she did. He need not worry she would turn into a hysterical female, insisting he do the honorable thing and marry her. She would prove to him that she had not set out to trap him. No matter how her heart bled to let him go.

"Of course," she replied with forced lightness even as her heart tightened into a painful knot beneath her breastbone. "I have no wish to marry."

His expression turned guarded, uncertain.

I have no wish to marry. True. She hadn't. Ever. So why did the words stick in her throat? Spending a night in his arms had not changed her ultimate goal. She wanted independence, craved a life abroad, to stand before the Parthenon and see with her own eyes if it was as magnificent as everything she had read. She longed for the freedom her mother enjoyed. Not nights of passion with a man that reduced her will to ashes.

"No regrets, then?"

"No regrets," she vowed.

Turning, he pressed a moist kiss to her palm. "This is all we'll have," he whispered against the tender flesh. His eyes met hers over her palm.

"I'm in no position to offer more than tonight."

For a moment, she allowed herself to wonder, *what if.* What if he *wanted* to marry her? Not because his grandmother wanted him to, but because he wanted to. Would she accept? Would she cast aside her dreams, sacrifice her hopes? The delightful weight of his body atop hers was answer enough. For night after night of this? Night after night of him? Her mind shied from answering the question. Instead, she released a chest-shuddering sigh, relieved that she wouldn't be given a choice—relieved and saddened.

His hand traced the line of her collarbone, the brush of his fingertips chasing away her troubled thoughts. That hand lowered, trailing a fiery path between her breasts and she trembled.

"Don't worry. I'll handle Grandmother," his low voice reassured her, most likely mistaking her shudder for anxiety over what his grandmother would say when they returned home. "We have tonight." His husky voice rumbled over her, a caress in itself. A slow lick of heat curled in her belly at his promise.

A single night.

She arched beneath his hand, thrusting her breast into his ready palm. Her hand circled his neck, dragging his mouth down to hers.

This would be all they ever had. It had to be enough. She would make it so.

Chapter 21

Portia and Heath had just cleared the threshold of Moreton Hall when Lady Moreton swept down on them like a carrion bird in pursuit of fresh kill. Her darting eyes—quick and hungry—assessed them, searching, looking for a point of invasion. No doubt she had been watching for their return from one of the upstairs windows.

The feral light gleaming in her eyes spiked unease deep in the well of Portia's heart. She shrank back, but Heath's hand on the small of her back stopped her from total retreat. He gave her a reassuring wink, and she melted at the small gesture before gathering herself tightly under control.

Tender feelings for him had no place in her heart this morning. Or ever again. Their intimacy ended the moment they crossed the threshold. A one-time affair, a brief foray into passion that must be put behind her.

"Where have you been?" Lady Moreton demanded, then waved a hand, granting neither one the chance to answer. "It's of no account now. You've been out all night together. Without a chaperone. The damage is done. You must wed posthaste."

Portia sighed, suddenly very tired. Tired of Lady Moreton's scheming and plotting and badgering. So much like her own grandmother with her insufferable expectations.

"Good morning to you, too, Grandmother," Heath greeted. "And yes, we're well—we found shelter from the storm, thank you for inquiring."

"Well, I can see you're both well," she snapped, that elegant, blue-veined hand fluttering in the air. "Now, I recommend you leave at once to procure a special license. I shall make the arrangements here while—"

"That won't be necessary," he interrupted in a controlled voice, smooth as polished marble.

"What?" Lady Moreton blinked rapidly, as if trying to rid some particle from her eye.

"We won't be getting married," Heath announced in a voice that brooked no argument.

Lady Moreton turned her twitchy stare on Portia. "You cannot mean to accept this, my dear."

From the corner of her eye, Portia saw Heath turn to study her, felt his unwavering gaze, his dark judgment as he waited for her answer. After everything, he still thought her a grasping, unscrupulous marriage-minded female. Her heart twisted. Yet if she were honest with herself, perhaps a small part of her did want to marry him.

Yet not like this. Not against his will.

Moistening her lips, she said as firmly as she could, "My lady, it's really for the best that I leave."

"For the *best*?" Lady Moreton's voice splintered the air of the great foyer. "Where's your dignity? You're ruined, you stupid girl!"

Portia flinched and closed her eyes slowly in one long fortifying blink, retreating into that dark cave she resided when her family lashed her with the barbed whips of their tongues.

"That will be enough," Heath's voice rumbled beside her, the pressure of his hand at her back warm and comforting, a lifeline drawing her from the shelter of the cave.

"I was afraid of this," Lady Moreton muttered, her head bobbing up and down like a buoy in tossing waters. "That is why I sent for the vicar."

"You what?" Heath dropped his hand from her back and stoically faced his grandmother. "So he can wag his tongue to all in the district about affairs that are none of his concern?"

A cold draft swept over Portia. "Why would you send for the vicar?" she heard herself asking.

Heath answered without looking her way. "She means for him to *persuade* us, isn't that so, Grandmother."

"Persuade?" Portia echoed.

"Portia. Dear." Lady Moreton seized both her hands with her chilled ones. "Mr. Hatley is a man of God. Surely he will help you and Heath see reason, convince you both to wed. For the safety of your souls if nothing else."

"Oh, let's be honest," Heath sneered. "You've sent for Hatley to force my hand."

"Did someone say my name?" a voice pealed through the vast foyer with the clarity of a bell.

Portia turned to watch the vicar descend the stairs. Dressed all in black, with a wide cleric's collar, she retreated a step as if the devil himself approached and not a man of God.

"Mr. Hatley," Heath greeted, his voice flat, void of warmth.

"I understand congratulations are in order," the vicar boomed in a voice bred for the pulpit.

"I'm afraid you've been misinformed," Heath replied. "My apologies. You made the trip out here for nothing."

"I told you he would be resistant," Lady Moreton

chimed, moving to stand beside the vicar. Together they presented an imposing, united front.

Mr. Hatley smiled. A patronizing curve of moist, over-fleshed lips. "Come now, my lord, be obliging. I can't say I endorse Lady Portia's methods"—he paused to waggle his brows at Portia in a look that could only be described as a jeer—"but you've been well and truly caught, lad. Time to own up to your responsibilities and marry the lady." Mr. Hatley winked at her and added in less than discreet tones, "You said you would bring him to heel and right you did, my lady. *Right you did.*"

Horrified, Portia shook her head, opening her mouth to deny she had ever purported to do such a thing. Those were his words. Not hers. Yet she knew with a deep pang in her heart that Heath would take this as the final, irrefutable proof that she was a liar, a heartless manipulator.

Even as he turned on her, eyes full of disgust, she knew nothing she said would ever convince him otherwise. Still, she had to try. "Heath—"

"Don't," he cut in, the single word a knife to her heart. As if in reflex, she pressed a hand against her chest, looking away from his scornful gaze, unable to bear it. "I'm weary of your lies."

"I told you we should have sent her back," a cheerless voice rang out.

Portia followed the sound, her eyes landing on

Constance, grim and unsmiling at the top of the stairs.

Chest tight as a drum, she looked back to Heath, braced to hear him second his sister's opinion. He said nothing. His eyes remained locked with hers, chips of ice that nothing could thaw. His stare imprisoned her; she wished she could look away, escape the intensity of cold gray eyes that chilled her very heart and froze her blood.

"Leave us, Constance," Heath said. "We've audience enough."

"But Heath—"

"Leave us!"

From the corner of her eye, she noted Constance's departure, relieved for that at least. Yet she had eyes only for Heath. She stared at him, praying that he would see the truth in her gaze, that he would see *her.*

"I'm aware of your reservations, my lord," Mr. Hatley inserted, heedless of the damage his thoughtless words had wrought. "I've counseled your grandmother on the matter for quite some time. Your concerns for spreading your family's disease are commendable."

Portia tore her gaze from Heath to watch the vicar's fat lips smile in a denigrating manner. He continued, "But such things are in God's hands, my lord. Not yours."

She glanced back at Heath to see how he took this pronouncement.

"God's hands?" Heath ground out, the muscles along his jaw knotting dangerously. "I'll not leave it to God's hands, sir." Each word fell hard and swift from his mouth, cracking on the air like a volley of gunfire. "As I recall, God did not intervene when my brother screamed from his crib. For nigh on two years, he suffered—his screams filling this house."

Her hands twitched at her sides, the urge to reach out, lay a hand on his tense shoulder and offer comfort, burning her palm. Yet she knew he would reject the gesture. Reject her.

In a voice still hard and unrelenting, he demanded, "Do you know what it's like for the screams of a child to fill your head night after night? To watch blood and puss ooze from sores that you could not stop his little hands from clawing?"

Portia's throat constricted, blocking the sob that welled up from her chest. Were such the side effects of porphyria? Is that what Heath had to look forward to? The thought made her heart clench in pain and bile rose up in her throat.

"I've seen God's work, Mr. Hatley," Heath went on in a low voice, subdued, a quiet thread of anguish on the air. "And I'll not leave my fate or that of my family's to His hands again. Not if I can help it."

The vicar's face swelled and reddened. "Very well. Might I suggest you consider of the young lady, then?"

Heath looked her way. She suffered his scrutiny, certain that he had no wish to consider of her just then. His cool gaze flicked over her as if she were a stranger and not the woman he had loved so thoroughly the night before.

"Heath," she murmured, desperate to reach him, to gain a glimpse of the man she had seen last night. The man she had taken into her body and held against her heart. She didn't want to part from him like this, with bitterness and misunderstanding between them. Didn't want last night to become a blight in her memory.

"Heath," she said again, her voice low with appeal. "Look at me. You can't believe I would—" She stopped and swallowed past the lump rising to choke her.

Something that looked damnably close to guilt flashed in his eyes, and she knew, like her, he was thinking of last night, remembering their less than innocent time together. He remembered and regretted. Damn him. No regrets, he had said. *Liar*, her heart cried as her hands knotted at her sides. He would not taint last night, would not sully the memory with regret. As if it were something he wished to take back and erase.

She shook her head swiftly, her heart beating like an angry drum against her chest.

Heath turned from her and addressed the vicar. "I am thinking of her. And I strongly suspect I'm the only one."

"Oh, Heath, that's absurd," Lady Moreton cut in. "You've ruined her. Only one thing can protect her now."

The vicar patted Lady Moreton's arm. "Don't overset yourself, dear lady."

Seemingly mollified, the lady gave a delicate sniff and pressed her lips together, nodding for the vicar to continue.

"Am I correct in saying that you two stayed the night together?" Hatley inquired evenly. "Alone?"

"We were caught in the storm. I couldn't very well have forced Lady Portia out into such inclement weather for the sake of propriety. She has only recently recovered from an ague."

"Precisely," Portia agreed, nodding, gladdened for the sound logic.

Mr. Hatley inclined his head. "Yet if you had no intention of marrying the lady, you should have braved the elements, my lord. Better to have risked her life than her soul."

A small hiss of breath escaped her lips at this heartless comment. Yet should she feel such surprise? Mr. Hatley's attitude was typical of Society. A lady's virtue was of more value than the lady herself.

Heath, however, did not seem to value this attitude. His upper lip curled in a sneer as he said, "I'll pretend you did not say that, sir, and ask you to take your leave before I say or do something truly regrettable."

"Heathston," Lady Moreton cried in shrill, affronted tones, her hands opening and closing in front of her as if she could grab a handhold of control, power. Something. "You dare address Mr. Hatley in such a fashion."

"Oh, I dare." His eyes glittered a glacier gray and Portia felt their chill right to her core. "That and more if he doesn't take his leave."

Portia blinked, thinking she had misheard him. Surely he had not taken offense on her account. He, who thought her the lowest sort of female?

Mr. Hatley made a small bleating sound and his face reddened even further. "Perhaps," he started, addressing the countess even as his eyes narrowed on Portia, "Lady Portia's brother should be notified of recent developments. I am certain he would like to weigh in on the discussion."

Portia's stomach rebelled at the obvious threat. If Bertram knew she spent the night unchaperoned with the earl, he would insist they wed.

"Get out," Heath ordered, his voice lethally soft.

Almost as from nowhere, Mrs. Crosby appeared, the vicar's hat and coat in her hands. Mr. Hatley collected his things, his fat lips squashed tightly with censure.

Mr. Hatley shrugged into his too small coat with maddening slowness. His fat lips trembled from suppressed speech, and Portia could well imagine the tirade he fought to hold back. At the door he stopped. His voice rang out with high sanctimony, "I will pray for you, my lord." His small, vapid eyes shifted to Portia. "And you, too, my lady. For what it's worth."

The moment he scurried out the door, Lady Moreton swung on Heath, her slender frame shaking like a reed in the wind, radiating a fury so thick, so palpable, it clogged the air. "What have you done? What have *you* done? You know he'll tell everyone!"

Lips compressed in a flat, ominous line, Heath turned his back on Lady Moreton. He glared at Portia in a way that made the hairs on her nape tingle. She angled her head warily, eyeing him up and down as she slid back a step.

"Why are you—"

He snatched hold of her hand, cutting short her question.

"Come," he ordered, pulling her along, her feet slipping along the damnably slick marble floor.

He thrust her into the library, slamming the door behind them.

Twisting free, she crossed her arms over her chest and watched him pace the vast room like a great caged cat. Her muscles tensed, wary that at any moment he would turn and pounce on her as if she were a sparrow to be devoured in one breath.

His feet burned a trail on the Persian carpet and she studied him as one might a spectacle at a traveling show. Finally, he stopped and faced her. The look in those smoke eyes of his sent a bolt of terror directly to her heart.

"Why are you looking at me that way?" she asked, inching back, stopping when she bumped into the large mahogany desk. Her hands grasped the hard edge behind her.

His broad chest rose on an inhalation. "You wanted this to happen. Did everything in your power to see it come about," he accused, his words dropping like heavy stones in water, swift, resolute, intractable—sinking into far-off depths where they could never be retrieved. "Your reputation is in shreds now. The vicar will see to that. Your family will demand satisfaction." He gave a stiff nod. "Very well. We shall wed."

Her heart constricted in her chest. Earlier she had entertained the notion of him proposing, of him *wanting* to wed her. But this had nothing to do with *wanting*. Quite the contrary.

"What?" she asked, the word weak and pathetic to her ears—horribly inadequate for her spinning emotions.

He shook his head tiredly, as if beleaguered with a thousand demons instead of simply her. "You wanted this. From the moment you arrived you've been my torment."

She pressed a hand to her breast, feeling the mad thumping of her heart against her palm. "Your torment?" Never had she thought to have that much power over anyone. Least of all him.

"Yes, you," he growled.

She laughed a brittle, hollow sound. "You give me too much credit."

"You won't convince me this was not your purpose. I heard what the vicar said. You told him—"

"A twisting of my words! He is the one to suggest that 'I bring you to heel.' What else was I to tell him? That I wished to remain here to escape Town and enjoy your library? He would have thought me daft."

Heath moved forward so quickly she hadn't time to react. He grabbed her by the arms and gave her a small shake. "Enough. I've heard enough of your lies." His features twisted into a tight grimace. "You're a brilliant actress, I'll give you that. I almost believe you. Very affecting really. Yet you said it, didn't you?" His eyes raked her. "Nor can you deny what you did—lifting your skirts for me most willingly, no different than any other prostitute selling herself for the right price."

"Bastard," she cried, certain she would strike him if he wasn't restraining her.

He made a slight tsking sound. "Come now, you've won. We'll wed. But know this. You'll regret the day you ever trapped me."

Portia froze, didn't move, didn't so much as flicker an eyelid. She simply stared at the man in front of her, realization rushing over her with a suddenness that robbed her of breath. She didn't know him at all. Not in the least. She had thought she understood him, understood what drove him in life, but she hadn't a clue.

His hands on her arms stirred up all sorts of feelings. Feelings she had no business experiencing. Feelings she had reveled in a short time ago. Strange the changes a few hours could bring. Her body felt as confused as her mind. The tenderness he had shown her last night was nowhere in evidence, and she couldn't help wondering what was real—the lover from the night before or the brutal, unfeeling man before her now. She could not reconcile the two.

"I won't marry you," she whispered, her voice a croak caught somewhere in her throat. Never would she bind herself to this stranger—a man who stomped on her heart as if it were nothing more than a rug beneath his boot.

"It's done. We've no choice. Even I underestimated my grandmother. I did not think she would send for the vicar. Even now, word of your ruin flies on the wind." He released her arms and resumed his pacing, moving with the fury of a storm sweeping across the moors.

She watched him in silence. Too numb. Too shocked to speak. Dully, she registered that he had continued with his tirade.

"It won't be a real marriage." He sliced her with a glance. "Last night was a mistake we won't repeat. The risk is too great."

Mistake. The word gouged her low in the belly like the swipe of a claw. So much for no regrets. Hot tears burned the backs of her eyes. She quickly spun around and walked to the window, staring out at wind-rippled heather as she fought to gain control of her emotions.

"I won't marry you," she repeated, more for herself than him.

And still he talked, as if she hadn't spoken, as if she were of no account at all. "I can't disregard that we spent the night alone together. I deluded myself to think I could. I know my duty." He snorted at this last bit.

"Duty?" She whirled around, too angry to hide

the tears spilling hot, silent trails down her cheeks. "Don't tell me you actually believe that overboiled sausage? So what if he wags his tongue? No one will hear of last night. Gossip in the wilds of Yorkshire is of no consequence in Town."

"I'll not risk it—as you undoubtedly suspected when you situated yourself so appealingly at the lodge."

She swiped the air with her hand. "You're the most vexing man I've ever met. Do you think yourself such a prize that I would stoop to such lengths to trap you in marriage?"

"No, I merely think you desperate and unscrupulous." He gave her a puzzled look. "Why must you continue this pretense? This is what you've wanted. Now you're getting it. Your family will get their money."

Her clenched hands shook in front of her. "I am tired unto death of defending myself."

"Very well." He gave a stiff nod. "Then cease your playacting."

Portia stomped her foot, the sound muffled on the thick carpet.

Heath turned for the door.

"Where are you going?" she demanded, uncaring if he wished to hear her or not. This was her life, her fate hung in the balance, and he *would* listen.

"I have arrangements to make," he replied in an annoyingly tired voice.

Arrangements. Portia didn't need him to clarify his meaning. He thought he alone decided whether they would wed. That she had been brought here to garner his approval and she need not be asked or consulted. As if he could simply announce his intention and she would follow along meekly. It made her ill. It made her furious. It made her feel suddenly very . . . drained.

"I've not agreed to anything," she said in a weak voice.

He tossed a disgusted look over his shoulder. "No? What was last night, then?"

Cheeks afire, she tossed one last question at his retreating back, the one question she wagered could halt him in his tracks. "What of the curse?" Perhaps he need only be reminded of the reason he had no wish to wed. "You can't have forgotten that." Not when it has guided his life. Every action, every decision.

He stopped and turned. Something flickered in his eyes. The pain that always lurked there, the knowledge of the bleak future waiting for him. "It will be an in-name-only marriage, naturally. We'll never repeat last night. The risk of getting you with child is too great."

An in-name-only marriage. As she had suggested to him days ago. Except then she had not considered herself in the hapless role of wife. She had thought some poor creature that did not want much from life would accept such a marriage—and be glad for it.

"As flattering as your proposal is, I must decline."

"Wake up, Portia. You haven't the luxury to refuse. Not after last night."

"I can, and I do," she replied, loathing his superior attitude, loathing that he could refer to last night as if it were a horrible incident he wished to undo.

"I'm sure your family will disagree."

Her family? Portia gave herself a hard mental shake. No. She felt certain Grandmother would never force her. Threaten, bully, cajole, and make life in general miserable, yes. But never force. Bertram, however, was another matter. He saw her as a means to an end—little more than a prized ewe to be sold to the highest bidder. He would have forced her to marry long ago had Grandmother allowed him. If word reached him of this, Portia would have a battle on her hands.

"My family doesn't decide my fate. This is between you and me," she said tightly, looking him steadily in the eyes.

He shook his head, that mirthless smile fixed to his face again. Her fingers itched to wipe it clean. "There is no you and me, Portia. Never will be.

We'll simply wed and spend the rest of our lives learning to abide each other."

With a heavy heart, she watched him open the door and stride from the room. Not once did he look back.

His words whirled in her head until her stomach grew queasy. *No you and me.*

Foolish perhaps, but she thought there had been.

Chapter 22

~~~~~~~~

Heath poured himself a glass of brandy and downed it in one swallow. Never had he needed a drink more. He hadn't made it as far as the stairs before he detoured to his office. The special license could wait until later. There were times when a man not only deserved a drink, but he needed one. Or in his case, a few.

"I thought you'd turn up here."

Heath swung around and eyed his sister sitting primly on the sofa near the fire.

"Been waiting long?" he asked.

She raised one shoulder in a half-shrug. "Ever since you slammed into the library." She nodded to the drink in his hand. "The kind of day you've had would drive anyone to drink."

"Not you, Con," Heath replied. "Nothing ruffles you. You're the perfect little package of starch."

Pain, raw and shining, flashed in his sister's eyes and Heath felt a stab of guilt. It couldn't be easy for her either. Thirty-one years old and no husband. No children. No life to speak of save visits to the orphanage and afternoons embroidering with their grandmother.

"Sorry," he muttered beneath his breath, turning for a refill.

"I warned you, Heath."

"Come to give an accounting of all my mistakes, Constance?"

"Unnecessary. You know where you erred."

His lips hugged the edge of his glass as he racked his brain, trying to recall the precise moment he first erred in regard to Lady Portia. He laughed once, a short bark. It seemed he had misstepped from the start. He shook his head, marveling at his stupidity. He should have sent her packing the moment he learned her name.

"What are you going to do about her?"

Heath shrugged, downed his glass, and answered in matter-of-fact tones, "Marry her."

Constance's jaw dropped. "You jest." Her eyes widened as she eyed Heath's grim expression. "You cannot mean to risk—"

"I'll marry her, but I'll not risk anything." Heath's voice vibrated with anger. The same anger he had felt upon discovering Portia, naked and ripe for him at the lodge. Never again would he take such a risk. Never again would he be that weak to succumb to the heaven he found in her arms. To do that was a straight path to hell.

Constance gaped, the dark slashes of her brows raised high. "Oh, you've got to be the biggest fool I've ever met. You think you can marry her and not once touch her? I've seen the way you look at her. Even I recognize you have feelings for the girl."

He shook his head fiercely. "On the contrary. I'm *feeling* quite indisposed to the chit. She's a heartless, greedy little witch who has done nothing but lie to me since she arrived here. I'll have no difficulty avoiding her bed. You'll see. The curse will not carry on. Not through me at any rate."

"Careful you don't underestimate her. She'll likely not accept the type of marriage you're offering. Most women wouldn't."

"She'll have no choice."

Just then the door burst open and Mina rushed into the room, face flushed and eyes shooting sparks as she demanded, "What have you done to Portia?"

Ignoring that Mina had finally deigned to speak to him, he replied wryly, "Come crying to you, did she?"

"Of course not. She's in her room packing." Mina paused, as if to see if this statement impacted him in the least.

"Indeed?" he asked, wondering what game Portia was about now. Did she want a pretty proposal? Words of enduring love? Him on bended knee? Well, she would not have it. He would not be as big a fool as either one of his parents who cared only for each other—of loving and hurting each other.

"Her driver has already brought their coach around to the front."

Heath poured himself another glass, doing his best to not let that bit of information rattle him. She couldn't mean to leave. Not when she had succeeded in getting the proposal she had set out to win.

"No doubt she expects me to stop her." He waved his glass in a small circle, indifferent to the sloshing fluid that dribbled over his fingers. "Expects that I shall fling my body in front of the coach if need be."

"No! I do!" Mina slapped a palm against her chest. "She expects nothing from you. From the moment she arrived, she never has, you bloody ass."

"Mina!" Constance rebuked.

He scowled at his younger sister, unaccustomed to hearing such rough language from her. Usually she wouldn't dare. No doubt more evidence of Portia's influence.

"You cannot really mean to let her go, Heath," Mina insisted, voice full of entreaty.

"Good riddance," Constance grumbled. "Let her leave."

"Shut up!" Mina cried, voice shrill, hands shaking at her sides. She swung her gaze back on Heath. "You can't let her leave. You can't." Her small fists knotted and Heath suspected she might take a swing at him. "She's the only friend I've got."

Heath turned, suddenly unable to bear the torment in his sister's face. Another sin to lay at Portia's door. Not only had she tied him in knots, she had quite thoroughly, completely, captured the heart of his sister. She had managed to leave her mark on all of them in a short time, and it annoyed the hell out of him.

As his sisters erupted into argument, he inched toward the window. The curtains were pulled back, permitting the faint morning light to trickle inside. His eyes landed on the waiting coach, Portia's ill-kempt driver leaning against its side, a bored expression on his face.

What manner of ploy was this? She would not leave. Not after accomplishing what she set out to win. Him. Or rather his wealth.

Then he spotted her, watched the straight line of her back as she descended the stone steps. She stopped at the bottom, rigid as a tin soldier while she pulled on her gloves in quick, efficient movements. He stared overly long at those pale hands, remembering their elegance, their petal softness.

The driver pulled the door open. Her maid clambered in first. Portia moved to follow, then stopped. Slowly, she turned. Their gazes collided. She lifted her chin as if daring him to stop her. He held his ground, careful not to reveal his bewilderment, careful to mask the silent question burning through his head.

Why are you leaving? What do you want from me?

He had agreed to wed her. Something he never imagined possible. And why did she wear that bloody wounded expression on her face? He inhaled deeply through his nose, but the air felt too thin, not nearly enough for his suddenly too tight lungs.

If she meant to go, he would not stop her, would not chase after her like some love-struck fool. He had agreed to marry her, had made his offer. That was enough. All she could expect of him. All he could give. He would not behave as his father—hotheaded and swept away with love to the exclusion of all sense.

He could not force her to accept his offer. He would feel no guilt, no regret.

Her gaze drilled into him for a moment longer, her expression unreadable, her stance still rigid, soldierlike. Then she was gone. A blur of skirts ascending into the carriage.

He watched, the blood wringing from his heart until it ceased to beat. His gaze followed the coach as it clattered away, longing for another glimpse of her. His eyes scanned the dark curtain at her window, searching for the sight of hair the color of jet, skin like cream.

At last the carriage turned the bend. Out of sight. Out of his life. He scowled, vowing he would have her out of his mind just as easily. In no time at all, he would not even recall her name.

Chapter 23

Portia stood in the dim foyer of her home and wrinkled her nose at the unsavory stench clogging the air.

"Finch!" her voice resounded in the emptiness, bouncing off walls of faded rose wallpaper and floating to mingle among the great canopy of cobwebs clinging to the domed ceiling. She squinted through the gloom at the cobwebs, marveling at how they had increased in her absence.

The shabbiness of her surroundings struck her full force. Especially since her stay at Moreton Hall, where everything gleamed and smelled of fresh lye, where light filled every room, where servants bustled about, busy making Moreton Hall spotless. A home.

Sighing, she tugged her bonnet free and rubbed the bridge of her nose. Several days in the coach, with only the most necessary stops, and her joints felt stiff as an old woman's. A warm bath, edible food, a familiar bed—she'd feel restored in no time. Physically restored, at any rate. Emotionally, might take a bit longer. Likely forever.

"Finch!" she called again, projecting her voice so that it reached the servants' wing. The old butler never lurked far from the door. He was anything if not reliable. Loyalty alone had kept him from departing when the servants' wages had diminished to naught.

"Where is the ol' goat?" Nettie muttered.

Shaking her head, Portia dropped her reticule on the round marble-topped table in the center of the foyer, pausing when she caught sight—and smell—of the rotting flowers situated in the center. At least a week old, the flowers were no longer identifiable. Their fetid odor tainted the air and her nostrils quivered in revolt.

"I don't know," she answered, gazing at the brown, shrunken blooms, slow dread filling her heart.

"Suppose I'll have to lug these to our rooms," Nettie grumbled with a kick to Portia's trunk.

"See to your luggage," Portia replied, tearing

her gaze from the decaying flowers. "I'll have someone fetch my trunks up later."

Without another word, she hurried up to the second floor, hoping to catch her grandmother at tea. Her pulse thrummed frantically as her feet flew up the stairs, beating out a rhythm on the steps that matched the tempo of her heart.

That she did not come across at least one servant as she hurried to the drawing room heightened her unease. Where was everyone? The house seemed preternaturally still. Not a single sound save the whisper of her footsteps on the carpet and the anxious rasp of her breath.

"Grandmother?" she called, pushing open the partially closed door and stepping into the drawing room. An empty room stared back, dark and musty. The drapes sealed out all light and made her feel as though she had stepped inside a tomb. Turning, she headed for the salon, Astrid's room of choice.

Upon entering, Portia did not find Astrid with her usual gaggle of Society matrons, duchesses like her mostly, all as cold and reticent as herself. Instead an altogether different breed of visitor occupied the room's confines. A stranger. A Goliath of a man wearing an ill-fitting jacket.

They sat side by side in a double chair-back settee that looked dangerously close to collapse. Portia glanced about the room, thinking to spy a maid tucked away in a corner, serving as chaperone. No such luck. Crossing her arms, she narrowed her gaze on the pair. True, Astrid did not rank among her favorite people, but Portia had never marked her the sort to cuckold Bertram. She was a stickler for propriety.

The stranger withdrew his great paw from where it fondled one of Astrid's curls. He moved slowly, the backs of his fingers skimming Astrid's shoulder as though loathe to relinquish his hold.

Astrid rose hastily to her feet, her muslin skirts rustling softly on the air. Her guest followed, unfolding his monstrous frame from the settee, an expression of mild annoyance on his blunt features. The walnut wood legs creaked in relief to be freed of his considerable burden. At least Astrid had the grace to look discomposed, flushing as she patted her honey blond curl, as though she needed to make certain it still hung there and he had not taken it with him.

"Portia," she greeted, a tight smile fixed to her face. As if nothing untoward occurred. Yet her voice gave her away. Usually modulated and dulcet in tone, it shook the barest amount. "I did not expect you home so soon. How was your trip?"

"Uneventful," she murmured, managing not to choke on the colossal lie. *Uneventful*. The single word said enough, would serve to answer the question burning in Astrid's eyes. *No, she had not nabbed the wealthy groom she had been sent forth to snare.*

Astrid's slight shoulders sagged a bit, but she soon recovered and straightened her spine. "Forgive my manners, Mr. Oliver. Allow me to introduce my sister-in-law, Lady Portia."

Mr. Oliver's gaze shifted to Portia. He assessed her from head to foot, coal dark eyes shining with a feral gleam. She felt instantly wary, like a hare caught in the hound's sight. He stepped forward and bowed over her hand.

"Delighted," he murmured, eyes trained on her face.

Her wariness intensified. She was no beauty to produce such an immediate reaction in men. Only one man had ever treated her as though she were anything beyond the par. The same man, she quickly reminded herself, that had so devastated her heart. Reclaiming her hand, she inclined her head in stiff greeting.

"Sister-in-law," he murmured, swinging his avid gaze to Astrid. "It escaped my attention that your husband possessed a sister. And such a lovely one."

Portia drew a shuddering breath. *Possessed.* He said the word as if she were just that—a possession.

Astrid gave a slight shake of her elegantly coiffed

head at him. A slight motion, almost impercepti-
ble, but Portia noted the gesture.

"Thank you for calling, Mr. Oliver," Astrid said,
all ice and vinegar again. The duchess Portia
knew well. "I shall send word if I hear anything."

A nasty smile twisted his lips. For a moment,
she had a glimpse of a man with whom she had
no wish to tangle.

"You'll be seeing me soon, Your Grace." He
turned to Portia. "A pleasure, my lady." With another clumsily executed bow, he murmured, "I'll
show myself out."

Portia waited for the door to shut before round-
ing on her sister-in-law. With a hand propped on
her hip, she asked flatly, "Who, precisely, is he?"

Astrid smiled heartlessly. "Always the blunt
one. No wonder you can't catch a husband. Gentlemen don't care for such straightforwardness."

Portia expelled a heavy sigh. When Astrid had
first joined the family, Portia felt the sting of her
words daily. She had even retaliated in kind. Yet
that was then. Unable to summon forth a scathing
retort, she only felt a bone-deep weariness.

Her sister-in-law eased herself onto the chaise
with a natural elegance that Portia had always envied. She watched as Astrid carefully positioned
the pillows at her back. Finally she looked up, saying with the mildness of one remarking on the
weather, "Your brother has left."

"Left?" Portia felt herself frown. "Left for where? When will he be back?"

"Perhaps I am not being clear." Smoothing both hands over her striped muslin skirts, she straightened her spine. "He has left *us*." Another pause. "Abandoned us, to be accurate."

Portia sank onto the chaise, mouth working in bewilderment before she choked, "How can that be?"

Astrid looked out the window. "He absconded with the jewelry. Mine, your grandmother's, even the little he found in your room. He should be well out of the country by now."

Portia shook her head. It didn't make sense. True, they were well in the dun, but why would Bertram wish to leave all the privileges of his rank for life abroad? Here, at least, he had a roof over his head. Creditors here couldn't lay claim to their property and would grant him much more latitude than those on foreign soil.

Even if they couldn't afford to outfit their own pantries, there would always be parties where he could eat his fill of lobster bisque and salmon pasties.

"It would seem his only choice," Astrid added coolly, as if she could read any one of the dozen questions whirling around Portia's head.

Portia looked more carefully at Astrid's face,

searching beyond the neutral mien, the remote gaze. There, beneath the calm façade, lurked a bone-deep sorrow. The type of pain one couldn't hide, no matter how hard they tried. Bertram's abandonment had cut deeply. No mistake about it.

"He's not coming back. To do so, he must face the House of Lords on felony charges. Lord Ashton paid me a visit yesterday morning and apprised me of the situation." Astrid's upper lip curled ever so faintly. "Your brother didn't even have the courtesy to leave me a note. I had to hear it from someone else."

"What did Lord Ashton say?"

Astrid gave her head a small shake. Composed again, she continued. "Apparently, Lord Ashton and several others in the House of Lords suggested to Bertram that he quietly depart." Her lips curved humorlessly. "You can't hang someone if he's not in the country, after all."

"Hanging? For what offense?"

"It seems we cannot ever accuse your brother of being unenterprising." Astrid smiled coldly. "Bertram got mixed up in forging bank notes. I suspected something was amiss. He was still losing at the tables." She snorted. "Everyone knew that. Yet he always had the blunt for the hells."

"Forgery," Portia breathed. *A hanging offense.* No wonder her brother ran. His peers would feel pressured to mete out the same sentence they had so uncomprisingly been issuing of late given the recent rise of forgery.

Recalling Astrid's guest, she queried, "Who is Mr. Oliver? How is he involved in all this?"

"He's the lender to which most of Bertram's debt is due."

"We cannot be held accountable for Bertram's debts."

"True, but neither can we feed and attire ourselves. And it's not as though we've anything to sell. Bertram already sold off everything that isn't entailed."

"So what does this Oliver fellow want?" Portia asked, unable to forget the man or his measuring gaze.

"Simon Oliver is a socially ambitious man. He wishes to move in more elevated circles."

And no circle was more elevated than that of Astrid and her friends. Simon Oliver could do no better than gaining acceptance among Astrid's august set.

"And that is *all* he wants? An introduction to the *ton*'s drawing rooms?" Portia snorted and crossed her arms, unable to forget the sight of his large hand on Astrid, unsightly against the pale glow of her skin. "I don't think so. Out with it, Astrid."

Almost instantly, the ice queen vanished. Bright splotches broke out over Astrid's fair skin, a rare display of emotion for her taciturn sister-in-law.

"And what is it to you?" Her nostrils quivered. "Why am I even explaining any of this to you? As I recall, you've bigger plans. Shouldn't you be off arranging a grand reunion with your mother?" she mocked. "Oh, that's right. You haven't heard from her in what? Two years?"

"Twenty months," Portia automatically corrected.

"Yes, well. Perhaps you'll run across your brother in your travels. Send him my regards, would you?"

"Astrid—"

"No," Astrid broke in. "You care only for yourself. Selfish. Like your brother. What a pair you are."

Portia winced. No one had ever laid that particular accusation at her feet. She had never thought it possible. Yet to be compared to her brother . . . Her stomach rolled, rebelling at the thought. Portia had long grown accustomed to her family's rebukes and criticisms. She could have expected Astrid to hurl almost anything upon her head. Yet not this.

"*I* am selfish?" she demanded, her temper taking over whether she willed it or not. And along with her temper came weariness. Weariness of the expectations, of being relied upon to save the family from the mess her brother had created.

"Yes, selfish," Astrid continued. "You might have gulled your grandmother, but not me. I know you've deliberately sabotaged every chance for a match."

Portia gasped. "I wouldn't say I *deliberately*—"

"Well, you hardly went out of your way to be appealing." Astrid nodded briskly, decisively. "If you possessed one shred of responsibility, you would have made a match that benefited the family. Do you think I had a choice? No. Father bade me wed Bertram and I did." Derision laced this last bit. "And I shall continue to do what duty requires, even if it means tolerating that jackanape's hands all over my person."

"You would permit Simon Oliver liberties?" Portia demanded in horror, watching Astrid raise her forgotten teacup to her lips, noticing the slight shake of her hand. She took a sip, blinking her eyes fiercely, as if tears threatened.

The realization dawned, gradual and unwanted— Astrid was more affected than she would have Portia know. Not such an ice queen, perhaps. For the first time, she truly saw Bertram's wife. Saw her as woman trying to survive forces beyond her control and cling to what dignity she could. A heart beat beyond that icy exterior, bleeding from wounds of its own. Had Portia never bothered to take a hard look before? To see beyond the outer shell?

Astrid set her cup back down with a clack. Her chest lifted with a sharp breath and her eyes, glittering with resolve, met Portia's. "Simon Oliver has made his desires clear. Along with gaining entrance into Society, he desires my . . . company. And I find I'm in no position to refuse." She spoke so coldly one would think her impervious, unbothered to offer up her body as services rendered. Yet Portia had seen the way that hand trembled and knew differently. "I know my duty," Astrid repeated. "I'll take care of everything."

Portia lowered his gaze. *Duty.* Duty drove her to make such a sacrifice. Could Portia permit her? Could she stand aside and let Astrid whore herself so that she could enjoy her independence? So she could cling to a dream, a fantasy that her mother would one day return for her?

"Someone has to," Astrid added. "Especially now that your grandmother is ill."

Her head snapped up. "Ill?"

"Yes, ill," Astrid replied, her voice sharp, clipped. "She's an old woman, Portia. Old women fall ill. Unfortunately, we haven't the funds to pay for a proper physician. We must appease ourselves with Cook's home remedies."

"Where is she now?" Portia demanded, surging to her feet.

"Resting."

Portia swallowed and blinked back the burn of

tears. Tears of shame and self-loathing. Astrid had it about right when she called her selfish. She felt every bit that. And more. A mirror had been held up to her face, and she didn't like what she saw—a selfish, immature girl who clung to impossible, romantic ideals.

"I'll do it," Portia announced with far more bravado than she felt. Her heart fluttered like a wild bird in her chest, panicked at her words, at their significance.

Astrid frowned, her expression dubious. "I don't understand—"

"I shall wed."

Astrid stared. It took a full moment for her to respond, and when she did it was in a voice full of mockery and scorn, its sting wholly felt. "Of course you will."

"I will. You have my word."

Astrid studied her, from the hem of her gown up to her unblinking gaze. "You're serious. Now. After all this time, you're agreeing to marry. Why?"

Portia looked away and fought to swallow the painful lump that rose to choke her. Her thoughts drifted to Heath. She closed her eyes and the delicious memory of his body pressing into hers surged forth. A memory so achingly real that a burning sob scalded the back of her throat, threatening to spill.

Sighing, she shoved him from her head, her heart, watching yet another dream—the dream of *him*—spread its wings and take flight. Even during her journey home, she had clung to the thin hope that she would see him again, that he would follow her, begging forgiveness, taking back all the terrible words he had flung at her and mend her bruised heart with sweet words. Dangerous thinking. The man had brought her nothing but grief.

She had refused his proposal—if what transpired between them in the library could even be deemed a proposal of marriage. That ugly scene still made her face heat. *You lifted your skirts for me most willingly—no different than any other prostitute selling herself for the right price.* A part of her hoped that he would somehow appear and erase those cruel words. Foolish, she knew. Words could never be erased. Nor would he ever try to do so. The hard, unforgiving glint in his eyes had attested to that.

Did her pride simply no longer exist?

Portia moved to the window that Astrid had looked out moments ago. There she gathered her resolve, wrapping it tightly about her heart as she stared unseeingly ahead. In time she would forget, her body would eventually cease to yearn for a man who had ravaged her heart and soul.

She touched the glass, cold and lifeless beneath her palm, and willed her heart to grow equally cold, numb. Dead. Lifeless in its own right. Then it could go forth and wed someone for which she felt nothing.

With that sole conviction, she willed Heath from her head . . . and let go of her other impossible, unattainable dream. Her dream for autonomy, freedom—for a mother's promise.

Astrid shamed her, made her realize she had no desire to follow Bertram's example and—if she were honest with herself—her mother's example, too. Like them, she had fled duty, responsibility, never once giving thought to the effect it had on others. Astrid. Her grandmother. The tenants in Nottinghamshire.

"Duty," she whispered, blinking rapidly against the sting in her eyes. Lifting her gaze, she turned and met Astrid's wide-eyed stare head on. "Tell me what I need to do."

A thick gloom permeated her grandmother's chamber. The drapes were drawn tight, only the barest thread of afternoon light creeping from beneath the worn damask. Portia hovered in the threshold, eyeing the figure beneath the counterpane, still as stone—death—atop the bed.

Her grandmother's cane was propped nearby, within arm's reach, as if she might wake at any moment and reach for it, rise to her feet and heap the familiar, long-standing rebukes upon Portia's head: *Feckless female. Over-the-hill spinster. Incorrigible bluestocking.*

Sadly, Portia wished she would. She would savor the sound of those denouncements if it meant her grandmother was whole again.

Portia approached cautiously, her feet shuffling slowly over the worn, threadbare carpet. A tight wheezing sound carried from the bed, rhythmic and repetitive as a metronome. Her grandmother's chest rose and fell deeply, as if each breath were pulled—heaved—from some place deep within her chest, from a chasm where life clung by a fragile fist.

Portia stopped at the side of her bed, a sharp gasp tearing from her lips, harsh and ugly in the still of the room. She had not steeled herself for the sight. Her grandmother did not rest there. No. That imposing lady had disappeared. Only a shell of her former self remained. Loose skin hung off the bones of her face, sagging lifelessly.

Portia sucked in a lungful of the room's stale air and rubbed her arms briskly, turning away, unable to look at the inert form on the bed and reconcile her to the vital woman who had bullied her . . . and loved her—at least as much as the crusty old Dowager Duchess of Derring could.

Portia glanced about the silent room. She could

not remember the last occasion she had entered these rooms. As a child, she had not been allowed. And later, as an adult, she had taken pains to avoid the old termagant, feeling nothing save keen disappointment in her presence.

"Grandmother?" she whispered, reaching for the hand limp at her side, the skin thin as parchment. Portia handled it carefully, treating it like fine crystal.

"Grandmother," she repeated, her throat suddenly thick. "Don't worry. I'll handle everything. You'll see."

For a moment, those lids flickered, as though struggling to open. Portia's heart leapt and she squeezed the lifeless fingers. "Grandmother? Can you hear me?"

For the barest second those lids cracked to reveal a pair of pale blue eyes. They stared at Portia with familiar intensity. Yet unfamiliar was the satisfaction, the approval, glimmering there. Grandmother had heard her vow. Heard and understood.

Any lingering doubts vanished. Her course was charted. She would join the Season and do what her family had desired of her five years ago. Her own desires no longer signified.

Chapter 24

~~~~~~~~~~~~

Heath yanked off his jacket. His vest and shirt quickly followed.

"What are you doing?" Della asked, rising from her desk, a curious smile playing about her lips.

"What does it look like?" he asked.

Ridding a certain female from my system.

Proving, once and for all, that Portia has no hold on me.

So what if she left, returned to Town and her life, to the plethora of suitors waiting for her. He would not suffer, would not expire like a tree lacking water or sunlight. Her removal from his life brought nothing save a keen sense of relief.

A mirthless grin curved Della's lips and he had the oddest sense that she read his thoughts.

"Looks like you're undressing."

"Precisely," he said, his fingers pausing at his trousers as he raked her a glance. "And why are you not?"

"Because of the look on your face." She flicked a hand in his direction. "You should see your expression."

"What are you talking about?" he snapped, touching his jaw.

"You look as if you're girding yourself for battle rather than making love."

Heath stared, unable to refute the accusation. He didn't *want* to make love to Della. He hadn't wanted to do that since Portia entered his life.

Groaning, he dropped onto the sofa and rubbed his face with both hands. He had come here in an attempt to exorcise Portia from his mind and body. Damn fool. Nothing could ever do that. The girl was in his blood.

"Heath, talk to me."

He muttered into his hands, "I'm in trouble, Della."

"The duke's daughter?" she asked flatly.

He nodded, glad she didn't say Portia's name aloud. Bad enough that it whirled around his head, a steady, ceaseless mantra to which his heart kept beat.

"You love her."

He opened his mouth to deny it, but found that he could not. *You love her.*

Did he? Had he fallen victim to the one emotion he had vowed to deny himself? God knew he *wanted* her. Could it be a simple case of desire? He had wanted other women and withheld himself. All but Portia. She had been the one he couldn't resist. When it came to her, something greater than lust drove him. But love? Had he learned nothing from his parents?

Love brought out the worst in people, gave them free license to abuse each other. Yet Heath could never imagine hurting Portia—at least not as his father hurt his mother, not as they had hurt each other. Perhaps that wasn't even love. He only knew that his parents had married for love, and then set about making each other miserable. Strife ruled their so-called love match, a hell on earth everyone, offspring included, inhabited. If he did love Portia, he had all the more reason to purge his life of her and save them both from the inevitable day when they turned on each other.

"You love her," Della repeated, her voice quieter, a thread of resignation to it.

"No," he answered forcefully, as if his denial would make it not so. Leaning down, he snatched his shirt off the floor. "I've no future to offer her. That much hasn't changed." He shrugged his arms back into his shirt with rough, angry jerks.

"Stuff and nonsense."

He blinked. "What?"

"Your future is not as bleak as you think." Her eyes clouded, avoiding his, looking somewhere beyond his shoulder.

"How so?"

She turned slowly, presenting him her back as she moved to the wingback chair near the hearth. She lowered herself into its soft depths, her skirts a murmur on the air. Her fingers clutched the arm as if in need of support, the tips whitening around the healthy pink of her nails. "I suppose you'll want to send me away."

"What are you talking about?" he demanded.

She wet her lips and closed her eyes tightly. "There's no risk of you becoming mad."

"What?"

"You're not in danger—"

"I heard what you said. Yet I fail to grasp your meaning?"

"I found a letter from your mother."

His gut tightened. "Where is it?" he growled.

She averted her gaze. "It was addressed to your father. I assume he received it; I remember you telling me that your father stayed here near the end. That he was too volatile—"

"Yes, yes," he cut in, not wishing for the reminder that his father, so far gone to madness, had to be removed from his family.

"Your mother must have sent it here." Her brown eyes gazed at him in silent plea. Heath stared, beyond speech, head spinning, trying to make sense of her words, trying to make sense of why she should gaze at him with such deep entreaty.

In a hushed voice, she continued, "She spoke of your brother's death—"

He cut her off with a fierce swipe of his hand, his throat constricting. He shoved back the memories, attempting to block out the ugliness, the perpetual night that swirled around him.

His fists clenched at his sides and he had to remind himself to breathe. Despite his determination to keep the memories at bay, they surged forth anyway, a battering ram to the walls he had erected. Wound upon wound. Grief upon grief. The sight of his mother, facedown in a pool of her own blood rushed into his head, fresh as the day he had found her. The feel of his brother's little body, soft and frail in his arms, the thin chest expanding, lifting, fighting for a breath that was not to come, joined the image of his mother, both eating at his heart—his sanity.

Della rose from the chair. She paced before the hearth, arms swinging. The light of the fire cast her in a soft glow, gilding her fair hair to flaming copper. How he had once prized that hair, spent many a night running his hands through it. Now his hands ached for another. For hair as dark as slate, thick as a horse's mane, sleek as oriental silk. Even now, his treacherous palms itched for their fill of those silken strands.

"It was such a shock finding the letter. I—I did not stop to think. I worried about losing you and my position should you be free to marry. Selfish, I know. Especially since I suspected you had feelings for this girl." She shook her head severely, closing her eyes briefly. "I've been in torment from the moment I did it."

"The letter," he demanded. "Where is it?"

A long moment passed before she answered, "I burned it. I know I had no right. Please forgive—"

"You burned it?" Fury spiraled through him.

"I'm so sorry, Heath."

He took a step toward her and jerked to a stop. In one blink, he forced the tension to ebb. Shaking his head clear, he asked, "What did it say?"

She faced him. "Your mother was furious at your father, cursed him for his infidelities, blamed him for your brother's death, for his own condition"—she squared her shoulders, adding—"and hers."

"Hers?" He blinked, not understanding.

"The disease—" Della stopped abruptly and closed her eyes as if gathering courage. Her chest lifted with a deep inhalation. "Your mother was afflicted, too."

"My mother had porphyria?"

"No, Heath." Della's eyes drilled into him. "The pox. Your father infected your mother with the pox."

Heath stared.

Della angled her head, her eyes searching his face. "Did you hear me?"

Oh, he heard her. Simply could not quite wrap his head around it. Not when he had been told otherwise nearly all his life.

Syphilis. His father went mad from syphilis?

Heath finally broke the silence with a harsh laugh. "You're mistaken."

"No, Heath. Your father was quite indiscriminating in his liaisons. Your mother was clear on that point in her letter. She cursed him for bringing the disease home—"

"My brother—"

"Was infected through your mother," she finished for him. "In the womb."

He lunged forward and grasped Della by the arms, giving her a swift shake. "No," he ground out, unwilling to believe that his whole world was built upon lies, upon the likelihood of a fate that was not his. If he wasn't Mad Moreton, then who was he?

"Heath," she said softly, reaching up to grip

one of his hands, her slender fingers surprisingly strong upon his. "You know it makes sense. The symptoms of porphyria and the pox are similar. The welts, erratic behavior . . . madness."

"No," he argued, a dangerous rage unfurling low in his gut. Rage at his father and mother for the lives lost and years stolen—for the brother born without a hope for life. Rage at his mother's funeral, conducted in the dead of night with no rites spoken over the body.

Rage smoldered in his veins, so intense that he had none left for Della. He looked upon her numbly, muttering, "Grandmother said it was the king's madness." Dragging a hand over his jaw, he released a pent up breath.

Della's lips twisted. "What would *you* rather have people believe? That the Earl of Moreton caught the pox and infected his family? Or he suffered a blood curse over which he had no control?"

Heath surged to his feet and donned the rest of his clothes, his movements violent, angry. Like the burning surge of blood to his head. His grandmother had known the truth. Of this he felt certain. She had harbored his father's dirty secret and replaced it with another. One she deemed less scandalous.

"Where are you going?"

"To see my grandmother. I mean to have the truth from her lips."

"What kind of satisfaction will confronting her grant you? Not the kind you crave, I warrant."

"Oh, I'll be satisfied," he vowed.

"Go after her, Heath," Della uttered, her voice matter of fact, no less certain for its quietness.

He stopped. He didn't need to ask about whom she referred. One hand on the door, he faced her, his jaw loosening, preparing to speak—but he hadn't a clue what to say. "Della—"

"Don't. You don't owe me an explanation, Heath. There were never promises between us. Never love. I'm happy that you're free." She tried for a smile, but her lips quavered, elusive as water. "Even if being free means you're free to be with someone else."

He shook his head, a rush of emotion filling his chest. "She left of her own choosing. I gave her what she wanted. I agreed to marry her. I'm not about to chase after her. Nothing has changed—"

"Quit lying to yourself and go." A sad smile hugged her lips. "You're not your parents. You're stronger. You'll respect the woman you love too much to hurt her. Go. Before it's too late."

Heath turned and escaped into the night, telling himself that free or not, he would not go traipsing to London in pursuit of Portia. Even if he felt the life-long noose about his neck loosen and the breath flow freely from his lungs, his heart was still tightly sealed. Nothing would ever change that.

Chapter 25

"Her Grace was absolutely right." Simon Oliver's moist breath fanned against her ear. "You are a marvelous dancer."

Portia suppressed her shudder at the heavy hand digging into her waist, wondering what else Astrid had told him. Had she informed him his suit would be welcomed? That he need only ask and she would accept his proposal? They had discussed and decided as much. Regardless that he made her skin crawl, Simon Oliver was an ideal candidate. Especially for someone like her. The gentlemen of the *ton* had never pounded a path to her door, and Portia could afford no delay in acquiring a husband.

"Thank you, Mr. Oliver," she murmured, the fine hairs at her nape prickling once again. She twisted her head and looked about the dance floor, searching among the dancers. The feeling that someone was watching—had been watching her for quite some time—beset her yet again.

"Please, call me Simon."

"Simon," she murmured, dragging her gaze back to his.

Astrid would see such an invitation as progress. Portia's stomach tightened to know they had reached the point of familiarity.

"I must say you're a fetching bit of baggage tonight."

Portia winced at the artless sycophancy and followed his gaze down the front of her low-cut bodice—one of Astrid's gowns that had been altered to fit her. "Again, my thanks."

He grinned, his broad, square face the picture of delight. The waltz came to an end. Portia sighed with relief as he led her from the floor.

"Can I get you anything, my dear? A libation perhaps?"

"Yes, that would be lovely."

Simon Oliver had shadowed her all evening. The chance for a respite beckoned. As soon as he turned, she fled through the mad crush of guests. Lady Hamilton's soiree was a rousing success tonight, if the crowd full of flushed faces was any indication. Music, food and rum punch flowed freely. Hardly the kind of event her grandmother would have allowed her to attend—especially in a dress such as the one she wore. Portia had placed herself in Astrid's hands, and her sister-in-law claimed this to be an excellent affair to launch the *new* Portia.

In moments, she was free from the press of bodies, stumbling onto the balcony, down the stone steps and deep into the gardens. She strolled until she located an iron bench situated beneath a large oak. Settling herself there, she lifted her face for the evening breeze to cool her overheated cheeks.

The slow drag of footsteps over the graveled path seized her attention. She watched as a shadow grew out of the dark, broad-shouldered and loosed limbed, drawing ever nearer with the firm fall of each step. Finally, an image materialized.

The dark fall of hair. The angular, hawklike features. The storm-cloud eyes.

"What are you doing here?" she whispered, her heart expanding inside her chest.

"I'm here for you."

Shivering at his words, she demanded hotly, "How did you know I was here?"

He shrugged. "An easy matter. The right coin will earn you any information you want."

Indignation smoldered inside her. "You bribed my servants?"

"Only one."

"Were you even invited here?"

"No." His lips curved in a maddening grin. "But what's one more guest?"

She huffed and crossed her arms. He had sauce, she'd give him that.

He merely looked her over, his eyes staring overly long at her low-cut bodice. She fought the urge to lift her hand and cover herself. Never before would she have worn anything so daring, or in such a bold color. Astrid swore the deep red complemented her, made her dark hair all the more lustrous, her eyes brighter, her skin glow like cream. Given the stares she'd elicited tonight, the gown had served its purpose.

"Have you come to change my mind?" She gestured about her with a loose flick of her wrist, her seeming apathy surprising even herself. "Unnecessary, as you can see. What happened in Yorkshire didn't *ruin* me. I'm still able to hold up my head. You may return with a clear conscience."

He took his time in answering, his unrelenting scrutiny making her breath come fast and hard. As always. That much hadn't changed. Her reaction to him assailed her instantly, visceral and inescapable. Time and distance and a renewed purpose in life hadn't changed that. Disappointing. No, frustrating. She had decided to give up her dreams and foolish girlhood desires, to cease all shallowness and follow duty's path. No longer a weak creature of passion. Wisdom, responsibility and maturity ruled her now. She should be beyond *wanting* Heath.

With a shrug that seemed to mock the searing intensity of his gaze, he drawled, "It doesn't change what happened between us." His husky voice rolled over her, tormenting her, the slide of silk against her skin.

Her throat constricted. "I've put that behind me. Forgotten all about it, in fact."

"Liar," he whispered so softly she barely heard him. His eyes glinted with an angry light, as if her words alone, untruthful though he claimed them, sparked some kind of primitive urge in him to deny, to disprove.

"I have," she insisted, rising to her feet. Then, thinking to convince him that she had well and truly moved on, she lifted her chin and said, "Mr. Oliver has proved excellent company, quite wiping you from my mind."

His hands clamped down on her arms and he gave her a small shake. "Enough, Portia," he rasped. "I know you're angry with me. You've every right to be, but don't pretend you feel nothing."

"Oh, I feel something." Her anger arrived at last, flowing hot and swiftly through her blood. She struggled in his hands like a wild bird, her chest rising and falling with the tumult of her own emotions. "Something akin to hatred." She shook from the inside out, infuriated at the mere sight of him, at the treacherous fire in her blood that his presence stoked into an obliterating blaze.

He smiled, a dangerous curve of sensuous lips that made her still in his arms. "Hate. Love. The two are nearly indistinguishable." His hands slid from her arms. She started to step back but he caught her again. One arm wrapped around her waist, hauling her against him, mashing her breasts into his chest. "A fine line, I think."

"No," she moaned, arching away.

"My sweet little liar," he rasped in her ear. "You mean for me to believe you forgot me? Forgot how good we were?"

She nodded dumbly, pushing at the rock wall of his chest.

"I haven't forgotten. Not for a moment. You might have left Yorkshire but your memory did not. You have haunted me, Portia."

She fought against the hot thrill his declaration gave her, and shoved harder.

"I haven't forgotten," he repeated. "Not your

taste." His tongue circled the whorls of her ear. She whimpered, biting down hard on her lip to stop the betraying sound. She ceased pushing, her hands clenching the fabric of his jacket as if she clung to her salvation.

He continued talking, his voice mesmerizing, a fiery caress against her skin. "Not your nails on my back. Not your lips on mine. Not your sweet little body milking me."

Gasping, she lurched free, stumbling as if drunk. And perhaps she was. His words swirled in her head, making her dizzy, making her skin tingle . . . intoxicating her as no wine ever could.

"You remember," he pronounced, voice thick with triumph, his eyes gleaming with desire. "And you want more of the same."

Without thinking, her hand shot out, the loud crack of her palm against his cheek both satisfying and frightening.

He fingered the flesh there, and she tensed, waiting for him to retaliate.

"Striking me won't make it untrue," he uttered with maddening calm.

"Stay away from me," she warned, shaking from fury, from a whole nest of snarling emotions he stirred within her. "I don't know why you're here, but we said everything we had to say at Moreton Hall. We're finished."

"We've only begun."

She shook her head at him, hopeless fury filling her heart. "Go home, Heath." Without another word, she spun on her heel, half expecting him to pull her back into his arms. And absurdly deflated when he did not.

Traitorous body.

Defiant heart.

Both wanted what her head knew to be wrong.

She entered the ballroom, her gaze scanning the throng. Spotting Simon's face, she made her way to his side, determined, now more than ever, to gain a proposal from him. That—her head told her—was right.

Who cared what her heart said?

Heath stopped at the threshold of the dance floor, his cheek still stinging from Portia's slap. He hadn't precisely planned on what to say when he faced her, but he had certainly imagined things going better than a slap to the face.

Hell, he hadn't counted on seeing her in another man's arms. Nor in a crimson dress that clung to her like a second skin. He watched as she returned to the side of that behemoth. The man clasped her by the arm and fixed her close to his side with a familiarity that made Heath's blood burn and his hands clench at his sides.

Despite his avowals, he had followed Della's advice and *traipsed* after Portia. That he loved the chit, as Della claimed, had nothing to do with it. He simply knew his duty. He had compromised a gently bred lady. And with the curse no longer shadowing him, nothing stopped him from marrying, from carrying on the Moreton line, from filling Portia's belly with his child. The very possibility, one he had never permitted himself to consider, made his heart thud faster. But not, he told himself, because he loved her.

His gaze fixed on Portia. She tossed back her head and laughed at something the hulk next to her said. Chandelier light glinted off her dark hair. His chest tightened, his fingers itching to unpin the heavy mass and run his fingers through the silken tresses of gleaming jet.

Nothing stopped him from marrying.

Nothing except her.

He relaxed his hands, a calming assurance sweeping through him. Lady Portia Derring would be his wife.

With that overriding thought, he strode across the room.

Her face blanched when she saw him approaching.

He smiled grimly. "Portia," he greeted, making deliberate use of her Christian name, staking his claim for the benefit of the man looming at her side.

"Lord Moreton," Portia returned, her voice

breathless. "You're still here? I thought you left." She glanced uneasily at the man beside her, a smile wobbling on her mouth.

"I've come a long way for you," he announced, "I'm not going anywhere."

Her eyes flared wide, smile vanishing.

"Portia," the man beside her demanded, his lip curling in a sneer as he looked Heath over. "Introduce me."

Heath fixed a cold smile to his face, not caring for the way in which he ordered Portia about—not caring for the fellow at all. He dropped his gaze to the hand that clutched her arm, to the fat sausage fingers that dug into her red silk sleeve. Something tight and deadly coiled itself in the pit of his stomach. He wanted nothing more than to plant his fist into the bastard's face.

"Mr. Oliver," Portia began, her eyes darting about in a clear attempt to assess the attention directed their way, "May I introduce you to Lord Moreton."

Heath returned Oliver's stare with a cold one of his own, and the battle commenced. One fought without words or acts. A line had been drawn. The question remained who would cross it first. Heath's fists knotted at his sides, his joints aching from the pressure. He stepped forward.

"Heath," Portia whispered, dragging his gaze back to her.

Please, she mouthed, those blue eyes of hers glittering brightly, the plea there unmistakable.

Something loosened and unfurled itself inside him, and he found he couldn't deny her. Not when she looked at him that way.

With a curt nod, he turned and strode from the ballroom, the house, his mind busy planning their next meeting.

Portia exhaled quietly, watching Heath stride away and disappear through the crowd. An inexplicable tightness filled her chest, making it impossible to draw breath without discomfort. Irrational as it seemed, a part of her felt annoyed that he had left. Had he come all this way to give up so easily? She gave her head a hard shake. He had hurt her enough. He would not do so again. Best that he give up. She would accomplish what she set out to do, what she had promised Astrid and Grandmother. Marry and marry well. Provide for her family. Perform her duty.

And she would protect her heart in the process.

"Come, Portia. Let's take a stroll." With his hand at her elbow, Simon guided her out the balcony doors and deep into the gardens.

"Would you care to ride tomorrow?" he asked after several moments of silence.

"Yes, that would be lovely," she answered even

as her heart constricted over the lie. She could think of countless things she would rather do than ride in the park with him.

He pressed closer to her side. His fingers rubbed her bare arm where he held her, his thumb moving in wide circles.

Unable to bear his touch, she halted on the path and pulled her arm free. "We better return."

Simon stopped and squared himself in front of her. "Something tells me you wouldn't mind being out here with that Moreton fellow." His tone rang out with the petulance of a child's.

It dangled on the tip of her tongue to tell him that she loved that other *fellow*—or rather, had loved him. *Had*. She gave herself a swift mental shake. One did not love someone who brought only grief and pain—*who agreed to wed but never bed you*.

But there had been joy, a small voice whispered, for however fleeting.

"Lord Moreton is of no consequence to me, Mr. Oliver." She shivered at the sound of her voice, a thin thread on the air.

"Simon," he reminded.

Portia cocked her head and tried not to pull away when he drew her hands into his.

"Simon," she said haltingly.

"It lightens my heart to hear you say that, Lady Portia. I realize there might be some competition for a lady of your rank." In the gloom of the garden, his barrel chest seemed to grow, puff out like a great balloon. "I shall do whatever necessary to win you."

Portia resisted the urge to reclaim her hands and endured the tight clasp of his fingers. She must grow accustomed to his touch. If anything, she needed to encourage Simon's suit—do everything in her power to bring about a proposal. She had promised Astrid as much. And Grandmother.

Her mind drifted to Heath and the look on his face when he'd seen her with Simon. As if she had slapped him a second time. Absurd. She had no reason to feel guilty. She owed him nothing. And he hadn't offered her anything. Hadn't even brought up marriage again. And how could she wed him knowing he believed she had trapped him, knowing he thought the worst of her?

Forcing a smile her heart did not feel, she locked eyes with Simon. "You've already won me."

He blinked. "What are you saying?"

Ignoring the dull ache throbbing just behind her breastbone, she drew a ragged breath and released it, saying, "I am receptive to your suit, Simon."

He gazed at her a long moment before clarifying, "Are you saying you will become my wife?"

My wife. She cringed at his words, watching as all her dreams spun into oblivion. Oddly enough, it wasn't her mother or the sun-kissed columns of the Parthenon she saw falling to the wayside. It was Heath.

"Yes," she heard herself saying in a faraway voice, as if spoken by someone else. "I will marry you—" her voice broke and she swallowed, desperate for some relief from the noose tightening about her throat.

Chapter 26

Portia's gaze landed on the wrinkled letter. And she felt nothing. No leap of her pulse at the sight of it, no surge of hope within her chest. Nothing. After all this time, she had finally ceased waiting, ceased clinging to a foolish child's dream. Her mother was gone. Would never send for her. Would never return. Why rip open the letter as if it contained news to that affect?

Instead, she looked back at her reflection in the mirror. Light glinted off her inky dark hair swept up in an elegant coiffure that made her feel the utter fraud. She had never been the elegant lady, never felt she looked as Astrid did, natural among the glittering ladies of the *ton*. Yet tonight she looked every bit the lady, every bit the way the daughter of a duke ought to look. Her grandmother would be pleased. Of that at least.

Portia reached for a bottle of perfume and dabbed it behind each ear with fresh determination. The reminder of her grandmother lying insensible in her bed a few doors down, in need of proper medical care, the kind of care only money could buy, only hardened her resolve to follow through and marry Simon.

She set the bottle down and gazed at herself searchingly. Her hair gleamed but her eyes were dull. No light there. The eyes of a woman whose fate yawned grimly ahead.

Nettie appeared behind her in the mirror. Her eyes roamed approvingly over Portia. "You look lovely." Her eyes strayed to the discarded letter. "Will you not open it?"

"Perhaps later."

"Later?" Nettie looked back to Portia. The smooth skin of her forehead knitted in confusion. "But it's a letter from your mother."

"I know." Portia stood and gathered her shawl, draping it carefully around her exposed shoulders, her concentration already on the evening ahead. Simon waited.

She flicked the letter a last glance. "It can wait. I'm going to be late, and I detest missing the prelude."

Heath studied Portia from where he sat in his box. She sat cool, regal as a queen, lovelier than he had ever seen and never once glancing his way even though he knew she had spotted him when they first took their seats, before the lights had dimmed and the audience fell hushed. Their eyes had locked, hers flaring wide in frustration. And something else. Something that gave him hope.

That hulk, Oliver, hovered beside her, eyes fixed on her as if she were some exotic bird that might take flight any moment. It wasn't to be borne a moment longer. She was *his* wild bird. For him to pursue and catch. Yet how could he if she didn't allow him within a foot of her? He had called on her yesterday. Twice. And that sour-faced butler of hers had turned him away each time.

Heath surged from his seat and strode from his box, the carpet deadening his swift steps. No more. He would not let another moment pass without seeing her. Without explaining why he had followed her to Town. As he should have done at Lady Hamilton's ball. And if he could sort that out for himself in the next thirty seconds, it would be most convenient.

The lilting aria dwindled to an end and the *ton*,

in all their glittering finery, poured from their boxes for the interlude. He darted among bodies, desperate for a glimpse of her, for a word, another shared look to give him encouragement.

Then he spotted her. For once her Goliath did not shadow her. Her dark hair gleamed blue-black under the lights, a raven's wing captured in sunlight. The jade green of her gown lovingly cupped breasts that his palms ached to feel again. She spoke to a lady beside her, her hands fluttering with speech. Guided by impulse, he stalked toward her and grabbed hold of one of those hands.

"Heath," she gasped.

Without a word or greeting, he gave a nod to her gaping companion and dragged her behind him.

"What are you doing?" she demanded as he pulled her along the winding hallway, away from the din and press of heavily perfumed bodies. "Where are you dragging me?"

He marched forth, leaving the mad crush behind until only a distant thrum of voices floated down the corridor after them. Spying a door amid the wood-paneled wall to his right, he glanced up and down the hall's length. Satisfied no one observed them, he yanked it open.

"Heath," she scolded as he thrust her within, "I insist you—"

He silenced the rest of her words with the hot

seal of his mouth, suddenly forgetting what it was he meant to tell her.

"What are you doing?" she hissed, tearing her lips from his and backing away several paces. Her temper burned bright—bright as the eyes glittering down at her in the dim room.

She pressed her fingertips to her mouth, still tasting him on her burning lips. Against her fingers, she raged, "How dare you drag me in here. I told you to stay away from me."

Moonlight glowed through the single window high in the wall, the sole light in which to see his features, harsh and fierce with emotion as he charged, "And you think I would listen? We've much unfinished, you and I."

She dropped her hand. "We have nothing to finish. Nothing at all. I've heard everything I ever want to hear from you."

He stalked her, backing her against the wall. "You cannot mean to seriously consider another man's suit. Not after what happened between us."

"What I mean to do is no affair of yours," she snapped, shaking her head, confused. Why was he here? Why would he imply that what happened between them held any significance when he himself had declared it a *mistake*.

He laughed, a dangerous, mirthless sound that

made her skin tingle. Trapped in this closet, she was totally at his mercy.

She latched on to the single weapon available— her anger. Recalling his shabby treatment of her, his words: *you're no different than any other prostitute selling herself for the right price*—her anger sprang to life. "You've said everything you had to say."

"Matters have changed—"

"I don't see how," she replied, trying to step around him once again. "Let me pass."

"Not until you hear me out," he growled.

She pressed her lips shut and arched a brow, waiting.

He stared down at her for a long moment, as if testing whether she would remain truly silent. Inhaling, he announced, "I still want to marry you."

Still. He needn't sound so blasted aggrieved.

"As I said, much has changed." He dragged a hand through his hair. "There have been certain . . . discoveries. The madness cannot be passed. Not like I thought."

She felt her brows draw together. "But your father, your brother—"

"Were sick," he finished. "And showing all the symptoms of porphyria . . . as my grandmother wanted everyone to believe."

"I don't understand." She pressed her fingers to her temples where a dull throb had begun.

"Grandmother wanted everyone to believe my father had porphyria."

"He didn't?"

"No," he sighed, and she felt that sigh vibrate through her, stretch along her nerves. "My father had the pox." His words fell hard as bricks in the dense still of the room. "He infected my mother while she carried my brother." He paused as though searching for words less shocking than those he had just uttered. "He killed her. And my brother."

"Syphilis?" Portia demanded, her head spinning. "Isn't there treatment—"

"Either he didn't realize it until it was too late, or he was in denial. The latter, I suspect. In any case, it killed him. And there was little to be done for my brother. A babe born with the pox has no chance."

"I don't understand. Why were you led to believe—"

"Grandmother," he snapped, recalling his grandmother's tearful excuses when he confronted her. "She considered a king's disease more acceptable than a whore's disease." He laughed bitterly.

Portia nodded. "Your grandmother chose the more dignified malady," she mused, rather suspecting her grandmother would have done the same. Despite her anger—her desperate need to put distance between them—her heart ached for him. "I'm sorry, Heath. Sorry for the years you and your sisters suffered."

"It's done," he said with a lift of his shoulder. "I'm concerned with now, this moment. For the first time in my life, I have a future to look forward to." He grasped her by the arms, his eyes glowing with an unyielding light. "Do you know what this means, Portia? There's no reason I shouldn't marry."

"No," she said slowly, "There's no reason you shouldn't."

"Considering I've already ruined you, you're the best—"

"*Ruined?*" God, how she detested that word. "I'm not ruined. No one knows—"

"That doesn't change the fact that I'm honor bound to marry you."

"Stuff your obligation," she cut in. "I release you from it."

"You can't release me. Obligation is simply that. No one can release someone from their duty."

Duty. A word she had come to appreciate lately. She felt inappropriate laughter bubble up inside her. He offered her marriage. He could wed her, bed her, and beget children with her. All for duty. Not out of love, not out of need or desire for her, but out of what was expected of him. She pressed a hand to her belly, suddenly feeling ill.

And ironically enough, duty demanded she wed.

Yet not him. Not this arrogant, insufferable man who had already broken her heart once. Who couldn't even manage a dignified proposal. She would not give him the power to hurt her again.

"I have my own obligations," she said tightly, lifting her chin. "I've changed, too, you know."

His gaze flickered over her face. "Is that so?"

"I no longer shirk my responsibilities." She shook her head, feeling painfully foolish to ever have thought that she could, that she could have been that selfish, that she could have been so much like Bertram. Squaring her shoulders, she confessed, "My brother has left us, departed for foreign soil."

"He abandoned you?" The astonishment in his voice rang clear and Portia smiled grimly. Heath would not be able to make sense of such a thing— a brother, an eldest son, fleeing duty, leaving his family to face trouble alone.

"Where has he gone?" he demanded in affronted tones, as if he himself would fetch her errant brother home.

She laughed dryly. "He did not exactly leave a forwarding address. It's for the best, I suppose. Scandal was imminent if he remained. Bertram became involved in certain activities."

Heath stared at her for a long moment before

nodding, accepting the little she had told him and not pressing for more.

"With Bertram gone," her voice faded. "Well, suffice it to say things have become rather desperate." Humiliation stung her cheeks, sharp as a Yorkshire wind. It scraped her pride to make such a confession, to reveal her brother's abandonment, to disclose the weaknesses of her family—even if logic reminded her that his family had its fair share of flaws.

"Portia," he began, his hands flexing over her bare arms, the rasp of his calluses on her flesh fluttering her insides. "Let me help. Marry me and—"

"No," her voice rang out, sharp and inflexible. Automatic. Although she had accepted the notion of marriage, she could not accept the notion of marriage to Heath. *Let me help.* So now he would marry her out of pity as well as obligation? Could he humiliate her any more? Regardless of how he made her feel, how her body responded to him, she could not tolerate marrying him for those reasons. *And for what reasons could you tolerate marrying him?* Shaking her head, she shoved the question into the dark night of her mind.

"No?" he echoed, his angry voice reverberating in the confined space, eyes flashing in the glow of the moon. "Why am I not acceptable? I thought deep pockets were the only requisite? You said you've decided to wed. You *need* to marry someone capable of supporting your family. I'm willing. Why not me?"

Why not me?

She shut her eyes in one long blink, hating how logical he sounded—how illogical he made *her* sound. *Why not him?*

His face as she had seen him that last day in the library—his handsome features twisted in loathing—flashed in her mind. He'd hurt her, wounded her to the core. She could not let him do so again. She couldn't be that weak, that stupid.

Her lips moved numbly, spilling forth an explanation that had nothing to do with the one that squeezed at her heart, "Oliver Simon will not simply support us, he will also settle Bertram's debts."

His fingers dug into her arms, nearly lifting her off her feet. "*I* can do that."

"Why would you want to?" she bit out. "With Simon it's an even trade. I get something. He gets something. Business. Plain and simple."

The opera resumed, the music swelling until it pounded all around them, humming along the walls and floor beneath their feet.

"And what exactly does he get?" The question was loaded, rife with danger. Heath's gaze slid over her, indicating he had already formed an opinion.

It was the one question she refused to dwell on. Not when her nights were spent thinking about Heath, remembering his hands and mouth on her. "Mr. Oliver wants respectability, an entrance into Society."

"He smells of the docks."

"It's a practical arrangement. You and I—"

"Make a hell of a lot more sense that you and him."

She smiled tightly, wanting desperately to fling his words back at him. *There is no you and me.* Instead, she settled for, "We don't suit."

"No?"

The tiny hairs on her nape tingled and she knew she had provoked him too far.

The air in the tiny room changed subtly, thickened, grew electric. He snatched both her wrists and pulled them above her head.

"What are you doing?" she squeaked as he pressed the hard length of his body against her.

His unsmiling face looked down at her, watching her intently as he lowered his head. His head inched toward hers, but she dodged his mouth.

His eyes narrowed, lips thinning into a grim line. Releasing her wrists, he spun her about and crushed her into the wall. He grasped her hips in rough hands, pulling them out slightly from the wall. A shocked gasp escaped her as he nudged her thighs apart through her gown.

"What are you—" her voice froze, trapped in her throat as his hands came around to clasp her breasts. A hard bulge prodded at her backside through the volume of her skirts.

His fingers rolled, tweaked and squeezed her nipples into rock-hard points. Desire pooled low in her belly. A keening moan escaped her. She turned her face and rested one cheek against the wall, unable to move, unable to resist the seductive assault.

His hands dropped. She moaned in disappointment.

Then she felt him hike her skirts to her waist. He shoved down her undergarments. Cool air caressed her. His hand traveled over her thighs, her backside. A hissing cry escaped her when he bent and nipped at her exposed buttocks. His hand slid between her legs, fingers probing, pushing deep inside her.

She came out of her skin, sobbing as his hand plundered her. Then the hand disappeared. An anguished whimper ripped from her throat, swallowed by the music pulsing around them. She bit her bottom lip, waiting, desperate for what was to come, what she had thought she would never have again. Her body burned, ached, trembling like a leaf.

Hard hands fell on her hips, fingers digging into her softness, lifting her to accept the hot length of him sliding inside her. He penetrated her deeply and a scream welled up in her throat.

His hands shifted, angling her for deeper invasion, anchoring her for his thrusts. She clawed the wall, fighting for a handhold. Her knees felt like water. If not for his hands on her hips, she would have slid to the floor in a shuddering, boneless pile.

Cries tore from her mouth at his every plunge. He lifted her higher, the heels of her slippers coming off the floor. His own breath came hard and fast in her ear as he ground into her bottom.

One of his hands slid from her hip, kneading and squeezing her bottom possessively before sliding around, dipping, finding that pleasure spot between her quivering thighs that begged to be touched, stroked, set afire. She gasped as his fingers worked their magic, moving in fast little circles until she broke, shattered, convulsed between the wall and the man at her back that had become her entire world.

A few more powerful thrusts and he stilled, buried to the hilt. He pulsed within her, spilling his seed deep within her.

A mixed sense of elation and horror grabbed hold of her heart, squeezing tightly. The night at the lodge he had always withdrawn, always held himself in check. Not so now.

She lifted her cheek from the wall and gazed at

her hands splayed flat before her. Moonlight washed the walls, tingeing the flesh of her hands blue.

Strong fingers brushed the back of her neck. "Portia—"

"No," she choked, loathing for herself—for him—burning a bilious trail up her throat as she squeezed between him and the wall. Her hands shook as she bent and set her undergarments to rights. "Don't say a word."

Straightening, she risked a glance at his face and her heart constricted at the almost tender look on his face. If his words matched the look on his face, she was doomed.

Her unsteady hand touched her hair as she moved toward the door.

His hand clamped down on her arm. "Surely now you can see—"

"I see nothing save two people who haven't a shred of sense or dignity." She inhaled a great gulp of air. "Who just copulated like beasts in a closet."

The tender looked fled, a hard mask taking its place.

"Marry me and you won't have to worry about that. We'll be husband and wife." He scoured her with a dark look, one full of lust and promise. The smoldering fire in her belly flared to life, betraying her. "You can have this every night without threat to your sense of *dignity*." He uttered the word as if it were a jest, something that did not exist. And perhaps for her it did not. When it came to him she had displayed very little dignity. It was as if she lost the ability to think when he entered the room.

Marry me and you won't have to worry about that. We'll be husband and wife. No, but she would have to worry about much more. Her heart, her pride, her self-control—her future with a man who held the ability to wound her like the sharpest of blades. She would have to be daft to bind herself to him.

"You once told me that I didn't belong at Moreton Hall," she said dully. "Well, you don't belong here. Go home, Lord Moreton. I'm sure you'll have no problem finding a bride more suited—"

"Oh, we suit," he inserted, his voice as dangerous as a whip cutting air. His gaze trailed over her, insulting in it thoroughness, as if he stripped off her gown and stared upon her nakedness. "In the most fundamental way. Except you're too pig-headed to see it."

Shaking her head, she turned and slipped from the room. Hands clenching and unclenching at her sides, she told herself that he was wrong.

Heath didn't return to his box. He stormed from the theater and hailed a hack, calling out the name of his hotel as he bounded within the musty confines.

Perhaps he should listen to Portia and leave— let her marry her smelly dockworker. Although the image of her beneath the brawny fellow, taking him inside her body, invaded his head and soured his stomach.

How many times did she have to say no before he finally quit? He thumped his fist on the seat. He had affairs to tend to—his sisters sitting at top of the list. Now that he knew there to be no threat of madness, he needed to see about getting them married. Mina would be delighted. Constance . . . he was not so sure. Still, he had better things to do than traipsing after some female who spurned him at every chance.

But her body opened like a flower at his slightest touch. Closing his eyes, he dropped his head on the back of the seat. He could still feel her heat, the tightness of her snug around him. He had released himself inside her, gloried in it. It had been the greatest sense of liberation—a claiming of himself right along with her. The thought of a child growing in her womb even now filled him with inexpressible joy.

She wanted him as much as he wanted her. They both knew it. He would do whatever necessary to prove it.

* * *

Alone in her room, Portia undressed herself, her hands lingering over the places Heath had touched, kissed. Her mouth, her neck, her breasts. Her skin still tingled, still ached for him.

Before donning her nightgown, she sponged herself clean. Washing away the evidence of their lovemaking from between her legs, she tried not to notice how her sensitized skin reacted to her ministrations. Still, she wished it were Heath's hands there.

Mortified at the wanton she had become, she flung the sponge back in the bowl and quickly covered her traitorous body with a nightgown. He'd be gone soon enough. Once she and Simon announced their engagement, Heath would see that they were well and truly finished.

She moved to extinguish the lamp but paused when she spotted the letter. Her mother's letter.

A sigh welled up deep within her chest. Might as well read it. Releasing her sigh, she picked up the missive, bracing herself to hear all about her mother's exploits abroad—places seen, people met, things done. Then the letter would end with the "wish" that Portia could be there to share in it all.

Unfolding the parchment, she skimmed her mother's elegant, scrawling handwriting with a numb heart, feeling none of her former excitement and anticipation when reading such letters, so grateful for a glimpse into her mother's life.

Her heart stopped beating altogether when she came to the end, to the words that suddenly took life and leapt off the page, instantly breaking from resembling all the previous letters she had received over the years.

Her fingers went limp and the letter fluttered to the floor, gentle as falling snow. She looked down, staring at the letter that lay there as innocuously as a forgotten handkerchief, a white smudge on the dark blue and green swirls in the threadbare carpet.

The words her mother had written struck her like a blow to the face, robbing her of breath, ripping at her heart.

I've married, my darling girl. He's a wonderful man and we want you to join us in Athens.

Chapter 27

❧❦❧

"**H**ave you decided when we can announce our betrothal?"

Portia opened her mouth but no sound emerged.

Simon repeated himself.

Faced with the reality of becoming his wife, of allowing him the intimacies she had only shared with Heath—one word fell from her lips, "No."

Portia frowned. How had that slipped from her lips? It had certainly not been her intention to reject his suit. She had hardly given Simon a thought until he had showed up for tea today. Her thoughts had been too wrapped up in Heath and the mother who had *married*—who finally remembered she had a daughter.

For years, Portia had lived in wait for such a letter, longing for the day her mother would *want* her, would turn her promise into a reality. Her mother had sent for her. At last. Just when Portia had ceased to hope. Except it didn't matter. Portia no longer cared. She had been avoiding life, avoiding her duties and responsibilities for the sake of a dream. And now that the dream hovered within reach, she no longer wanted it. It was the dream of a girl, a little girl who had needed her mother. That girl no longer existed.

Portia needed something else now. Heath's face emerged in her mind. Aggravating, considering the way he had humiliated her in Yorkshire, but nonetheless there. Always there. And she was beginning to suspect he always would be.

Simon shook his head, looking as confused as she felt. "I thought you were eager to wed."

"I was—am." Portia paused and pressed her fingers between her brows where her head was beginning to throb. Suddenly, a sense of knowing filled her. Dropping her hand, she looked him directly in the eyes. "I cannot marry you, Mr. Oliver. I apologize for giving the impression that I could."

He stared at her a long moment, an odd little

smile fixed to his face. Clearly, he had not heard her.

"I cannot marry you," she repeated as gently as possible. "I thought I could, but I cannot."

"No?" he queried, rising swiftly to his feet.

"You must see we don't suit."

He looked down at her, his face flushed an unbecoming shade of red. "Your sister-in-law assured me you were agreeable to this match."

Nodding, she dropped her gaze to her hands. "You mustn't blame her. I thought—"

"You thought you could," he finished in a snarl. With surprising swiftness, he leaned down and circled her neck with his hand, exerting the slightest pressure as he said, "I'll not be made a fool, my lady. No one makes a fool of Oliver Simon."

That said, he released her neck and stormed from the room, flinging the door wide open. It crashed against the wall, the sound reverberating on the air for several moments. She sat there for a long moment, her hand at her throat, willing herself to cease shaking.

"Portia?" Astrid said, hurrying into room, her face pinched tight with concern. "What happened?"

"I—I—" Portia glanced back at the door, wondering if she might somehow call him back, yet knew she could not. Not when to do so pinched at her heart and made her feel as though she were betraying not only Heath but herself.

"Portia?" Astrid pressed.

"I refused to marry him," she blurted.

Astrid gave her head a small shake as if she had misunderstood. Pressing her hand against her temple, she cocked her head to the side.

"Astrid?" Portia asked, trying to catch a glimpse of her sister-in-law's eyes. Only she continued to look away, as if the sight of Portia disgusted her.

Portia leaned forward, her voice urgent. "Astrid, I will marry. I promised you and Grandmother that I would. Only not Oliver Simon." The image of Oliver's face, mottled red with anger, his beefy hand on her throat like a steel collar seized her and she suppressed a shudder. Right or wrong, she could not marry him. "Give me a little more time. I'll find someone else."

At this, Astrid laughed. A grating sound that sent a chill down Portia's spine. "Who else would marry you? You've nothing to recommend you save a family name that, thanks to your brother, is now in question."

"Astrid—"

"Have you not heard the whispers?" Astrid demanded, swinging her dark gaze back on Portia, the venom reflected there lethal as hemlock.

Portia shook her head, then stopped. She had noticed a few stares. Yet she had chalked that up to her new wardrobe, and the fact that Oliver Simon, not the most cultured gentleman, escorted her about Town. It had not crossed her mind that everyone whispered behind their gloves about the pathetic Derring women, abandoned, rejected, scrabbling for a way to survive penniless among the echelons of Society.

"Everyone knows Bertram fled in order to escape trial. We're the talk of Town. The destitute Derrings." Astrid's dark eyes shimmered suspiciously.

"I will find someone else," Portia insisted, already thinking of Heath and weighing how degrading it would be to seek him out, to ask him if he still wished to marry her—despite all her protests. Would she look the complete fool?

"All I need is a little time," Portia vowed.

Time to find Heath. To swallow what little pride she had left and tell him she would marry him. For duty's sake and not love.

Portia stared blindly into the dark, straight and rigid as a slat of wood, fingers laced tightly over her stomach. Two days and no sight of Heath. No sight of him since the theater when he had obliterated her will and reduced her to a shallow creature that lived and breathed for him and passion alone.

She had set Nettie to the task of finding him, of checking all the hotels and inquiring among servants. Nothing. Had he done what she had asked and gone back to Yorkshire?

She lowered her hand and brushed the swell of her stomach, the linen of her nightgown soft against her palm. She thought of them in that moon-washed room again, the wicked way they had made love and something told her it would always be that way with Heath. Mad or sane, there would always be a part of him too wicked to tame. And she didn't want him any other way.

Her balcony doors stood open and the curtains shifted, fluttering with a whisper in the wind.

Astrid hadn't spoken a word to her, and although Grandmother could now sit up in bed and take down some food, she still needed a physician's care. Portia didn't have time to play at courtship. Where was Heath? He couldn't have changed his mind. Couldn't have given up. Could he?

Sighing, she rolled onto her side, thinking of Heath, of her desperate need to find him, to marry him.

Marry Heath. A warmth suffused her at the very idea, at the nights they would have, the leisurely attention they could devote to each other's bodies. Frowning, she quickly tried to suppress the warmth with a cold douse of reality. He was still the man who had hurt her, who had crushed her in Yorkshire. Nothing would change that. There would be no love between them. She would not grant him such power over her, would not permit herself to fall in love with him.

But you loved him in Yorkshire. And you haven't stopped.

"No," she vowed aloud, her fist thumping the mattress beside her. "I don't—I won't!"

"Won't you now?"

She lurched up in bed with a gasp, her eyes searching the gloom for the source of that velvet voice. Her heart hammered in wild relief. *He had come.* That he had been so bold as to climb the trellis outside her window shocked her not in the least. This was Heath, after all.

"Heath?" she addressed the room, her voice a hush on the air as her eyes strained for a glimpse of him.

Silence. She shoved back the covers and swung her feet over the side. Her bare feet dropped down silently. She moved toward the robe draped over the footboard.

A hard hand shot out and gripped her wrist. "Leave it off. One less item I'll have to remove."

A secret thrill skated over her skin. He meant to have her here? With her sister-in-law two doors down? And her Grandmother directly across the hall? Portia opened her mouth to deliver a ring-ing set down, but the words never made it past her lips. His mouth crushed hers and her protest died in her throat.

She tangled her hands in his hair, pulling his head closer, deepening their kiss and parrying her tongue with his. He backed her up until she bumped the bed.

He broke their kiss and her eyes fluttered open. Her chest rose and fell with each savage breath that shuddered free of her lungs. His eyes glittered at her in the dark, twin spots of gleaming onyx.

"What are you doing here?" Senseless question, she knew. He gathered her nightgown against her hips even as she asked.

"I think it would be clear what I'm doing." In a single, swift move, he pulled the nightgown over her head. Night air rushed over and she shivered. "Did you miss me?" He breathed against her temple, stirring the fine hairs there.

She managed a strangled sound, a gurgled affirmation. *Miss him?* With every fiber of her being. His large hand cupped her bottom and lifted her high against him, snuggling her against his prodding erection. That hand rounded the curve of her bottom, sliding lower, fingers teasing, probing her entrance and ripping a gasp from her throat.

Then she was falling. His body came down over hers, surrounding her, pinning her to the bed. Instinctively her legs parted wider, allowing him to settle deeper against her. Their mouths fused together, a hot, wet melding of lips and tongues, of nips and long, deep drinks from the fountain of their mouths.

The dam broke at last and she let herself go, reveled in his mouth, his hands on her body. She had decided to marry him, decided to bind herself to him—had spent two days agonizing that she had lost her chance. Even without love, she could have him, have *this*.

An incredible sense of freedom, of power, seized her and her hands flew to his trousers. In a heartbeat, she freed him. Her hand closed around his hard length. His groan emboldened her. A shudder ran through him and vibrated within her as she stroked him—slowly, carefully at first, then in long, firm strokes that made him breathe harder. She rubbed her thumb over his tip, delighted at his low groan, at the bead of moisture that rose up to kiss her thumb and coat the head of him.

Releasing him, she shoved hard at his chest. He fell back on the bed. She hovered over him for a moment, wishing she could see the magnificence of his body. Memory would have to serve. Hands fumbling in her excitement, she removed his jacket, vest and shirt, at last exposing him to her roving hands. At least she could feel him. She traced the ridges of muscles along his stomach, the outline of each rib. And taste him. Dipping her head, she tongued his navel before licking her way down the thin line of hair.

She stopped, perched uncertainly. The rasp of his breath filled the air, encouraging her. Taking him in one hand, she placed a kiss at the tip of him.

"Portia," he croaked in a voice she had never thought to hear from him. Vulnerable. Lost. Totally at her mercy. It thrilled, aroused and prompted her as nothing else could. Slowly, like he was the most delectable piece of fruit she had ever sampled, she licked him.

His body jerked almost as if in pain.

She released him. "What? Did I hurt you?"

In response, hard hands clamped down on her arms. Before she could draw a breath she was on her back and he was driving into her, so deep he touched her soul.

His mouth slammed over hers as he plunged in and out, loving her in a way completely unlike their previous times together. The first time had been a reluctant loving, sad and resigned, shadowed by guilt. Their second time had been a punishment, his way of proving to her that she wanted him. But this was wild, uninhibited. He took what he needed, pounding into her ruthlessly and she didn't care because she wanted it too. Needed it. Needed him.

Her hips rose to meet him and she cried out as he drove harder into her, gripping her hips as if she were a lifeline, the only thing that kept him grounded to earth. Her heart swelled even as she reminded herself that this wasn't love. Only lust. Lust in all its thrilling, consuming thrall. Hopefully they would always have this.

And it would be enough.

This was more than lust. Heath knew it the instant he felt her shudder beneath him, felt her tremble and arch under him in the throes of her climax. His own climax followed fast and fierce. He reveled in the sensation of his seed spilling inside her—again. Knowing he *could* release himself without fear—knowing nothing would please him more than creating children with this woman.

She breathed heavily beneath him, the tips of her breasts pebble-hard and rubbing his chest in the most arousing way. He propped himself on his elbows and stayed just so, buried in her, never wanting to leave.

"Portia," he began, determined that tonight, once and for all, she would agree to become his wife. Why it burned within him with such importance, he dared not examine. He simply knew that he had to marry this woman, to wake up beside her every morning for the rest of his life. Never could he abuse her as his father hurt his mother. He'd cut his own heart out first. "Portia, I—"

"Portia? Are you awake?" A gentle knock sounded at the door and the two of them flew off the bed as if a red-hot poker prodded their backsides. Heath tossed her nightgown at her and made short work of straightening his clothing. He glanced at the thin line of light glowing beneath the bedroom door.

"Portia?" The woman at the door knocked again. "May I come in?"

Her small hands pushed wildly at his chest, shoving him in the direction of the balcony. It occurred to him that he could linger until that door opened and put an end to the question of their marrying. Yet he didn't want her to agree to marry him because she'd been compelled. He wanted her to *want* to marry him.

His eyes searched the dark, desperate for a glimpse of her face, desperate to say—

"Go," she hissed.

"Tomorrow," he managed to say before stepping onto the balcony and plunging into the night.

Portia dove beneath the counterpane a mere moment before Astrid strode into the room. She took a gulp and tried to steady her breathing and the erratic thumping of her heart against her chest.

"You're still awake?" Astrid asked, her expression surprised.

Her cheeks flamed. "Yes."

Astrid motioned to the side table and the goblet sitting upon it. "Why did you not try the tonic I sent up for you earlier?"

Portia glanced at the goblet, having forgotten all about it. Leery of Astrid's "tonics," Portia wrinkled her nose.

"It's my *special* tonic," she chided. "Will do wonders for those bothersome wrinkles you're starting to get at the corners of your eyes. One cup and you'll look much improved."

Portia picked up the goblet. Mostly to appease her sister-in-law, but also to distract Astrid from looking too closely at the rumpled bedcovers, or her mussed appearance, or to catch the lingering smell of sex, she downed the contents of the goblet. It tasted like wine but with an underlying bitterness that she puckered her lips against.

"Good girl." Astrid smiled and patted her hand with far more solicitousness than she had ever displayed.

"Astrid," Portia began as she settled against her pillows. "I know you've been angry with me—"

"Hush." Astrid waved a hand, averting her eyes

to arrange the covers around Portia. "Let's not talk about it."

"Please believe me when I say that everything will be fine. You have my word."

A vague smile played about Astrid's lips. For some reason the sight made Portia's stomach tighten. Unease settled between her shoulder blades, tensing her back.

"I know, Portia," she murmured evenly. "I'm not angry anymore."

Portia studied her closely, trying to gauge that smile of hers. The one that never reached her eyes, the one that Portia had seen her exhibit on countless social occasions. The one that hid something. Everything.

"Get some sleep." Turning gracefully, Astrid strolled from the room. The door clicked shut and darkness shrouded her again.

Portia bounded from the bed, hoping Heath hadn't left, that he lurked somewhere in the humming night outside her room. Standing on the balcony, she scanned the lawn below. Gripping the stone railing, she risked a loud whisper. "Heath."

Nothing. He had gone.

Deflated, she rubbed her arms for comfort and leaned upon the railing, the cool stone seeping through the thin cotton of her gown, chilling her.

A pleasant lethargy crept over her. Strange. Moments ago she had not even felt tired. Goose bumps broke over her flesh, but she still didn't move. Her legs felt heavy, leaden. She glanced down as if she would see fetters about her ankles. Turning, she pushed from the railing, suddenly eager for the comfort of her bed.

She dragged herself forward, her hand seeking the balcony door for support. Her legs felt steady as rubber. Blood rushed to her ears—made her head feel stuffed full of cotton.

She grasped the door, clinging to it, her fingers digging into the wood. One of her nail's splintered from the pressure as she tried to stop from sliding to the floor.

Her knees buckled and she fell, sliding down like a limp doll. She dropped to the floor, head whirling, spinning until black oblivion rolled in.

Chapter 28

Heath bowed low over Lady Astrid's hand, slender and delicate. Her skin was pale as cream, the blue veins visible beneath.

"Lord Derring, how nice of you to call." Her unswerving gaze reflected no such frailty. Her eyes, a dark coffee brown, were a startling contrast with her fair hair and skin. They looked straight through him, direct as any man's.

"My apology for not calling sooner, Your Grace. I've heard the Dowager is unwell." He lowered himself into the chair across from her.

Lady Astrid inclined her head slightly. "That is

true. Although she has improved markedly in the last few days."

"I'm greatly relieved to hear that. I know my grandmother will be most distressed to learn she has been ill." Unable to hold off any longer, he inquired, "And Lady Portia? Is she receiving today?"

"Portia?" Lady Astrid straightened where she sat, pulling her shoulders back as if preparing for something unpleasant. For half a second alarm flashed in her cool gaze. "You've come to call on Portia?"

"Yes. She and I grew acquainted in Yorkshire."

"Acquainted," she murmured, rolling the word around her tongue as if it were some strange sound. In a single, fluid movement she rose to her feet and strolled to a cabinet in the corner.

Her back to him, she asked bluntly, "What are your intentions concerning Portia?" She opened the lacquered door and removed a tray arrayed with a decanter and glasses. "Sherry?"

"No." He gave a swift nod, still mulling over her question. He supposed it fair. With Bertram gone and the dowager ill, Lady Astrid did have some right to know the depth of his interest in her sister-in-law.

"I intend to marry her."

At his declaration, she downed her glass in one swallow. Reaching for the decanter again, she asked, "Are you sure you won't join me for a drink, my lord?"

"Quite." Uneasiness tightened his gut. His statement did not elicit the reaction he expected.

"Does Portia know of your intentions?"

"I believe she will accept my suit." He damned well wasn't leaving until she did. After last night, she couldn't seriously consider refusing him. At least that's what he told himself, what his heart desperately whispered to his head.

The duchess downed her second glass with one swallow. She turned bright eyes, burning with emotion, on him. With a heavy sigh, she muttered, "Then you best go after her."

He rose slowly, his pulse quickening. "Go after her? Where has she gone?"

"Scotland. She left early this morning."

"Scotland?" he echoed.

"Yes." She grimaced. "Where else could she marry on such short notice?"

Portia woke to a throbbing headache. It pounded at the insides of her temples with fierce little hammers. She cracked open one eye, then the next. Hissing at the harsh invasion of light, she clenched them shut again.

A slight rustling sounded near her head. "Nettie, would you draw the drapes?" she asked, her tongue dry as sand in her mouth.

Before Nettie could respond, her world tilted and careened.

"Nettie," she choked, a hand flying to her mouth as she fought down her heaving stomach. "Chamber pot—quick!"

With more strength than Portia thought Nettie capable, she was pulled upright and forced into a sitting position. Much too quickly for her rebelling stomach.

"Ah," she groaned against her fingers, a vile taste rising in her throat.

"Open your bloody eyes and stick your head out the window you daft female!"

Her eyes flew open at the sound of the coarse command.

Simon Oliver stared back at her, looking both anxious and wary. She lunged for the window. Sticking her head out the flimsy drapes, she heaved the contents of her stomach, mindless of the rain soaking her as she watched the wet earth roll by beneath them.

Confidant that she would not be sick again, she fell back against the squabs, demanding weakly, "What have you done?"

She pressed a hand to the base of her throat as if she could still the wild thud of her pulse beating there. His eyes, feral and gleaming, fixed on that hand, watched it as a fox watched its dinner. "You thought you were finished with me, didn't you?" He leaned forward in his seat. "I warned you—"

"Mr. Oliver," she croaked, her tongue thick in her mouth. Pausing, she swallowed and tried to force words out of her dry mouth. "I insist you turn this carriage around at once. My family must be besides themselves with worry—"

"Your family," he cut in, the crack of his voice loud as the falling rain around them, "is in full support of our marriage. Who do you think helped me make off with you in the middle of the night?"

Portia sucked in air and jammed her eyes shut against the sudden spots filling her vision. "No. They wouldn't do that. Not Grandmother. Not Astrid." They would not have betrayed her, would not have resorted to such methods.

She must have spoken aloud, for Oliver suddenly sat on the seat beside her, his voice a serpent's slither in her ear, his chest a barrel pressing at her side. "I know nothing of any plans your grandmother may have had. Lady Astrid, however, came up with this. She said once we were wed, you would see reason."

Astrid. Portia knew her sister-in-law was angry, desperate even. She had felt it in her cold stare. Yet if she had just trusted Portia, given her a little time, she would have seen that she intended to honor her promise.

Heath. A dull ache began to throb beneath her

breastbone. An image of him filled her mind, her soul. When precisely had he become *everything* to her? When exactly had he turned into her every dream, her every hope for the future?

Oh, Astrid, how could you?

"No," she breathed, jamming her eyes shut, unwilling to open them and face the man at her side. Face the ugly truth that spilled from his lips and washed over her in wave after horrible wave.

"No," she repeated, as if the single word had the power to remove her from this awful reality.

Fingers hard as iron grasped her chin. "Yes."

Her stomach heaved anew. Swallowing, she opened her eyes to glare at her abductor, to stare him down as if every inch of her weren't trembling at the prospect of becoming his wife, at never again seeing Heath or feeling his arms surround her. Wrenching her chin free, she dragged herself to the edge of the seat until her shoulder dug into the carriage wall.

He slid after her, his small, dark eyes narrowing in predatory enjoyment. "A few hours in this carriage and marriage to me will be your only alternative." He nodded, his chin jutting forward in satisfaction. "I mean to see you keep the promise you made."

His hands grasped the hem of her nightgown. She shrank back as far as the wall vibrating against her shoulder would allow.

Still, he clung.

"Can't have you wed in this, can we?" His thick fingers worked fast. Two great, mauling paws gathered fistfuls of her nightgown. She slapped at his hands. Still he talked, lifting her gown higher and higher, heedless of her kicks. "Your sister-in-law packed a change of clothes. Nice of her, eh?"

If the hands on her nightgown weren't message enough, his leer left no doubt. He meant to ravish here right here, right now.

"Simon, please—" her voice broke into a strangled sob as his hands gripped her bare knees. Hard, brutal fingers dug into her tender flesh, forcing her legs apart, spiking unthinkable terror in the deep well of her heart.

This isn't happening. Pulse thundering in her throat, she thrashed her legs, desperate to fight him off even as her stomach rebelled, convincing her she was going to be ill again.

He dropped his full overwhelming weight on her—a mountain crushing the air from her lungs, shoving her so hard into the carriage wall that she feared her bones might snap from the pressure.

Grunting, she fought for breath, life, freedom. She writhed, struggling to free her hands from between their bodies. All the while her knees worked furiously, pumping, squirming, trying to shake off his foraging hands.

He leaned back ever so slightly to fumble with

his trousers, and her terror swelled, a deep burn in the pit of her stomach.

Time suspended. She froze, sealed in a tight bubble of astonishment. She gazed at him, the man bent on violating her: the wild tick in his jaw, the sweat sheening his nose and beading his upper lip, the open mouth and wet, furry-looking teeth.

Sounds heightened, building to a roar in her head. The excited rasp of his breath. The creaks and groans of the jostling carriage. The thundering beat of rain all around them. The fall of hooves on the wet road.

Her gaze shifted, darting about wildly, desperately, a sparrow in flight looking for a safe place to land. The sound of his trousers sliding, dropping, fired her to action. Her gaze fell on the door's latch, inches to her left.

With a prayer on her lips, she surged forth and kicked him full in the chest. Her hand flew to the latch, grappled with it for a heartbeat before it opened. A gust of wind flung the door wide. Rain pelted her face, impairing her vision as she looked out at the blur of trees flying past.

Squeezing her eyes shut, she jumped. Wind and rain rushed her. Earth rose up to meet her. She landed unevenly, her feet slipping on the wet ground. The carriage thundered past. She fought for balance but still fell, pain lancing her left ankle.

Half staggering, half crawling, she dragged herself into the thick undergrowth crowding the road. She pushed ahead, slapping at branches, ignoring the wet, the cold, the agony in her ankle. Branches clawed at her sodden nightgown, tore at her unbound hair. Still, she pressed on, determined to lose herself in the woods.

She struggled forward, wincing at the jar of her every step, her breath falling in violent spurts. She bit her lip until the coppery tang of blood ran over her teeth. Soon another sound rose over the rain and pound of her heart.

Voices.

Simon's. The driver's.

They grew closer, the heavy tread of boots on the forest floor reverberating through the trees.

"Portia!"

Close. Much too close.

Dropping on all fours, she crawled to the nearest tree and pressed her back against the rough bark. Tucking her knees to her chest, she tried to steady her gasps, to collect her thoughts. Her ears strained for the slightest noise, a voice, a movement beyond that of rain and wind. Unfolding her legs, she resumed crawling through the muck.

"Portia!"

She froze. The voice was close, so near she feared she had been sighted. Still as stone, she looked up. Her heart lodged in her throat. She eased back on her heels and pressed a fist to her lips, stifling the cry that threatened to spill.

Simon stood to her left, leaning against a tree not two yards from where she squatted in the mud. He stared ahead, not looking in her direction. Her heart beat wild as a drum against her chest. Surely he would see her white gown. She risked a glance down and released a silent sigh. Not a trace of white remained. Closing her eyes, she remained just so, making herself a part of the landscape, as still as any rock lying on the ground.

Simon pushed his wet hair back from his brow and looked left and right, his gaze skipping over her. "Portia!" he roared.

A shudder ripped through her. She clenched her hands, her nails slicing into her palms as she willed herself to become invisible.

With an ear-stinging curse, he set off again, calling her name in a voice that carried to the skies.

Once his heavy tread faded, she shoved to her feet and slogged back to the road. Bursting through the trees, she scanned the road. The coach loitered several yards to her right, its horses munching on the low-hanging branches of a hawthorne tree.

Heart hammering in her too-tight chest, she

hurried forward, careful not to startle the horses. Clambering to the driver's perch, she snatched up the reins and flicked her wrists.

The horses didn't budge.

"C'mon," she begged, flicking her wrists again. One horse looked at her, ears flattening with displeasure before resuming his feast.

At that moment, Simon burst from the line of trees, the driver behind him. Her stomach plummeted and a small whimper escaped her lips. Simon's face, mottled several shades of red, turned deadly when he spotted her atop the driver's perch. He charged the carriage with a bellow, spooking the placid beasts from their leisure.

She snatched the crop from the seat and whipped the horses. Under normal circumstances, she would never strike a horse so hard, but the sour taste of fear coating her mouth banished any reservations.

The crop served its purpose. The horses bolted, the force flinging Portia back on the hard seat.

"Stop," Simon shouted, waving his arms as the carriage barreled toward him. The horses didn't slacken their pace—and she wasn't about to move left or right to avoid the blackguard.

At the last moment, he dove clear.

She glanced over her shoulder to see him submerged in mud. He clutched one boot close to his chest, and his strained expression told her he had not dodged the carriage unscathed. Served him right.

Facing front again, she squinted against the slashing rain and tried to gain control of the animals and slow their breakneck pace. She rounded a corner, pulling on the reins fiercely.

Wincing at the sudden bite of wind and rain on her cheeks, she averted her face. And didn't see the horse and rider. Not until it was too late.

He materialized from the gray curtain of rain like a phantom, a specter magically brought to life. Rider and stallion both black as night.

She jerked on the rains, her scream trapped in her throat as her fingers yanked and twisted on the slick leather.

The horses' screams filled the air, shrill and eerily human. Blood roared to her head. Her heart plunged to her stomach as the carriage careened to one side, balancing precariously on its wheels. She kept a death grip on the reins, her lifeline, the only thing keeping her atop the carriage as her body lifted from the seat.

Her eyes met and connected with the oncoming rider for a single heartbeat. Recognition flashed in eyes as gray as the sky. Her heart leapt to her throat.

"Heath!" Her cry reverberated through the air, strange and faraway—as if someone else cried out.

Then her hands were empty, groping for reins, a handhold. Something. There was nothing. Nothing but wind.

She flew, toppling through the air as if her body were boneless, weightless. Trees and sky rushed past in a blur. The earth rose up to meet her in a dizzying whirl, a vast maw ready to swallow her whole.

Heath swung from Iago's back before the horse even came to a full stop. He skirted the capsized carriage, sparing only a glance for the shrieking horses that fought to be free of their restraints.

Bitter fear swept through him, flooding his mouth, burning his nostrils. "Portia," he called brokenly as he looked for her along the road. "Portia!" Terror seized his heart, wringing tightly.

Then he saw her, buried in mud, her crumpled form so small and lifeless at the edge of the road. He ran. It took only a moment, but he thought he'd never reach her. Never have her in his arms again. Never have the chance to say what his heart had known from the start. He loved her. Even when he had no business loving her, he hadn't been able to stop himself.

His hands shook, suspended over her for the barest moment before he touched her, grasped her shoulders and gently folded her into his arms, praying that God could not be so cruel as to place her in his life only to take her from him so quickly.

Rain pelted her ashen face as he stared down at her.

"Portia?" He brushed a hand over her cheek, relieved to feel its warmth. His fingers slid to her throat, to the pulse point that beat steady and strong.

"Portia," he said again, her name a sigh, a benediction.

Her eyes opened, blinking, looking up at him in confusion. "Heath?"

"Are you hurt?" he demanded, eyes raking her as if he could ascertain her injuries for himself.

"I'm fine, but I think I may have run Simon over with the carriage."

He laughed then, his heart loosening, expanding inside his chest. "I won't lose any sleep over that."

Her face crumpled. "You came?" she choked, a sob lifting her chest. "How did you know—"

He cupped her face. "Astrid told me everything. But that's not important." He struggled to swallow the lump in his throat. "We've wasted enough time. I've wasted years," his voice faded and he shook his head determinedly. "But I'm not going to waste another moment with you."

Her eyes devoured him, the blue brilliant and vivid through her glimmer of tears.

"I love you, Portia," he said, feeling an immense relief in uttering words he had thought himself incapable. Words that had been caged inside him for a lifetime, waiting to be freed, waiting for *this woman* to free them. "Marry me. Not because of duty, or because we should. Marry me because I love you." He stared into her wide, unblinking eyes and added in a growl, "Marry me, damn it or I will go mad."

Her sob fell then, loud and deep, and he felt it lodge in his heart. She flung her arms around his neck and pulled him close, burying her face in his throat.

Her lips moved against his skin, spiking a familiar haze of desire. "This isn't real," she murmured. "None of this real. I'm afraid to let you go, to find out—"

He pulled back and silenced her with a kiss that sent a lick of heat spiraling low in his gut. After a moment, he tore his lips free. Forehead pressed to hers, he said roughly, "It doesn't get any more real than this."

His eyes locked with hers, their gazes melding until he felt as if they were physically linked. In a ragged, desperate voice, he said, "I need to hear you say—"

"Yes," she blurted, without the slightest hesitation, her eyes drilling into him with an intensity that shook him. "I will marry you. And I'll spend the rest of my life loving you. *You* are my dream."

At that moment the rain increased, the skies dumping sheets of water on both of them. Heath lifted his face, relishing the water flowing over him, rinsing him clean.

"Heath," she murmured, laughter in her voice. He looked down at her rain-sluiced face. "It seems we're destined for muddy roads."

"My little mud pie," he murmured, trailing the back of his fingers over her wet cheek. "I suddenly find that I have a great fondness for muddy roads."

Epilogue

Six months later

Shielding her eyes with one hand, Portia tilted her head back to view the sun-baked white columns stretching into a cloudless blue sky. For a long moment, she could only stare, allowing the reality of standing before the Parthenon to wash over her, a warm balm to the soul.

A strong hand settled at the small of her back, capturing her attention. Turning, she looked up into Heath's face. So dear. So familiar. Warm wind blew his hair across one cheek. Her heart constricted at the tender look in his eyes. A look reserved for her.

The trip had been his gift to her—their wedding vows barely uttered before he had her on a ship sailing across the Channel. He had teased that they would need a relaxing honeymoon before returning home and suffering the come-outs of his sisters.

"Is it everything you dreamed?" The deep rumble of his voice slid though her like warm honey, the mere sound igniting her.

Her gaze skipped back to the structure that had endured two thousand years. She eyed a statue of Athena, staff in one hand, shield in the other. Its beauty alone pinched at her heart. The dignified hauteur of the goddess's face whispered to her soul.

She returned her gaze to Heath, her husband, and felt an even deeper tug on her heart—a louder call to her soul.

"No," she answered with a quiet certainty. Lacing her fingers through his, she squeezed his hand with hers. "But this is."